WHISKEY & WINE

Visit us at www.boldstrokesbooks.com

By the Authors

Vintage & Vogue

Whiskey & Wine

WHISKEY & WINE

by

Kelly & Tana Fireside

2023

WHISKEY & WINE

ISBN 13: 978-1-63679-531-7

This Trade Paperback Original Is Published By
Bold Strokes Books, Inc.
P.O. Box 249
Valley Falls, NY 12185

First Edition: November 2023

Credits
Editor: Cindy Cresap
Production Design: Susan Ramundo
Cover Design By Ink Spiral Design

Acknowledgments

This was such a fun story for us to write. Just like Lace and Tessa, we were best friends before we were lovers. We understand how much is at stake when you make that leap. Yes, it's exciting and beautiful. It's also scary as hell. So this is a big shout-out to everyone who hung in there with us as we navigated those days—especially Margaret who, at just the right moment, reminded us that life is messy. Without all of you, we wouldn't be here, and neither would this story.

We want to give a huge virtual hug to everyone we know and love in the wine world, especially our friends at J Wrigley Vineyards and, in Southern Arizona, Sand-Reckoner, Callaghan, Rhumbline Vineyards, and Dos Cabezas WineWorks. It's always fun hanging out in your vineyards and tasting rooms. You inspire us with your dedication, delight us with your world-class wines, and honor us with your friendship. A special thanks to Sarah, who let us pick her brain and helped us create the vineyard timeline that became the outline for this story.

Also, thanks to everyone at Bold Strokes for giving this newbie writing pair so much encouragement and support. Even more, thank you for making sure stories of, by, and for the queer community get told.

Finally, just a note. The books in this series are all set in Owen Station, which is a fictional town, loosely based on Bisbee, Arizona, a former mining town located just north of the Mexican border. We lived there for a bit and fell in love with the people, the history, the landscape. We're thankful to have been a part of that world and carry bits of it with us wherever we go. If you get a chance, go visit.

Dedication

To John and Jody—all dreams are possible

Prologue: 1917

M argaret was waiting for her inside the carriage house.
The horses had long since been moved out, of course,
to make way for Mr. Owen's automobiles. Indeed, he owned more
than one, although the roads were barely passable for the mules,
poor creatures, that were used to haul equipment down to the mines,
and copper out of them. However, Mr. Owen loved nothing more
than to make a show of his wealth. That is the only reason he insisted
on purchasing the latest fashions from Kansas City and Chicago. It
would not do for his wife to be seen in public in anything less—
regardless of what his wife might desire.

He was rarely at home those days, as he and other town fathers
were constantly huddled together, discussing ways to disabuse their
workers of any notion that by *striking*, they would somehow make
their lives better. Mr. Owen was persuaded that only intimidation
and threats of physical violence would be effective—and, if that
were to fail, he intended to organize a mass deportation. "I will rid
this town of vermin, if it's the last thing I do," he said, pounding the
table at dinner the night before last, making her jump. She pitied the
workers, as she was all too familiar with his capacity for vengeance.

She could not wait to make her escape.

As soon as she pushed open the heavy wooden door, she was
met by cool air—and Margaret, who stepped out of the shadows to
greet her with an embrace.

"Elizabeth! Come!"

Margaret took her by the hand and led her to a wooden bench that sat along the back wall.

"It has finally arrived." Margaret took a deep breath and pulled a small magazine from her bag. "This is the literary publication I have been telling you about—it was founded and is managed by a woman like us. She lives in Chicago but is planning to move to Paris with her…with the woman she calls her wife. There are others there, many others. They are living in the open."

Margaret's eyes were wide with wonder, sparkling with possibility.

"I have finally saved enough for both of us, Elizabeth. I just need to make the arrangements—so that we can get away quickly and quietly, without anyone realizing until after we have gone. Tell me—when is the next time Mr. Owen will be away?"

"I don't know for certain. He has talked of a trip back to Kansas City in the spring, to meet with investors. But he will want me to accompany him, of course."

"Oh my dear, that is the opportunity we need. I will go to Kansas City myself, then. It will be easier for us to be anonymous in a large city. We will make a plan to meet there. Then, we will escape together. And we will not stop until we are safely at our destination. Paris! The city of love and revolution, of freedom and art!"

Elizabeth took the small magazine Margaret was holding, opened it, and reverently turned the pages. If Mr. Owen found her with something like this, she did not doubt the punishment would be severe. The words on the pages were scandalous—and exhilarating.

For the first time that she could remember, she believed that a new life was possible.

CHAPTER ONE

I think you should give the butt plugs names."
Lace nearly choked on a pretzel. "Excuse me?"

She turned around carefully, keeping her arms tucked to avoid knocking a drink out of someone's hands. The bar at the Triple D was shoulder to shoulder and, between the all-women band kicking out another country favorite and the din of a hundred or so women trying to have conversations with each other all at the same time, it was hard to hear. But Lace heard *that*.

"I said you should give the butt plugs names."

Lace laughed. "I heard you the first time, Tessa. And hello to you, too. Why do butt plugs need names?"

Lace had been hoping to see Tessa that night, but she hadn't realized how much until Tessa actually walked in. She was maybe the only woman in the place, besides Lace's BFFs, Hazel and Delaney, who wouldn't be flirting awkwardly, trying to get Lace to take them home. Also, as usual, Tessa was all business.

"Everybody gives their vibrators nicknames. Ms. Pinky. Big Bertha. Rubyfruit."

"Rubyfruit?"

"You know, like *Rubyfruit Jungle*."

Lace shook her head and shrugged.

Tessa laughed. "Sometimes I forget you're younger than me."

"Only by five years!"

"*Rubyfruit Jungle* is only like the most important lesbian book ever written. Anyway, the point is people give their vibrators nicknames because it makes them seem more, I don't know, playful. Not serious or scary. They're just fun. Butt plugs need help."

Lace had to admit vibrators and dildos flew off the shelves at Frisky Business, the toy store she opened a few years ago, after she and Knox divorced. Butt plugs, not so much.

"Okay, I'm convinced. Want to help me name the merchandise next week?"

"A butt-plug-naming date?" Tessa grinned.

"A butt-plug-naming business meeting, you mean."

"Exactly what I meant."

Tessa Williams became one of Lace's favorite people almost from the moment she ambled into Frisky Business a year ago, all sun-kissed and crunchy, looking like she just walked out of a tourist brochure for Arizona wine country. Because, as it turned out, she had. She was looking for a gift for her daughter, who had just turned nineteen. Lace was surprised but tried not to look it. Tessa didn't look young exactly—too much life lay behind those eyes, for that— but there was no way she looked like she ought to have a kid that old. In what Lace would learn was typical, transparent-as-hell Tessa fashion, she said she'd gotten pregnant way too young. Madison was born in the middle of her first year of college. "It's normal to be horny when you're that age," Tessa said. "But I was horny, ignorant, and naive." Nobody had to worry about Madison being naive. Not with Tessa as her mom.

Yep, Tessa was great. Which was why there was no dating. Dating was for fun and sex. Lace could have that with literally anyone.

"By the way, this Rubyfruit Forest you speak of—"

"Jungle." Tessa rolled her eyes. "Rubyfruit *Jungle*."

"When was it written?"

"I don't know exactly. The seventies, I think."

"The nineteen seventies? As in, the middle of the twentieth century?"

Tessa nodded. "Technically, that would be the last *quarter* of the twentieth century."

"Maybe you're older than you look."

"Maybe you need to brush up on your math." Tessa punched her playfully in the arm. "Besides, you don't have to be old to know about *Rubyfruit Jungle*. You just have to know a little about queer history. And maybe read once in a while."

"Hey! I read!"

"Customer reviews and text messages don't count." Tessa laughed and then started elbowing her way up to the bar. "What can I get you?" she shouted over her shoulder.

"I'm good! Delaney's getting a round. Meet you back out on the dance floor in a bit?" Lace threw her thumb over her shoulder for emphasis, just in case Tessa wasn't sure she heard right.

Tessa nodded with a grin.

Lace could count on one hand the number of people who had ever seemed to get her the way Tessa did. There were Delaney and Hazel, of course, her two best girlfriends. And there was Knox, who had been her best friend since Coach picked her to be team captain instead of him in fifth grade—and who stayed her best friend, even after they divorced. She loved them all. But they'd known each other forever.

It was different with Tessa. She only knew the new Lace. Lace the business owner. Lace the sexuality educator. Lace the whiskey connoisseur. Lace the very soft-masc lesbian with the pompadour and a great sense of humor, who all the young ladies wanted to date. It was weird how much easier it was to be herself with someone who hadn't known her since before she could do algebra. Since before Dad died and Mom lost it. Before the mess with Knox. The hasty marriage. The miscarriage. The affair. Tessa only knew the Lace that Lace had spent a lifetime trying to become, not the Lace she used to be. So, when she was with Tessa, it felt a lot like freedom.

Tessa was new to Arizona. She had moved in a handful of years ago, after a messy breakup of her own. Her ex-wife kept the California vineyard, even though Tessa had been both the brains and the muscle behind it. Tessa took back her last name and her settlement, and bought a vineyard twice as big, right in the middle of the Sonoita Valley, a scrappy new winemaking region. She named it Mujer Fuerte, Spanish for strong woman. Tessa was making a name for herself in the wine world, and no wonder. She made great wines, plus she was a genius when it came to business.

And that's how it all started.

Tessa popped into Frisky Business on a late September afternoon just after harvest and asked for a vibrator recommendation. Before she left she had given Lace a dozen new ideas for merchandising, marketing, and inventory control. Lace was captivated. Tessa left her card, and a few weeks later, Lace closed the shop early and drove out to the vineyard. Tessa gave her a tour and a tasting on the house, and talked her ear off about why the high desert of Arizona was such a perfect place to grow old world style wines…with new world freedoms and creativity.

Since then, they'd been texting a couple of times a week or more. They quickly developed their own emoji shorthand. A dollar sign meant a big sale—for Tessa, that usually meant a new Mujer Fuerte wine club member. The little guy with his head blowing off meant they'd just had to deal with an especially annoying customer—for Lace, that usually meant somebody's ding-dong boyfriend using a dildo to pretend-measure the size of his own manhood. As if you could measure that with a ruler. Anyway, at some point, they started having lunch together, about once a month or so, whenever Tessa came into town for supplies or a haircut at Color Me Crazy, the salon Delaney managed. They'd each bring their own sandwich or salad, and eat in the back room at Frisky Business. Lace hadn't wanted everyone in town—and, by that, she mainly meant big-mouthed Delaney or nosy Knox—seeing them together.

Lace wasn't exactly sure why she had kept her relationship with Tessa a secret for so long. It seemed silly now. But Tessa was a new…friend…not just another fling. And that was something she thought her old friends probably wouldn't understand.

She was right.

"Hey, there you are!" Delaney was holding two whiskey glasses and handed one to Lace.

Lace took the glass, leaned in, and gave Delaney a kiss on the cheek. "Delaney, I love you."

"You should. First of all, I gave you that fabulous haircut. Second, I come here with you and Hazel once a month, even though there's not a man in sight. And, third, you've been keeping secrets from me—I saw you out there dancing with Tessa!—and I'm still talking to you."

Lace's cheeks felt suddenly hot. "I told you—we're just friends."

"Sure you are." Delaney waggled her eyebrows suggestively.

Even her friends thought they had Lace all figured out. Now they were going to have to process new information.

Yes, she could make a new *friend*. With a woman. What was the big deal?

It felt like coming out all over again.

"So, how long has this *friendship* been going on?" Delaney's eyebrows were plastered to the top of her forehead, and the twist of her mouth made it clear she wasn't buying it.

"I don't know. Not quite a year, I guess."

"A year!" Delaney's turquoise cowboy hat, perched precariously on top of a big bleach blond top knot, nearly toppled off her head. "I've been cutting her hair for at least that long, Lace. And neither of you thought to mention this to me?"

Lace shrugged and looked past Delaney to scan the room. A gaggle of sorority sisters down from Tucson for the weekend were huddled a few feet away, sucking on glasses of something that looked way too sweet, probably daring each other to do something. Anything. They needed stories to tell when they went back to their boyfriends on Monday. But, one of them, the one who looked the most terrified, froze when she accidentally made eye contact with Lace. Lace winked at her and smiled. She wanted to go over and tell her everything was going to be okay. Instead, she *thought* it really loud and willed the girl to hear her. She hoped the kid would have an easier time coming out to herself than Lace did.

It might have been easier if her family hadn't exploded right about the time Lace should have been figuring it out. After Dad died, Mom got into bed and didn't come out for three months—she was never the same, no matter what medication she took or how many therapists she saw. It was pretty hard for Lace to deal with her own issues, when her mother's issues took up so much time and space.

"Lace, are you listening to me?"

Delaney was glaring at her.

"What's the big deal, Delaney? It's not like I need to check in with you about every move I make. I have a life of my own, you know."

"You do not, Lace Reynolds. Don't be ridiculous."

Lace laughed. Delaney had a point. They lived in Owen Station, an old Arizona mining town tucked up in the Mule Mountains, about fifteen minutes from the Mexican border. The place swelled during tourist season and the business chamber did their best to draw in the crowds with ghost tours, art walks, and local music festivals. But true Owenites, the ones who lived and worked there, were in a parallel universe, where everybody knew everybody else—or, at least, everybody else's business. And, at Color Me Crazy, Delaney was right in the middle of all of it.

"Speaking of keeping tabs on our friends," Lace said, "where is Hazel, anyway?" Hazel had been part of the gang since grade school. She was the only one of them who got out after graduation. Went to the university in Tucson and got herself a girlfriend. But she came home to take care of her mom after the cancer diagnosis and never left. She worked at the library and bored pretty much anyone who would listen with random historical facts about the town. Lace adored her.

Delaney did a little happy dance. "Oh, you missed it! While you were out there playing with your *friend*, Sena showed up."

Sena was even newer to town than Tessa—although she had deep roots in the area. She was an Abrigo, one of the oldest and wealthiest Mexican families in Southern Arizona. Sena made quite an entrance, marching into Knox's coffee shop earlier that summer, introducing herself as a tech-whiz turned developer, talking about turning Owen Station into the next Silicon Valley, for women. For a hot minute it seemed like she and Hazel were going to be a thing, as weird as that seemed. Hazel helped start the town's architectural preservation society. It was a total opposites attract thing. So it wasn't too surprising when they had a big fight in the middle of Main Street. Hazel had been avoiding her ever since.

"Well, that must have been interesting."

"Interesting doesn't come close," Delaney squealed. "Hazel acted like an idiot and ran out. I made Sena chase her. They had a big fight in the parking lot. And then they seemed to make up. Then they went flying off somewhere in Sena's fancy little sports car."

"Sounds like you were tracking them pretty closely." Lace rolled her eyes.

"Of course I was! I hope Hazel finally gets laid tonight. That girl has been wound way too tight." Delaney's face suddenly sparkled like somebody sprinkled fairy dust all over it. "Plus, wouldn't it be wonderful if she just finally let herself fall in love?"

Lace laughed. "It's adorable when you go all hopeless romantic, Dee. Try not to float away while you're hanging out up there on cloud nine."

Delaney was opinionated, stuck her nose where it didn't belong, and loved a juicy piece of gossip more than she loved Knox's rhubarb pie—and no one loved Knox's pie more than Delaney. But Delaney loved her friends, most of all. Especially Hazel.

"You're teasing me, Lace. And that's fine. But you know as well as I do. Hazel has been through a lot, and she deserves a little love in her life more than anyone."

"More than *moi*?" Lace held her fingers above her head and did a little ballerina twirl—not an easy feat in her brown harness boots.

Delaney flicked her in the chest. "That's not what I'm saying. Besides, you *choose* not to fall in love. You won't even *date* anyone for more than three months."

"Three months is the perfect length of time for fun and sex. Things tend to get too serious after that. And what's fun about that? Besides, I get all the love I need from my friends." Lace held her arms out. "Come here and give me a hug."

Delaney rolled her eyes but let Lace embrace her.

"Alright, Lace. That's my cue. Usually it's Hazel and me leaving you behind to make your way home with a cute little someone. But it looks like I'm headed out on my own tonight. Are you good? Want me to stay?"

Delaney was always the driver on girls' night out. She loved pulling into the Triple D in her red Wrangler full of lesbians. Confused the hell out of everyone.

Lace smiled. "Stay if you like, Delaney. But I'm good."

"No, you're not. You're very, very bad. Which is why I'm outta here." She gave Lace a quick kiss on the lips. "That's all the action I'm going to get in this place. Have fun, my friend. Be safe!"

Delaney's exit opened the field. Three women immediately started moving toward Lace as if following arrows Coach drew on a whiteboard during halftime. Bridget was at three o'clock—they'd been in school together. She popped into Frisky Business once in a while and was very clear that she was looking for something long-term. Lace wasn't. A weekend lesbian was moving in at nine o'clock—unnaturally blond, clothes too tight, a touch too much makeup. Maybe mid-forties. Botox made it hard to tell. Down from Scottsdale, probably. And, no doubt, a husband at home. No thanks. But coming straight at her, through the crowd and across the dance floor, was the lead singer of the band. Mid-thirties, maybe a little younger. Long, auburn hair, which she wore in loose waves, perfectly framed an adorable, round face. Her short, crocheted dress hugged her hips and a generous belly, and those boots looked like they'd been out riding a time or two. Lace saw the other two closing in and made a snap decision to punch up the middle while she still had time. She met the singer at the edge of the dance floor and greeted her smile with one of her own.

"Nice set."

The singer grinned. "You've got a nice set, too."

"Why thank you, ma'am." That wasn't where Lace was going, but she was certainly open to it. And she was already having fun. A sense of humor was a serious turn on. "I haven't seen you before. First time in Owen Station?"

"Yep. We're from Portland—the band and me. We're all friends from college. Been playing together locally for about a decade. But this is our first tour. Hence, we're *here* in the middle of nowhere."

Lace looked around. The Triple D, located about eight miles outside of Owen Station and a universe away from Phoenix, was a stop for a lot of new bands. It had been around forever and was a legend in the queer community across three states, but it looked like it hadn't been cleaned since 1992. Rumor had it the mirrored back bar came from an old saloon in Tombstone, where Doc Holliday was known to throw down, shoot 'em up, and lose way too often at the poker table.

"Well, welcome to nowhere—and one of the last lesbian bars in the state." Lace spread her arms out and bowed dramatically.

"One of the last lesbian bars anywhere, you mean. It's the real reason we're here. We don't get a chance to play gigs like this too often."

Lace nodded. "Can I get you a welcome drink? Not much in the way of top-shelf liquor. I'm always complaining about the whiskey options. But they've got all the basics, and there are a couple of local beers on tap."

"Nah, thanks. I'll have a cold bottle of water waiting for me on stage, and we're just about to go back on. I don't drink and sing. But I'll let you buy me one at the end of the night." The singer tugged playfully at the collar on Lace's upcycled vintage Western shirt. "Unless you're already going home with somebody else?"

Lace smiled. This was her happy place. "I'll meet you at the bar when you're done. Barb, the grisly barkeep behind the stick, keeps a couple of stools open for me at last call."

The singer kissed her on the cheek and then brushed her lips across Lace's ear. "I can't wait."

Lace watched her hop onto the stage, take a swig of water, and grab a mic. Then the girl—Lace realized she hadn't asked her name—closed her eyes and started to sway as the band began to lay down a muddy groove.

"That looked successful. She's cute." Tessa appeared and stood beside her, grinning. "They really do just fall all over you, don't they?"

Lace grinned back but felt her cheeks get warm. "What can I say? I'm irresistible."

"You're something, alright." Tessa leaned sideways and used a shoulder to give her a friendly push.

They were standing on the edge of the dance floor, which was starting to fill, and talking loud enough to be heard over the music.

"So, how's your night going, Tess? Meet anyone interesting? Or have you spent the evening giving Barb advice on how to clean up this old bar and double her revenue in a month?"

"Very funny."

"Seriously, though. She could use your help."

"You're not wrong. But all I'm looking for tonight is a fun time on the dance floor."

"As sweaty as you are, it looks like you found it."

Tessa laughed. "It'd be a helluva lot more fun if there were more line dances, where I can just do my own thing out there, without worrying about whether or not my partner can dance." She leaned in so Lace could hear her, but nobody else who might be in earshot. "It's amazing how many people can't dance, but still want to lead."

"Are you talking about dancing or life?"

Tessa laughed. "Both."

"Maybe you should stop looking for those type A types."

"I don't go looking. They just sort of find me." Tessa shrugged.

"That probably doesn't have anything at all to do with this sexy girl-next-door vibe you have going on. I'm loving the cutoffs with those fancy blue cowboy boots."

Tessa tipped her Western hat. "Why thank you very much, Miz Reynolds. I'll take that as a compliment. All I have to say is, it's a good thing I can follow just about anybody."

Lace laughed. "Is there anything you *can't* do?"

But Tessa didn't laugh. Instead, a flash of something crossed her face. The old disco ball, which had been spinning during the last set at the Triple D for decades and was all of a sudden in fashion again, was throwing weird shadows everywhere, so maybe it was just that. But Lace didn't think so. When, after a minute, Tessa didn't have a snarky comeback, didn't say anything at all, in fact, Lace knew there was something going on.

"Hey." She gave Tessa a quick scratch on the back and leaned in closer so Tessa could hear her without having to shout. "What's going on? Did I just step in it somehow?"

Tessa turned to look at her. "No. It's nothing you said. I just. It's Madison." She shot Lace a crooked smile. "I guess I'm not feeling like my usual I-can-do-anything self."

"Is she okay?" Naturally, Lace jumped to the worst possible scenario.

"Yeah, yeah." Tessa touched Lace's arm and smiled appreciatively. "She's okay."

Lace exhaled slowly. How did parents do it?

"We just had a big fight this afternoon. She told me she's moving out."

"Oh, shit, Tessa."

"Yeah. It's big."

They stood side by side for a long couple of minutes. Lace had stopped listening to the music, and she was barely aware of the dancers in front of them. She just felt Tessa beside her, in pain, worried about her kid.

Finally, she leaned over. "So, do you want to dance? Or do you want to get some fresh air?"

Tessa looked at her and tilted her head. She was squinting and had a weird look on her face. Confusion, maybe. Like she was puzzling something out. Lace wasn't sure if she had asked the right question. But then Tessa nodded slowly. "Let's head outside."

Lace nodded back, took her hand, and led her through the crowd toward the front door. When she pushed through it and out of the congested bar, it was immediately easier to breathe. It was still summer and Owen Station was having unusually high temps during the day, but the desert cooled off at night.

"Where'd you park?"

Tessa tipped her chin in the direction of the back lot and Lace led them around the building, toward the truck. It was an older model, but Tessa kept it looking brand new. Lace loved the sticker on the back window. A laughing skeleton, holding a wine glass and watching a butterfly, said "Would you look at that—my last flying fuck." Tessa told Lace she stuck it there not long after the divorce, as she was packing up to leave California.

Lace opened the tailgate and let Tessa hop up first. She followed and they sat on the edge of it together, legs dangling.

The moon wouldn't set for another couple of hours, but the sky was dark enough for a spectacular display. Scorpio shone above them in the middle of a blanket of stars. Lace could have sat there looking at them all night.

Tessa broke the silence first.

"I've always been so worried about her, you know. Ever since she was born. I was so young. I had no idea what I was doing."

Lace knew the big picture but had never heard the details. "What about her father? Was he around?"

Tessa blew a sarcastic laugh through her nose. "No. I grew up fast when Madison was born. He did the opposite. We haven't seen him since she was about three months old."

Lace tried to imagine nineteen-year-old Tessa. Not much younger than Madison was now. "Were you in love with him?"

"Oh, I suppose I thought I was. What do you know when you're nineteen?"

Lace laughed. "Fact."

"I didn't really date in high school. I was too serious."

"No." Lace grinned, using her shoulder to give Tessa a friendly bump.

"Yes, I know that's hard to believe. I was just really focused on getting good grades and getting the hell out of town, but when Billy asked me to go to prom with him our senior year, well, he was captain of the football team. Everybody was shocked, including me. Turns out I had been right to stay focused on school all those years. The minute I got distracted, I got pregnant."

The parking lot was beginning to clear. A group of Swifties piled into the SUV next to them, rolled down the windows, cranked their music, and kicked up gravel as they peeled away. Tessa leaned back and looked up at the sky.

"I had a scholarship to UC Davis—a full ride. I wanted an ag degree, even though my family thought I was nuts. They were all farmers. Generations of them. And none of them had ever been to school. Besides, what's a girl need college for? My mom told me to find a farmer, settle down, and learn how to cook big meals for the workers. Anyway, I packed up my things and got on the bus to Davis not knowing. I thought I was missing my period because of the stress—being away from home for the first time and all that. By the time I realized what was happening…"

Lace waited.

"Billy told me he knew a place. Told me to get rid of it," Tessa said softly. "But I couldn't do it. Madison was born at the end of winter break."

"Wait, wait, wait. Billy *Madison*? You didn't!"

Tessa laughed. "No, I didn't. Not on purpose, anyway." She got quiet again. "None of it was on purpose. I mean, I'm not sorry. I love Madison more than I ever thought it was possible to love anyone. But it was hard, you know? My mom said they would help only if I came back to the farm. They said I proved their point, that I was never going to be anything but a wife and a mother."

Tessa paused and looked out into the darkness. "I stayed in school and tried to make it on my own. But I couldn't do it. I ended up leaving the program. I just couldn't handle being a full-time student, a mom, and making enough money to support us both. I got a job cleaning tanks at a big winery and took classes online."

"You did what you had to do, Tessa."

"I know. But I've always worried about her, you know. I wish she had a mother who didn't make so many stupid mistakes."

"You're kidding, right? You're the most not-stupid person I know!"

Tessa laughed. "The *most not-stupid person* you know? Whoa, take 'er easy there, Pilgrim."

Lace's mouth dropped open. Tessa's impersonation of one of her favorite Western movie stars was spot-on. Lace responded with one of her own. "Wait just a minute, little lady, are you telling me you're a John Wayne fan, too?"

Tessa laughed harder. "Of course I am. You are, *too*?"

"Well, duh. And, anyway, you know what I mean. Madison is so lucky to have you as her mom. You're the original mujer fuerte, as strong as any woman I've ever known. And she's going to be just fine, Tess. She's not a little kid anymore. She's almost twenty. She's smart and she's stubborn. She'll figure it out, just like you did."

A big van with a rainbow-colored peace sign on the side pulled up in front of them and the passenger window slid down. The singer.

"So, here you are!" She didn't look pissed, even though she had a right to be. "Looked for you at the end of the set. Looks like you found another last call. Catch you next time!"

They took off before Lace could respond.

Tessa leaned against her. "Oh shit, Lace. I'm sorry."

Lace shrugged. "No worries. I wasn't feeling it tonight, anyway. But it does leave me without a ride home."

"You're on my way. Come on. I'll drive you."

They hopped down, and Lace flipped the tailgate closed. They talked all the way back to Owen Station. When they pulled up to the house, Tessa pulled a bottle of her favorite Mujer Fuerte red out of a case in the back seat and Lace grabbed a couple of glasses. They sat in the Adirondacks on the front porch, talking until the moon set. Tessa headed off to the vineyard a little before sunrise. And Lace realized something.

That was the first time she had ever spent the night with a woman...just *talking*. It was weird.

And it was nice.

CHAPTER TWO

The air was crisp, but the sun was shining. Exactly what the vines needed to rest. Just like Tessa.

After a long, slow, hotter-than-hell summer, harvest had come early. And, when it came, it came hard. Tessa had never been through one like it. With the help of Jeremy, her vineyard manager, and a crew of workers she had grown to love and trust, she got through the brutal long days and nights, and pulled in more fruit than any of them thought possible. Then, finally, the grapes were in and the vines could begin to relax. For what seemed like a minute that fall, the fields were a tapestry of brilliant oranges, yellows, and reds. Then the first hard frost snapped, and the leaves browned and dropped to the ground. Now, the vines looked dead. They weren't of course. They were just sleeping. Soaking nutrients from the soil up through their roots. Being reborn, in a way. Getting ready for the next season of growth.

Tessa measured her life this way—in seasons—just like every farmer. And it had been a long one. She had hardly had time to breathe. And she hadn't been out dancing since that surprising summer night, when she stayed up talking with Lace until the sun came up.

Madison moved out at the end of the summer, not long after the big blow up. Right before harvest, it couldn't have been worse timing. Tessa was not thrilled. But she had to admit it was time for the kid to be on her own. Living in three hundred square feet, in an old Airstream, on a vineyard in the middle of nowhere, with your mom, wasn't exactly a twenty-year-old's dream. Besides, Tessa had raised Madison to be a strong woman, hadn't she? How could she be angry when Madison decided to actually act like one?

Tessa helped her find a little apartment in Owen Station. Madison found the roommate, a guy who worked in a tasting room down the road. He seemed nice enough, had a boyfriend, and paid his half of the rent on time. It had been hard, but like so many things, in the end everything seemed to be turning out for the best. Plus, it was kind of nice having her little house-on-wheels to herself. Bleu, her very protective, five-year-old Australian shepherd, was a much less demanding housemate than Madison had ever been. And, once they weren't living together, Tessa and Madison got along really well.

She hadn't been to town much at all since Madison got settled. She went in every other month or so for a haircut and to pick up provisions. And she would always make a point of seeing Lace for a quick lunch. Even though they had already been friends for a year or so, that night after the Triple D, sitting on Lace's porch sharing wine and stories, something changed. Lace stayed on the phone with her during her ninety-minute drive back to the vineyard, to keep her awake and make sure she got home safely. Since then, they were on the phone, or at least texting with each other, every day. But they didn't actually see much of each other. Tessa had just been too busy. Sometimes she was so busy she forgot to eat.

She did make time for the things that were really important, though. There were three she never missed.

Weekly dinners in the Airstream with Madison.

Playing her guitar for thirty minutes every morning, while the coffee brewed, before the sun came up.

And movie nights with Lace every other Sunday.

Tessa had been looking forward to it all day.

"Hey, Mom, can you add the new cheese board to the system, please. It wasn't in there when I tried ringing it up."

"You got it!"

Tessa was working beside Madison under a canopy up on the hill, where they had set up an outdoor tasting area. It was a little unorthodox. They were the only winery in the area that didn't have an indoor tasting room. But Tessa loved being able to share her wines right in the midst of the vines. The view was spectacular, and the omnipresent wind helped keep things cool, even on the hottest days.

Madison was clearing the counter after a tasting for four old friends. They had come from different states to attend their fortieth high school reunion and a holiday mariachi festival. Decades ago, they had been in their school's band together—and credited that experience with their success at work and in life. Madison got them to sing one of their favorite songs, which drew applause and cheers from a couple dozen very appreciative customers.

As much as Tessa loved the excitement of harvest, she was always grateful for this season, when even the wines were pretty much tending themselves, and she could be in the tasting area more often.

Tessa whistled to herself—a new song she was working out on the guitar—while she added the cheese board to the point-of-sale system. And as long as she was in there, she checked the numbers. They were having a killer day—a lot of which was due to Madison, who sold eight new wine-club memberships before three o'clock. Tessa had fired off a dollar sign emoji to Lace each time.

Tessa's pocket buzzed. It was Lace.

How's your afternoon going? Is Madison still killing it?

Always. Tessa added a string of emojis. Fire. Fist bump. Wine glasses. Dollar sign. Three different smiley faces.

Madison FTW!

Tessa smiled. Lace and Madison had formed a mutual admiration club. They had only spent a few hours together, on those rare occasions when Madison had tagged along into town and Lace invited her to join them for lunch. But Lace sealed the deal when she pitched in to help Madison move last summer, filling her Bronco with boxes of Madison's things, and carrying them up two flights of stairs to the apartment. Plus, Madison said Tessa was happier now that she had a "best friend." Tessa just laughed—like they were in kindergarten or something.

How about you? Tessa typed. *How'd the IBF go?*

IBF was Lace's shorthand for the "It's Been Fun" conversations she had with the women she dated. They happened about once every three months.

Three little dots danced on Tessa's screen while Lace was typing.

She loved the rabbit.

Tessa laughed. At the end, Lace always shipped them whatever their favorite toy had been. It's no wonder she was still friends with most of the women she dated. She was honest with them right up front—they would have fun and lots of sex for three months—and they would not get serious. Because how could it be fun if it was serious? That was Lace's motto, anyway.

Tessa took a good look around. She was tucked under a sun sail, overlooking her vineyard, with the majestic Patagonia Mountains as a backdrop, pouring wine beside her daughter. Wine she produced with her own hands. From fruit she grew herself. Life couldn't have been much better. And she wouldn't have traded it for anything.

But she would be lying if she said she wouldn't love to have Lace's life, at least for a weekend.

"Earth to Mom."

Tessa laughed. "Sorry. I guess I spaced out."

"You did look deep in thought."

Tessa put her arm around her daughter. "I was just thinking about how thankful I am for you."

Madison kissed her on the cheek. "I love you, too, Mom." Then she went back to work.

A white couple in their thirties stepped up to the counter—a counter Tessa had built herself using reclaimed barn wood and a few old wine barrels. The man had a sleeping baby strapped to his chest.

Tessa put a menu in front of them. "Welcome to Mujer Fuerte! We've got a nice tasting menu. Two whites, a rosé, and two reds. For twenty bucks you get 'em all, plus a Mujer Fuerte glass to take with you. If you buy two bottles, the tasting is free."

"We'll both do a tasting. But I don't know what we'll take home, if anything." The woman wasn't scowling, exactly, but she wasn't smiling, either.

"Everything okay?" Tessa looked at them sideways as she set up the tasting glasses and poured the first white. She'd seen enough faces across the counter that she could tell when something was up.

The man brushed his hand gently over the baby's head and glanced at his wife. "Yeah, everything's fine. We've just been having a little debate."

"His parents asked us to bring wine to dinner," the wife blurted. "They're having turkey. He insists we should bring white. But we're not just having turkey, are we? I think a white gets lost in the middle of a big holiday meal."

"She wants a red. But that feels like too much. I mean, turkey's a white meat, right? White meat. White wine. It just makes sense." He snuck another glance at his wife. "Honestly though, honey. I don't want to fight about it anymore."

"We're not fighting, David. I just don't want to mess this up. You know how your mother is."

About half the people Tessa served that day were stocking up for the holidays. She had broken up more than a few of these arguments. "How many wineries have you visited so far today?"

"One too many."

"Three."

"And how many answers have you gotten to this question?"

"Four."

"Ouch. No wonder you're frustrated." Tessa leaned a little closer to them and smiled. "I'll let you in on a little winemaker secret. There is no right or wrong choice. Drink what you love."

The two just stared at her.

"I'm serious! My advice is, while you're tasting each of these wines—" She waved her hands over the tasting bottles. "Imagine yourselves sitting at the table, enjoying all of your favorite holiday foods."

"With my mother-in-law glaring at me."

"All the more reason to have something in your glass that makes you smile."

That made them both laugh.

"So, close your eyes and imagine the flavors. Then taste the wines. Pick the one you think will put a smile on your face. If you each have a different favorite, take them both. And if all else fails, throw in a rosé. That's my personal favorite. It goes with anything."

The wife let the corner of her mouth tick up and, for the first time since they arrived, she looked like maybe she didn't want to hurt someone. "I bet you sell a lot of wine with this strategy."

"I don't know about that. But I do help end a lot of fights."

"We weren't fighting." The wife stood on her toes and gave her husband a kiss.

Tessa poured their next taste and stepped over to say hello to the trio of first-time visitors Madison was serving. She was introducing them to the Mujer Fuerte story. Their story.

"I pretty much grew up running through grape vines. My first memory is toddling through barrels." She paused when she saw Tessa. "And here's the winemaker now. This is my mom, Tessa!"

Tessa gave a little hello wave, and Madison kept talking.

"We got our start in Marin County. It's not as famous as Napa or Sonoma, but Mom's wines consistently won gold and silver. But, then a few years ago, we needed a..." She glanced at Tessa. This part of the story was always the hardest.

The move from California to Arizona, after Tessa sold her share of the vineyard to Olivia in the divorce, was as hard on Madison as it was on her. Maybe harder. Madison had been in the middle of high school, a tough age no matter what. All the drama at home, and then being uprooted away from her friends, made it that much harder, especially because, just like always, Tessa's family was no help at all. They hadn't approved when she got pregnant. They didn't support her when she decided to raise Madison on her own. They were dumbfounded when she married Olivia. And when she got divorced, all they had to say was, "We told you so." Maybe one of these days it wouldn't feel so tender. Tessa felt thankful that, in spite of all their ups and downs, she and Madison had each other.

Plus, it was beginning to feel like they were building a *new* family, in this new place. Lace was a big part of that, even if they didn't actually see each other very often.

Tessa put a hand on Madison's shoulder and gave her an assist. "We needed a fresh start," she told their new guests. "So we moved here!"

That was all the help she needed. Madison picked up the story from there. "Yep. And we love it. We especially love making wine in Arizona. The high desert is a great place to grow old-world grapes. The climate, the elevation, the soil. It all works. But, in some ways, because this is like the Wild West of winemaking, we have a lot of freedom to try new things. We're growing varietals here that you just don't see many other places in the country, and we're making blends that are surprising everyone, not the least of which because they are delicious. And my mom is starting to rack up awards all over again!"

Madison could bring these wines to life for their customers almost as well as Tessa could, and she often sold more bottles. Today was no exception. Tessa was thankful. Each day felt precious as she watched Madison begin to spread her wings.

Thanks to Madison's command of the tasting area, Tessa was able to clock out from behind the counter early. She called Bleu and headed into the vineyard for one final walk-through.

Days were short at this time of year, and the sun was low in the sky. It wouldn't be long before the sky was ablaze in tangerine, eggplant, magenta, and sunflower yellow. Tessa had never understood the line about purple mountains majesty until she moved to Arizona and found herself surrounded by the Patagonias, the Santa Ritas, and the Mules. Majestic was no exaggeration. It all seemed a little lost on Bleu. She kept her nose to the ground and her ears alert, keeping watch for predators. But it wasn't lost on Tessa.

Dried leaves crunched beneath her boots as she and Bleu walked up one row and then down the next. She looked for any sign of distress or disease and made mental notes about where more pruning was needed. Tessa couldn't imagine any other kind of life. It was good hard work, spent mostly outdoors, soaking up the sun and breathing fresh air. But they were long days. After about an hour in the vineyard, she headed up to the wine barn. Madison had already cleaned up the tasting area and gone home. But Tessa wanted to spend some time with the wines before calling it a day.

Even during the slower seasons, there were always things that needed to be done. The crew had been racking, filtering, and bottling whites and rosés that week, but late on a Sunday afternoon, the barn was empty. She puttered around, checking their work and tasting the reds. They needed much more time in barrel before they were ready. She made notes about which varietals she thought she would want to blend.

And she made a decision about her next experiment—she always had one going. Most of the time, she experimented with some unlikely blend, two or three grapes that no one would think of putting together. Sometimes they worked and ended up in bottles. She was always disappointed when they didn't. Tessa was driven to be the best at whatever she did, and never quite felt like she measured up, no matter how many blue ribbons she won. She no doubt had her family to thank for that. They questioned every decision she ever made, never once acknowledged her successes, and never stepped in to help when she could have used it. But Tessa was a farmer. When bad things happened, you kept going, made the best of what you had, and waited for the weather to change. Besides, she told herself, she always learned something from those experiments that went wrong.

After a few hours in the barn, Tessa was beat. She was more than ready for a good old-fashioned Western, a bowl of popcorn, a glass of her own wine, and Lace on speaker.

Her phone buzzed in her pocket. It was another text from Lace.
Still on for tonight?
Tessa laughed. She wouldn't miss it for anything.
Yep. Headed back with Bleu now.
When works? I'm just closing up shop.
8:00?
Lace responded with a thumbs up.

Tessa had been watching Westerns for as long as she could remember. One of her earliest memories was sitting next to Great-Gram, snuggled on the couch, watching one John Wayne flick after another on Sunday evening. Dad was out doing evening chores. Mom was in the kitchen, of course, cleaning up after a huge midday meal. Pot roast, over-cooked veggies, copious amounts of gravy, homemade biscuits. Tessa rushed through it, knowing that the couch, a movie, and time with Gram would be next. Gram loved the old Hollywood stars—Doris Day, Gene Autry, Henry Fonda—once upon a time she had wanted to be one.

After all those years, when Tessa grabbed the old Hudson Bay point blanket on the end of her bed, she swore she could still smell Gram's perfume.

This new Sunday evening ritual with Lace had become just as special. At first, she couldn't believe that Lace loved Westerns as much as she did. But they could swap famous, and not-so-famous, movie lines all night long.

Once she got home, Tessa moved fast to get ready. Chores. Shower. Food prep for the week. Dinner dishes in the drying rack. Bleu fed and watered. Then she padded into the bathroom to put her hair up in a scrunchy and grabbed her favorite flannel pj button-down top and new organic cotton joggers. Like most Californians, she used to think Arizona was always hot. She soon learned that, especially at that time of year, up in the mountains, there were huge swings in temperature from day to night, and the forecast was for frost.

Tessa filled the hopper in her pellet stove and hit the ignition. It was efficient, clean, and heated her little home in a few minutes. Bleu took that as her signal. She jumped on the bed, knowing that popcorn was next, and Tessa would soon be climbing in beside her.

With Bleu watching her every move, Tessa slid open the pantry—which was a ten-inch-wide pocket closet, next to the kitchen stove, which was next to the small fridge, which was next to the couch, which was next to the bed. The Airstream's efficiency made up for it being so small. She pulled vegetable oil and a bag of local popping corn out of the pantry. She made it the old-fashioned way, on the stove top, then topped it with home-churned, cultured butter from the 4-H fair. The final, not so old-fashioned addition was specialty salt, made by a local vendor using Mujer Fuerte wine.

Everything Tessa needed or wanted was basically within arm's reach. It was simple and, wherever possible, it was local. She and her ex had a sprawling, three-thousand-square-foot house, filled with every imaginable luxury. Yet it had never seemed like enough. Why had it taken so long to realize you can't build a happy life with *things*?

The final detail before she could climb into bed, click on the TV, and call Lace? Choosing a wine. That wasn't hard. In such a small space, she kept only a few of her favorite bottles. She settled on a glass of Isabelle's Blend, named for winemaking pioneer, Isabelle Simi. Isabelle was a teenager when her father became an early victim of the Great Influenza pandemic. She took over her family's Sonoma County vineyard, surviving the pandemic first, and then Prohibition. It was a well-balanced, red blend of Grenache, Mourvèdre, and Graciano, and it paid homage to an honest-to-God heroine of the wild, wild West. It was a perfect choice for Western movie night with Lace.

Her phone rang just as Tessa was tucking herself into bed. She answered on speaker mode.

"Hey! How was your day?" No matter what time of day it was, Lace always sounded like it was high noon. Upbeat and ready for anything. That voice had picked her up through the rockiest times over the past year, especially when things were so bad with Madison.

"My day was *long*. Bleu and I were up bright and early. And Madison had me hustling in the tasting area."

Lace laughed. "How many memberships did she end up selling?"

"I don't know. More than a dozen."

"That girl is fire. If you ever get tired of her, send her my way. I have a feeling she could move my merchandise just as fast."

"I have no doubt. And how *was* the toy business today?"

"Oh, you know. I'm living the dream. I spent today researching everything new in the vibrator world. Did you know every year the designers at Pantone, some company out of New Jersey, pick a *color of the year*? And everyone uses it for everything? And I do mean everything. "

Tessa laughed. "Um, yes. I do know that. My ex had the whole house repainted the new *it* color scheme every year."

"That's insane."

"Tell me about it."

Bleu wiggled up from the end of the bed to lie right beside Tessa. She was pretty sure that dog always knew when she was even thinking about her ex. Olivia had been the life of every party. Everybody liked her. Except Bleu.

"Well, apparently, you're not in the adult toy big leagues unless you're carrying vibrators in the *it* color."

"That's hysterical. I'm picturing people buying vibrators to match their new bedroom paint color, or their new, trendy-colored underwear. I guess if it blends in, there's less chance of the kids finding it when they're digging through your drawers."

"Why would kids be digging through your drawers?" Lace sounded horrified.

"Seriously? Madison was always digging through mine, usually looking for clothes or jewelry to borrow."

"Well, you do have style."

Tessa laughed. "I'm a farmer, for God's sake."

"A very stylish farmer."

Something that sounded like a train flying down the tracks burst through the phone, snapping Bleu's ears to attention.

"What in the—*Lace*!"

The noise stopped. "Oh, sorry! Didn't mean to shake that right in your ear."

"Well, it wasn't in my ear, but it was loud." Tessa laughed. "And it sure got Bleu's attention."

"Oh, hey, Bleu!" Bleu cocked her head and stared at the phone, wagging her tail-less butt. "Sorry about that, baby!"

Those two loved each other from the moment they met, and Tessa almost always let Bleu tag along on those rare occasions when she actually got to see Lace in person.

"So, do tell. What cocktail are you mixing up tonight?"

"A new one. I just found it on the website of a women-owned distillery, named after the first Black master distiller on record. Right after the Civil War, he worked for and taught Jack Daniels everything about making whiskey."

"And, let me guess, the white guy got all the credit."

"Of course—and all the money—which is why Uncle Nearest is the most famous distiller most people have never heard of." Lace was almost as serious about whiskey as Tessa was about wine. "Tonight I'm making a cocktail called Second Act. It has a popcorn garnish."

"Sounds perfect for movie night."

"My thought exactly. It's made with crème de cacao and egg whites—"

"Sounds a little fancy for someone who likes their whiskey neat."

"I can be fancy."

Tessa laughed. "No, you can't. Also, did you say egg whites? Didn't your mama tell you raw eggs can kill you?"

"No. My mom and I used to eat half the raw cookie dough before it even got into the oven."

"Well, that could explain some things."

Tessa heard Lace putting all her movie fixings together. "So, where are you going to watch from tonight?" Unlike Tessa, Lace had options.

"I'm all set up in my living room. Comfy couch. Crackling fire in the fireplace."

"Is Mrs. Owen coming to movie night again?"

"Not sure. No sign of her yet." Lace believed old Mrs. Owen, the First Lady of Owen Mansion, was still hanging around.

"Well, let's get going already! I am so excited for this." Tessa already had the movie all cued up. "The last time I saw *Calamity Jane,* I think I was about eight years old. It was with my great-grandmother. She was on the lot with Doris Day once, on the same day she was. She never met her. Didn't even see her. But Gram told that story all the time. She called it her 'brush with fame.' My parents would roll their eyes every time she talked about it."

Lace laughed. "I think I watched this movie a half dozen times before I was ten. I even dressed up as Calamity for one of Delaney's notorious Halloween parties a few years ago. But I haven't seen it in forever."

"What's your favorite scene?"

Lace thought for a minute. "I loved how bad ass Calamity was, especially when she went to the big city on her own. And how she wasn't afraid to just be herself."

"That is so good. I also love the scene where she sings 'Secret Love.' I think that might be my favorite scene from any Western— maybe any movie ever. You know who she was singing that about, right?"

"Of course I do!"

"Don't get all huffy. You didn't know what *Rubyfruit Jungle* was. I thought maybe you just didn't know your queer history."

"I didn't need a history lesson to know Calamity was in love with her best friend, Katie, even when I was a kid. I mean, they fixed up that little house together and painted their names on the front door. It was epic."

Tessa tossed a buttery piece of popcorn in the air, which Bleu caught, and then she popped one into her own mouth. "I also really love that scene when the saloon owner—what was his name— blurted out the word *gender* on stage, after *Mister* Francis Fryer performed in drag."

Lace didn't respond.

"Are you still there?"

"Yeah, sorry. I'm here." Lace's voice was soft. "I was just thinking that I was about ten when I really understood what was happening in that scene. That was the first time I ever thought about how gender maybe isn't so...static."

Tessa pictured Lace in her Chucks, a short-sleeve button-down, and that sassy pompadour, in all her masc energy, striding down the street, busting into a room, bursting with confidence, telling silly jokes, just loving life and everybody in it. It had probably taken a long time to become the Lace that Tessa knew.

"Alright, my friend. Let's get to it. Are you ready?"

"Let's do it."

One hundred and one minutes later, Tessa clicked off her TV and put down her empty glass.

The movie was even campier than Tessa remembered, even though she still teared up when Calamity sang "Secret Love." She couldn't even imagine what it would have been like for lesbians, living in fear and in secret, back in the 1950s, to see themselves on the big screen. To see themselves, portrayed by Doris Day no less, on the big screen. But the movie was problematic in other ways.

"Wow. That hasn't aged very well, has it?"

"No."

Silence hung between them.

"What the hell with the Native Americans?" Tessa's head hurt.

"It was horrifying."

"Do you remember thinking that when you watched it before?"

"When I was ten? No. I mean, I knew those actors didn't look or sound anything like the Native American kids I went to school with. I just remember thinking it was a dumb joke—like the Cavalry guys who couldn't shoot straight and the cowardly cowboys."

"It doesn't seem at all funny today."

"No, it doesn't, especially in light of everything we've just been through in Owen Station."

Living ninety minutes outside of town, and being in the middle of harvest, Tessa only heard about the events that happened at the end of last summer. Lace called it a racial reckoning and it had a huge impact on her.

Tessa scratched Bleu's ear. Glass clinked on the other end of the phone, and Tessa knew Lace was starting to clean up.

"Lace…"

"Yeah?"

"Thanks for watching with me, and for always making me think about things in a new way."

"You're welcome, Tess. I'm sorry revisiting your favorite movie tonight wasn't what either of us hoped."

Tessa gathered up her dishes. "That's okay. It's a good reminder of how far we've come, in a lot of ways."

"And how far we still have to go. I mean, let's be honest, there are a lot of neighborhoods in this country today where Calamity and Katie wouldn't feel safe painting their names on their front door."

Tessa sighed. "You're right. Not even if they used that year's *it* color."

Lace laughed. "On that note, I'm going to say good night."

After Lace signed off, Tessa cleaned the kitchen thinking about their conversation. It had been a long time since she had a friend who could make her both laugh and think. In fact, she couldn't remember ever having a friend exactly like Lace.

When she stepped outside to let Bleu have one last go, she looked up. It was a crescent moon so the stars were brilliant against the dark sky. She really did love her life. But that night she felt very far away from everyone and everything, and she remembered the night she spent out on Lace's front porch. She needed to figure out a way to have more of those. And as she padded off to the bathroom, before she climbed into bed, she realized she was humming "Secret Love."

Her phone vibrated on the nightstand just before she drifted off. It was a text from Lace.

Can't get that song out of my head.

Tessa texted back a laughing emoji.

But she couldn't, either.

CHAPTER THREE

Lace grinned as soon as she glanced over and saw the text from Tessa.

OMG! OMG! OMG!

Then dozens more hit her phone, from Knox, Hazel, Delaney, Sena, Ricki, at least six of her last girlfriends—everybody.

Lace had scraped a thin layer of ice off the windshield and run up to the post office to ship yesterday's orders before the store opened that morning. She was doing everything she could to beat holiday shipping deadlines and keep her customers happy. When she hopped back into her old Bronco, Walt was reading the news on KBIS, Owen Station's community radio station, which managed to stay alive with the help of a mostly volunteer staff. And it seemed like the whole town—including Lace—had heard him read the news at the same time.

Frisky Business had just been voted best adult toy shop in the state.

That's when her phone started jumping all over the passenger seat.

Four more texts from Tessa all said the same thing.

OMG! OMG! OMG!

Her sixth text was just emojis—fireworks, fist bumps, and those little dancing women. Lace pulled out onto the road to head back to the Owen Mansion and told her phone to call Tessa. It didn't even ring.

"Oh my God!" Tessa yelled.

Lace just started laughing.

"This is amazing, Lace! Oh my God, I'm so proud of you!"

"I'm pretty proud of myself."

"You should be!"

Lace shook her head and laughed again. It was unbelievable.

When she started Frisky Business, it was more therapy than anything else. Somehow she'd gotten into her mid-twenties before she realized she wasn't into men. Like, at all. But growing up in an Italian Catholic family, in a small town, she hadn't known much about *anything*. Plus, at exactly the moment she should have been figuring it all out, Dad went and got himself killed. And Mom had a breakdown she never recovered from. Lace spent her early teen years trying to prevent the inevitable. She became Mom's best friend, her therapist, her priest, and eventually her caretaker. Until there was no space left for Lace to think, to grow, or just to *be*.

Knox rescued her.

It was her idea to go all the way, after their senior prom. She was curious as hell. And he was crazy about her. When she told him she was pregnant, he married her instead of heading off to the university like he had planned, and got a job at the truck stop outside of town. He wouldn't even hear about anything else. Even after the miscarriage, he worked his ass off. He opened Banter & Brew, a cute little coffee shop right on Main Street. He got his real estate license. And he made sure she got a degree. It was online, and it taught her everything she needed to know about marketing. When she finally broke down and told him about the affair, well, not an affair exactly. It was more like gigantic, twenty-four hour, "I'm throwing my life away" fuckup. She had a fling with a gorgeous, blonde biker with flowing hair, a gentle touch, and a sexy-as-hell leather vest. She had come into town for the weekend. She was somebody Lace had never seen before and would never see again. It felt like a safe place to experiment.

It was anything but safe.

When Lace didn't come home that night, Knox was out of his mind worrying that she was dead in a ditch somewhere. It was

Lace's way of trying to get it out of her system, convince herself that the feelings she had been having weren't real. It didn't work—and it nearly broke Knox. It broke them both.

It was months before he could get through a conversation—with anyone—without breaking down in tears. Lace ran Banter & Brew for him, pretty much on her own, those days. She would come home and find him curled up in a ball in bed. He refused to eat. He wouldn't see or talk to anyone. She started to think maybe it was her who caused her mom's breakdown. First Mom, then Knox. She was the common denominator.

Finally, she convinced him to come with her to therapy. They saw somebody in Tucson, who they wouldn't have to worry about bumping into in the dairy aisle. It helped them understand each other—and themselves—a whole lot better.

Knox had given Lace the only emotionally safe place she could find, at a critical time in her life. Lace gave Knox somebody to take care of, somebody whose wounds were even deeper than his own.

It was so messed up. And, honestly, they were still working that shit out. But it did explain why their physical relationship had been awkward as hell. Knox was actually relieved to understand why.

He forgave her.

"You couldn't be more honest with me than you were being with yourself," he said.

God, she loved him. She still did. And that's why she could never forgive herself.

She dedicated herself to helping others find the happiness she hadn't been able to give Knox. And she never wanted anyone else to ever have to go through what they had been through.

He didn't either.

So, when Lace came up with the idea for Frisky Business—a body-positive, sex-positive, adult toy shop that focused on education for people of all orientations and identities, but especially for the queer community—Knox was all in.

"Are you going to stop laughing and say something?"

Lace realized she had forgotten Tessa was on speaker. "I'm so sorry, Tessa! I just can hardly believe it myself."

"Well, you better believe it, my friend. This is real. And this is big!"

Lace finally let it all sink in. "I had no idea there even was such a thing as a best adult toy shop in Arizona!"

"Well, it sounds like it's something the *Arizona Weekly* does at the end of every year. They run a survey or something and make a best-of list for everything. It's huge to get on that list, Lace! And, oh my God, this is going to be such a big deal for Owen Station. Did you hear Walt say no place in town has ever been on that list before! He said people in Phoenix don't even know anything out here exists."

"He's not wrong about that." Lace started laughing again.

"It is so great to hear you so happy, Lace. I swear to God! I know how hard you work to make other people happy. How you lose sleep over having the right products, what you're teaching in your workshops, whether you are reaching enough people. I know how much you give away, too, doing free sex ed for high school kids, giving away condoms and dental dams at every town festival. I know how much you care about your work and how important Frisky Business is to you."

"It means everything to me, Tessa." And it felt really good to know that Tessa knew it, too.

Lace pulled into her driveway and turned off the Bronco, but she didn't hop out. She just sat there, looking up at her house—her shop.

"I don't know if I ever told you this, Tess. Knox helped me buy this old place. After the divorce. I told you it was basically falling down, so I got it for next to nothing. He not only invested his own money in it, he invested his time and labor, and helped me fix it up. I moved into the back rooms and turned the front of the house into the shop. I think our friends all thought we were nuts."

"Well, you have to admit, opening an adult toy shop in a town the size of Owen Station might seem kind of—"

"I know, I know. But Owen Station has always been a bit unconventional. Back in the wild, wild West days, when the mines first opened, there were more bars and brothels here than anywhere west of the Mississippi. We still get lots of tourists coming to town looking to cut loose for the weekend. Some of our bars, like the Miner's Hole—you know, Ricki's Place—"

"Yes, I know Ricki *and* the Miner's Hole. I might live ninety minutes away, but I'm not a hermit."

"Right, right. I know. Ricki's place has been around for more than a hundred years. Her great-grandfather won it in a poker game."

"I know all that, Lace. Some of those places look like they haven't been cleaned in that long, too."

"Fact! The point is, Owen Station has always been kind of a wild place."

"But still, I think you were very brave to buy Owen Mansion and open Frisky Business here."

Lace thought about that for a minute. Then she pulled her keys out of the ignition, grabbed her bag from the back seat, picked up her phone, and started up the drive to the house. It was almost like having Tessa right there with her.

"I guess maybe it was. I mean, it was a pretty intense first couple of years, that's for sure. There were some months I was barely able to pay the bills. Knox helped me get through the leanest times. But then, when the virus shut everything down, I moved as fast as I could to get an online shop up, and moved most of my educational programs and support groups online. I never imagined how much that would change things, how many more people I would be able to reach."

"And now that everybody in the state knows how awesome you are, that store of yours is going to be booming!"

Lace balanced the phone on her shoulder and smiled as she stuck her keys in the door. "Don't you have some grapes to stomp or something?"

"Don't be silly. Crush happened months ago. Haven't you learned anything yet?"

"You know I'm a whiskey girl."

"Oh, I know. I also know you have a cush job. I've already put in three hours this morning, ordering replacement vines and going over the equipment to see what repairs have to be made. Let me guess, you're just getting to the store."

"Actually, smarty-pants, this is the *second* time I've been to the store today." Lace pulled open the heavy wooden front door and stepped into the shop, making the bell over the door tinkle. She put it there to let Mrs. Owen know she was coming.

"Any sign of her?" Tessa knew the drill.

Lace laughed. "Well, her favorite red dildo is bouncing around the floor again, as usual."

"I don't know how you live with ghosts." Lace thought she heard Tessa shudder through the phone.

"Not *ghosts*, plural. Just one. Old Mrs. Owen has lived here a lot longer than I have. She was the original owner, remember? I'm just thankful she lets me share the space with her." Lace picked up the dildo, turned it off, and made a mental note to charge it. It wouldn't be good to make Mrs. Owen mad.

Then Lace dropped her bag behind the counter. "As I was saying, I was in very early this morning, putting together a huge holiday shipment and taking it to the post office. Because, you know, nothing says happy New Year like new nipple clamps."

"That's what I've always said."

"Seriously, this time of year is nuts for me. I don't know what I'll do if you're right and business really does start booming."

"You'll have to break down and hire someone, that's what you'll do."

It was hard to imagine that. Employees were complicated, just like relationships. At some point there was always some kind of drama. So, in her dating life, Lace let people know right up front. She never dated anyone for more than three months. They had fun. They had sex. And they had a happy good-bye. Lace still kept in touch with most of the women she had dated. She made them feel appreciated and special and they loved that. But it never got serious. Lace had tried that once and failed. She was never doing that to anyone else, ever again.

She kept things simple at work, too. It was way easier to manage the schedule, even if it meant more limited store hours, so she could handle it all herself.

Lace moved through the store, flipping on the lights. "Not everyone has a Madison, Tessa."

"That's true. Madison's great. She's pretty much handling all of our holiday sales and shipping this year. But she's not my only employee. I couldn't do what I do without a crew."

"I don't know how you do what you do, period. I have to remind myself sometimes that you're a *farmer*, not just a winemaker."

Tessa laughed. "Yes, I'm a farmer. Where do you think all those grapes come from?"

"It's just weird, that's all."

"You're weird."

Lace laughed. "I love hanging out with you like this."

Lace held her breath. She *did* love hanging out with Tessa. But she'd never said anything like that before. It sent a tingle through her shoulders and down her back.

Was it strange to say something like that to your friend?

Lace had no idea. She'd never had a friend like Tessa before.

There were Delaney and Hazel, of course. They had each other's backs. If Lace needed something, she knew she could call them and they'd drop everything to be there for her. But they never just hung out on the phone. They didn't text each other a dozen times a day. They got together for lunch once in a while. Went to the Triple D for girls' night once a month. Celebrated birthdays and holidays together, that kind of thing. But this?

She hadn't had this kind of friend since Knox. Since *high school* Knox. She'd lay on her bed, talking to him for hours, until her mother yelled at her to get off the phone and come watch TV with her or listen to her cry. Mom hated being alone. Almost as much as Lace hated having to be her mother's mother. Knox was her refuge back then. But that was a long time ago, when she was a kid. Younger than Madison was now.

Lace was grown. Was it strange to want to spend all day on the phone? Because, literally, Lace could have. She wanted to talk to Tessa about everything and anything and nothing. She *did* love it.

But actually saying it out loud felt weird.

Tessa was so quiet, maybe it felt weird to her, too.

Lace pulled out the dust mop. She liked to run it across the floor every morning before opening. But also, pacing was what she did when she didn't know what else to do.

"Well, I should probably let you get back to your *farming*. Or whatever you're doing today."

"Yeah, I should probably go. Madison's in the winery, probably wondering what happened to me. As soon as we heard Walt say Frisky Business, we screamed, and then I grabbed my phone and went running outside to call you. Bleu thought I lost my mind." Tess laughed. "She's been following me while I've been walking up and down the rows talking."

"I'm pretty sure that dog is used to you acting strange."

"That's funny. I'm like the most boring person I know."

"Boring? What are you talking about?" Lace moved back and forth across the floor. If that dust mop had been a lawn mower, the rows would have been perfectly straight.

"Did we forget the part about me being a *farmer*? Up before the sun. Work all day. Drop into bed exhausted. Get up and do it all over again the next day. About the only thing that ever gets a farmer excited is the weather."

"What's so exciting about the weather?" Lace paused to look outside—it was another crisp, December day—she wouldn't have been surprised to see a few snowflakes. "Don't you people have a book to tell you what the weather's going to be all year? What's it called?"

"By you people do you mean farmers?" Tessa chuckled. "The book you speak of is called the *Farmer's Almanac*. My grandfather swore by it. But farmers haven't used it for decades. It makes long-range predictions across huge regions that just aren't very helpful or accurate. Lots of non-farmer people still swear by it, I guess. Kind of like the horoscope."

"Hey, I totally follow my horoscope. I read it every day."

"You know what I say about horoscopes? If you keep firing bullets, you're gonna hit something eventually."

Lace stuck the dust mop back in the closet. "I'm telling my psychic you said that."

"If she's really psychic, she'll already know I said it, right?"

Lace laughed.

It was crazy how often she laughed when she was with Tessa.

"Speaking of the paranormal, any more signs of Mrs. Owen?"

"I keep telling you, Tessa, spirits aren't *paranormal* in Owen Station, or anywhere in this part of the country. In the Southwest, they're just *normal*. Every building in this town is haunted. You get used to it. But no. No more sign of her yet."

Lace set her phone down on the counter. "Hey, I'm putting you on speaker, so I can start opening things up in here."

"No problem."

"Can you hear me?"

"Yeah, I can hear you. *Can you hear me, Mrs. Owen?*" Tessa yelled.

"Very funny."

"Okay, I should go, anyway."

"We said that ten minutes ago."

"I guess we did, didn't we."

Through the phone, Lace could hear Tessa breathing and the crunch of her boots as she walked. No wonder she looked so healthy. The girl never stopped moving.

"How are the vines looking?"

"Why, Lace Reynolds. What a beautiful thing for you to think of to ask."

"I'm teachable."

"Apparently so. The vines look great, as a matter of fact. I was just thinking about how much I love this time of year. Up here, it looks like everything is dead. Or asleep, anyway. The grapes and leaves are all gone, all you can see are the trunks and canes. But underground, the roots are soaking up nutrients, keeping the vines strong, getting ready for spring."

"I love when you talk farmer to me."

Tessa laughed. "You're ridiculous."

"I try."

"Seriously, it's beautiful out here. Cold. But beautiful. I should have brought my pruning tools. There's still a lot of work that needs to be done."

Lace was listening but she was also getting the shop ready to open. She counted the drawer and made sure there was enough cash in it to make change—for the handful of shoppers who still used cash. Then she moved around to the front of the counter to freshen up her point-of-sale products.

"Hey, Tessa."

"Yeah?"

"What do you think people would be more likely to grab as a last-minute gift, a Ride 'em Cowboy Condom Sampler Pack or the Swashbuckler—it's a mini vibrator in the form of a necklace."

"A vibrator necklace! Seriously?"

Lace stopped moving and focused on the phone on the counter, as if Tessa was actually standing right in front of her. "Yeah, *seriously*. Why? Is that too weird?"

Tessa laughed. "No! That is sexy as hell. If your honey wore that out to dinner with you, you wouldn't have to guess what she wanted for dessert. Do that one."

"Alrighty then. The Swashbuckler it is."

Knox had invested in Frisky Business, and he was always there for Lace to bounce ideas off of, if she had a big decision to make, like when she opened her online shop. But he had his own businesses to run, the coffee shop and his real estate agency. And, lately, he and Sena were working together as she bought up one old building after another, with plans to bring new women-owned high tech businesses to town. Even before Knox was so busy, though, Lace wouldn't have asked him questions about things like last-minute holiday gifts. He would have turned all red and stammered and not been very helpful. And Lace didn't have anybody else. Not even a sales or stockroom assistant. She was on her own.

"What did I ever do without you, Tessa?" Lace smiled.

"I have no idea, Lace. But I'm really hanging up now. Madison is probably cussing me out."

"Okay. Talk to you soon."

Tessa clicked off and Lace picked up her phone. There were thirteen voice messages—Hazel, Sena, two from Delaney, Ricki, Walt, who probably wanted an interview, Triple D Barb, one from a

Phoenix number she didn't recognize, and five from Knox. Lace had seen the calls all come through while she was on with Tessa. She shoved the phone into her back pocket. She'd listen to the messages later. Right now, she needed to flip that closed sign around.

The last thing she did before unlocking the door was open the tablet she used to track inventory and take payment. It was also where the online orders showed up.

In the past hour and a half, there had been one hundred and twenty-three new sales. That was one hundred and twenty-two more than she had at the same time the day before.

"Oh my God." Her stomach dropped and she suddenly felt like it was three hundred degrees in the shop. She tried to pull her phone out of her pocket, but her hand was shaking so much it was hard to grab it. Finally, she got a hold of it and herself. Mostly.

Her face unlocked the screen. She opened the messaging app, clicked on Tessa's name, and hit the dollar sign emoji ten times.

The phone rang immediately.

"Are you kidding me? So fast? What happened?" Tessa's voice was pitched higher than Lace had ever heard it.

"I've had a hundred and twenty-three orders in the past ninety minutes."

Tessa screamed. "Madison! Lace just got a hundred and twenty-three orders in the past ninety minutes!"

In the background, Lace heard Madison scream. Now they were both screaming. "Oh my God! Oh my God!"

This was not helping.

Lace took a deep breath and tried not to throw up. "Tessa, what am I going to do?"

Tessa got very quiet.

"Okay, Lace. Listen. I know you're freaking out. You probably should be. But it's going to be okay. I promise."

"I don't see how, Tessa. It's been five minutes since I looked. I'm afraid to see how many more orders there have been since then." Lace dropped her head and closed her eyes. "This could ruin me."

"I know it's scary. Growing too fast is one of the biggest problems a small business can face. Been there, done that. We had something similar happen to us in Marin County. A national wine magazine included us in a story. We thought it would be fun, bring in some new clients. Did it ever. It almost killed the business—and me. But I learned some things. I can help."

"How can you help, Tessa? I know how busy you are. You have the vineyard and the tasting room and Madison and bottling and, I don't know, all the farming stuff you do, and it's the holidays and—"

"Lace, stop. Really. Just stop. And take a deep breath."

Lace did as she was told. She breathed in through her nose. And exhaled through her mouth.

"Take another one. This time, fill your lungs. Breathe in through your mouth."

"Okay, I'm breathing." She wasn't sure she could keep breathing, but at the moment, Tessa's calm voice was enough to help her focus.

"Madison has things under control here. And her roommate James is helping out for the holidays to make a little extra money. Jeremy and the crew can handle the work that needs to be done in the vines for the next few weeks. I'm going to call my fulfillment center and tell them they just got themselves a new client. They're small and they're local, just outside of Tucson. So they can be more flexible. It's a crazy time of year, of course, but I trust them. And I give them enough business, I'm confident they'll be willing to help out, even at this time of year. As long as we can get the inventory to them, they can get your orders shipped out."

Lace couldn't even respond. She didn't know what to say. And she didn't think she could open her mouth without crying.

"Are you there, Lace?"

Lace nodded. Then she realized Tessa couldn't see her.

"Yes," she squeaked. "I'm here."

"Okay. As soon as I talk to Fred at the fulfillment center, I'm coming to you. I'll be there in ninety minutes. When I get there, we'll dive into your books and see what we've got to work with. It's a balancing act when you scale up quickly. I'll help you put together a good cash flow projection, so you don't get into trouble. In the meantime, I want you to pull sales reports for the past six months and highlight your most popular products—that's where we'll start building up your inventory. Grab the orders that have come in so far this morning. As long as you've got enough product on hand, you and I will get those out the door today. And, Lace, this is important. Are you listening?"

Lace was pacing back and forth across the floor, running her hand through her hair. She was having a hard time tracking everything Tessa was saying, but she *was* listening. In fact, Tessa's voice had become a lifeline. It was like that long pole lifeguards hung on the wall outside of public pools. Tessa was using it to make sure Lace didn't drown.

"I said, are you listening?"

Lace nodded at the phone.

"If you're nodding at me, Lace, I can't see you."

"Oh, God. I'm sorry. Yes. I'm here. I'm listening."

Tessa talked slowly and clearly. "As soon as we hang up, I want you to turn off your online store. Put a message up saying the site is temporarily offline, and give them the option of signing up for the mailing list. Thank people for visiting and tell them to check back later, or read their email for the latest updates. Do you hear me? Do this as soon as you hang up."

"Turn off the store?"

"Yes, Lace. Turn off the store. It's just temporary, until we can get a handle on this. Got it?"

"Yes."

"Can you do that?"

"Yes."

"Okay. I'll be there in ninety minutes. Try to breathe."

Tessa ended the call and Lace was alone. Except she wasn't. Tessa was coming. Tessa would help make sure everything was going to be okay.

CHAPTER FOUR

Tessa probably should have just grabbed a blanket and curled up on the couch. Lace was offering. Insisting, really. They were both bleary-eyed after poring over financial statements and inventory lists, placing orders for new stock, and making a plan to get Frisky Business through the next few weeks of what was going to be the holiday season from hell. Or heaven, depending on how you looked at it.

Tessa looked at her phone. It was three o'clock. In the morning. They had just made the online store live again. And there was nothing more they could do, at that point, to get Lace ready for what was coming next.

Tessa needed sleep. They both did.

"Thanks for offering, Lace. But I don't want to give Mrs. Owen any ideas by sleeping on her couch."

"Mrs. Owen is harmless. Besides, this is *our* couch. She's learned how to share."

Tessa never knew how much of her joking about Mrs. Owen was for real, but a little tingle went up her spine every time Lace talked about her. And she definitely did not want to find out in the middle of the night, while sleeping on Mrs. Owen's couch.

"Seriously, thanks. But I've got to get home to Bleu. I don't know why I didn't bring her with me. I was in such a hurry to get here this afternoon, I took off without even thinking about it.

Madison put her in the barn for me before she left for the night, but the poor pup will be worried sick about me."

Lace frowned. "Well, I'm worried. I am so thankful you came. I couldn't be doing this without you. But I wish you didn't live so far out of town."

"It beats living in town and driving ninety minutes back and forth to work every day."

Lace shrugged. "That's true. But Madison does it."

"She only does it four days a week, most of the year." Tessa smiled as she shoved her laptop, cords, and notebooks into her bag. "Besides, Madison's a lot younger than I am."

"All the more reason for you to crash here tonight."

Tessa laughed and stuck out her tongue. "Thanks for that. But I'll tell you what, if I don't go potty and deposit the three gallons of coffee I drank tonight, I *will* crash, somewhere out on Route 88, and that won't be pretty."

Lace's brow tightened and her mouth shrunk two sizes, but somehow she managed to squeeze out words. "Don't even joke about something like that."

Tessa's breath caught in her throat. "Oh my God, Lace. I am so sorry. I wasn't thinking."

Lace snapped around quickly, so that her back was to Tessa. After a minute, she brought her hand up to her face and seemed to wipe her eyes. Then she shook her head, cleared her throat, and turned back around.

"I'm sorry, Tessa. I guess I'm feeling a little emotional tonight."

"And tired."

"Yes, and tired. But I know you were just kidding." Lace grabbed Tessa's elbow lightly and gave it a little shake.

"Of course I was. I'm tired, too. But that's no reason to be so insensitive. Really, I am so, so sorry."

Lace's chocolate brown eyes were moist. "It's okay. Let's not talk about it right now. I don't think I can take much more tonight."

Tessa felt bad all the way home. Lace had told her about her dad's car accident the summer before she started high school, and that he didn't make it. She never said more.

It was strange to see her so overwhelmed. Lace wasn't bubbly, exactly. She was too solid—both physically and emotionally—for that. But she seemed unsinkable.

Like a buoy.

In the murky waters of Clear Lake, where Tessa had learned to fish, buoys warned you about dangers beneath the water—jagged rocks, shoals, turbulence—but you couldn't necessarily *see* what was under there.

What lay beneath Lace's buoyant personality and ready smile?

It made Tessa feel a little sick to her stomach that she had never wondered that before. She had leaned on Lace more times than she could count over the past year. But never once, until now, had Lace asked for more than advice about a new product line or what to do with kale or how to tell Delaney to stop gossiping so much. She had never asked for *help*, never let herself be so vulnerable. It was a new side to Lace. And Tessa had almost blown it.

She made an intention right then and there, flying—carefully—down Route 88, to pay more attention.

It was cold in the Airstream when Tessa finally got home. Bleu was happy to be delivered from the barn and relieved that her person was safe. She jumped up on the bed while Tessa lit the stove and got coffee ready for the morning. The sheets were warmed when Tessa climbed in.

Her phone buzzed.

Are you home yet?

Tessa closed her eyes, feeling horrible that she hadn't texted Lace to let her know. So much for being more intentional about paying attention to Lace's feelings.

Yes. Just climbed in bed. I didn't text because I didn't want to wake you.

She followed with three sad emojis, and then watched the little scrolling dots, waiting for Lace to respond. It seemed like it was taking forever. After a few minutes, they disappeared. Tessa put her phone on the nightstand and punched her pillow into shape.

Then the phone buzzed again.

I couldn't sleep until I knew you were home safe.

That was Lace. Always thinking about others.

I'm glad you let me help you tonight.

There were no thinking dots this time. Lace responded quickly.

I don't know what I would have done without you today.

Tessa looked at those words for a minute before responding.

How many times have I said that about you?

Lace was quick to answer.

A million. I'm amazing.

Tessa laughed out loud, and Bleu looked at her sleepily, one eye open and one eye closed. Tessa clicked on the little heart reaction to show Lace she agreed—she really was amazing.

Good night, Lace.

Good night, Tess.

Tessa slept hard but not nearly long enough. The sun rose late at that time of year, seven-thirty, but it still came way too early. She pulled the blanket over her head wishing she could catch at least another hour. She hadn't missed a sunrise, or time with her guitar, since the last time she was out all night. She would definitely be giving Lace crap about that later in the day.

Just as she filled her travel mug with steaming coffee, Knox's special roast, and a splash of organic milk, she heard a truck coming up the road. Madison was early, which was good because Tessa had a list of things to tell her before she left for town. Sena was expecting her at Banter & Brew at ten o'clock.

But when she stepped outside, with Bleu on her heels, it wasn't Madison pulling up. If she hadn't been so tired, she would have known it couldn't have been, because the pickup truck in front of her trailer was louder than a jet engine, and almost as big. The six-by-six monstrosity was a dually on crack, with an extended platform to allow *three* axles, twenty-inch off-road tires, a flatbed large enough for a family of four to live in, and a pair of giant rubber balls hanging off the hitch. The logo sprawled across the side of the truck—a bull, wearing a jersey with the word STUD stamped on his chest, holding a barbell in one hand and drinking a gallon of milk with the other—told her the day was going to get worse before it got better. The absolute *last* thing in the world she had the time or energy for that morning was Spencer Taurus, the notorious owner of Spencer Taurus's Udder Distribution—STUD, for short—and her neighbor.

Bleu stood at Tessa's side, ears flat, a low growl coming from deep within her chest. The heavily tinted driver's side window slid down and Spencer grinned a giant, fake smile. The sun glared off his bald, white head and his beady eyes darted down at Bleu, who growled even louder. Then he slowly turned his attention to Tessa. "Hey there, little lady. How do ya like my new wheels—all six-by-six a'them. Just picked this baby up. Cost me three hundred thousand chalupas. Whaddaya think?"

"I think it's ridiculous. And now that we have that out of the way, what do you want, Spencer?"

"Just as friendly, as ever, I see."

Tessa shrugged. "What do you expect? I'm going to throw a party for the guy who's sucking up all the groundwater in the neighborhood? I don't think so."

"Alrighty then, I'll get right to it." He shoved some papers through the window at her. "I've filed a complaint to get that outdoor playground of yours shut down."

"What playground? What are you talking about?"

He waved his hand in the direction of the tasting area. "That! There were too many people there all weekend. Cars were coming and going all day long."

"Of course there were. Cars bring people. And people buy wine. It's called business."

"Well, it's too noisy and it's bothering my cows. And the way I read the county regs, you can't just put up a tent and serve liquor outside like that."

Tessa's head shot back and she stared at the sky, trying to take it all in. She took a deep breath and glared at the small man in the big truck.

"First of all, the way *you* read the regs? Since when are you a lawyer? Second of all, your *cows*? The way you have those poor animals—thousands of them—crammed into feedlots, unable to even move. It's inhumane. You don't give a damn about them."

Spencer started to argue but Tessa held up her hand.

"Finally, what the hell do you care what I do on my property? Isn't that exactly what you said to me when I told you the stench from your operation is making my customers sick, and that mega-well you're planning to drill will dry up my well, and every well on this road?"

Spencer tried talking, but Tessa pushed her still-raised hand in his direction. "I'm not finished, Spencer. I need you to hear me say this. You can take your complaint-filing, lawsuit-threatening, well-drilling *ass* and shove these papers"—Tessa pushed the papers back through the window—"right up inside it. Now, kindly get the hell off my property."

"You have no idea who you're messing with, little lady." He revved the absurdly loud engine. "Me and the guys at the county are thick as thieves—fishing, hunting, drinking buddies. You'll be singing a different tune when they show up here, 'stead of me. Don't say I didn't warn you."

Then he made a fast U-turn and his fat tires spat gravel as he sped back down the drive.

Tessa was shaking, and not just because it was cold enough for the vines to be covered with frost. Bleu had stopped growling but hadn't left her side. She looked up at Tessa, concern in her eyes.

"It's gonna be alright, girl," she said, bending to scratch beneath Bleu's chin. But she wasn't sure it would be. Spencer was the richest guy in the county. He inherited his wealth from his daddy, who got it from his daddy, and so on. Spencer was using it to build the biggest dairy operation in the Southwest, starting right next door. He had ten thousand dairy cows, but that was just the beginning. He was buying hundreds and thousands of acres to expand his operation, an operation that would use more water in a week than Tessa would use in a year. And he was spending hundreds of thousands of dollars digging wells half a mile deep. Eventually, if he wasn't stopped, he would suck up all the groundwater in the county. And no one with the power to stop him seemed to care.

Tessa's bravado might have fooled Spencer, but it didn't fool Bleu. She licked Tessa's hand and pulled at her sleeve. "Okay, okay. Let's get going."

Tessa opened the truck so Bleu could hop in, and they headed down to the wine barn together. As always, the place was organized and clean. Her vineyard manager, Jeremy, cared almost as much about Mujer Fuerte as she did. Once he had found out she was leaving Marin County, he practically begged her to take him with her. He liked Tessa's ex—everybody did—but there was no way he was going to work for her. Olivia might have been the bankroll that got things started, and kept them going during the lean years, but she didn't know a damn thing about running a winery.

The barn was so cold Tessa could see her breath, but she zipped her jacket up to her chin, shoved her hands deep in her pockets, and stood looking around. She had spent every cent she got from the divorce settlement buying that land, a fortune's worth of equipment, and building the barn. She put a small commercial kitchen in it, so they could offer tapas and cheese boards, and designed a cozy office where she and the team could meet. But she hadn't included a tasting room in the plans. That first year, before the barn was built, she threw up a couple of sun sails at the top of the hill, overlooking the vineyard, and started tasting wines outdoors. People loved it. And then, when everyone was avoiding indoor public spaces, they loved it even more.

Fuck Spencer.

If she had to, she'd carve out part of the barn and move the tasting room indoors. She had worked too hard and invested too much to let that little weasel wreck it.

She turned the thermostat up in the office so it would be nice and warm when Madison got to work in an hour, and she chased Bleu up onto the couch. She would keep Madison company in the tasting area and, when she wasn't, she would roam the vineyard, scaring off predators.

By the time Tessa turned onto the highway, she was already thirty minutes behind schedule. She glanced over at the phone on the passenger seat. Lace hadn't texted yet. Hopefully that meant she was still sleeping. She would need rest for the days ahead.

She got her phone's attention. "Call Sena Abrigo."

Sena answered on the first ring.

"Hey! Sorry to call you. I know how much you hate talking on the phone, but I'm driving."

"I don't *hate* it. It's just so two thousand and ten."

Tessa slowed down as a road runner darted across the highway. "Two thousand ten wasn't that bad."

Sena snorted. "Wasn't it? Zuckerberg snagged *Time*'s person of the year. Space-X launched *Falcon 9*—and made sure we'd never hear the end of Elon. Could it have been a *worse* year?"

Tessa sped back up. "Does Hazel think you're sexy when you whisper tech-talk in her ear?"

"I don't kiss and tell."

Tessa smiled. Sena had wandered into Mujer Fuerte the summer before, on a particularly bumpy day for her, and a slower one for Tessa. They worked their way through a tasting, and then Tessa shared a bottle from her first winery—the vintage that had put her on the winemaking map—and her story. It was an unusual move. Tessa didn't typically get so personal with customers, especially ones she just met. But there was something about Sena that day. It was clear that she was a force to be reckoned with. She had a plan to turn Owen Station into a tech mecca for women. And she had the means to make it happen. But she also seemed so isolated, lonely even. Vulnerable. Tessa invited her out to the Triple D one night—the night she and Lace stayed up talking until sunrise—and they stayed in touch. Later, after she and Hazel got together, Sena thanked Tessa for changing her life. That seemed a little dramatic. It was just a bottle of wine and a conversation.

Then again, the right conversation at the right time with the right person could make a big difference. Like that night Madison said she was leaving, when Tessa realized that, of all the people in the world she could think of to talk to, there was no one she wanted to be talking to more than Lace.

Tessa stretched her neck back and forth, trying to get a kink out. She really needed more sleep. "Speaking of annoying rich guys, I'm going to be late to our meeting," she said as she grabbed for her travel mug full of coffee.

Sena sighed. "I figured—even if I totally don't understand what that means. What do rich white guys have to do with your being late? Everything okay?"

"Yeah, I guess. I just had a visit from my asshole neighbor."

"Stud?"

Tessa almost spit coffee out of her mouth laughing. "Oh my God, please don't call him that. That's exactly what he would want."

"Okay, well, what's the little weanie's name, again?"

"Spencer." Tessa spat it out.

"What hornet's nest is he whacking this time?"

"I'll tell you about it later. I'll be about thirty minutes late."

"Got the whole morning blocked out for you. I'll see you when you get here."

Tessa took another swig of coffee. She had had this meeting on her calendar for weeks. Sena had asked for it. She had recruited a couple of new tech start-ups to town. Sena called them early adopters. And she thought Tessa could help them get off the ground. Tessa objected at first—what did she know about technology? But Sena said they didn't need help with technology. They needed help with *business*.

Tessa could do that.

Suddenly, the phone started quacking next to her and she just about jumped out of her seat. "What the *hell*?" Lace's picture was on the screen. And the phone kept quacking.

Tessa answered. "Did *you* do that?"

"Do *whaaat*?" Lace sounded like she was trying too hard to sound innocent.

"Make my phone quack when I get a call?" It sounded so ridiculous when she said it, she started to laugh. "How'd you even know my passcode?"

"Madison's birthday? That was an easy guess."

"You *did* do it!" Tessa smacked the steering wheel. "Last night when I couldn't find my phone for a minute."

Lace laughed. "You shouldn't leave it lying around where just any old, exhausted, overwhelmed business owner with a junior high sense of humor can find it."

Lace was just the medicine Tessa needed after a night that was way too short and a morning that started with Spencer STUD Taurus. "You're a piece of work, Lace Reynolds. And, just what I needed. It's been a helluva day."

"It's not even ten thirty."

"Exactly." Tessa scowled.

"Want to talk about it?"

"Not really. You talk, instead. How are things at Frisky Business this morning?"

"Fantastic! I got a great night's sleep. More than two hundred new people have signed up for my newsletter. And another fifty-plus orders have come in since we flipped the website back on last night."

"This *morning*. We flipped it back on at three o'clock *this morning*." Tessa was feeling it in her bones.

"Right! I know. I've already talked to Fred at the distribution center, got confirmation from my vendors on the orders we put in last night, and I feel ready to take on the holidays!"

"I am so glad, Lace. You're gonna kill it. Just one more thing to do, though. Hire some part-time help to make sure you've got coverage in the store for extended holiday hours."

Lace groaned. "I was hoping you forgot about that part of the plan."

Tessa rolled her eyes. "I did not. You shouldn't, either."

Lace didn't respond.

"I'm on the edge of town and just about to go through the tunnel, so I'm going to lose my signal. You know, I'm meeting Sena at Banter & Brew this morning. I'll call you later." Tessa paused. "Put a job description together and call Walt. Get that ad on the radio asap."

"Aye aye, Captain."

It was ten thirty-eight when Tessa walked into Banter & Brew. She was running on three hours of sleep and it had already been a full morning. She hoped the rich aroma of Knox's freshly roasted coffee and the usual cacophony of voices would be enough to perk her up. A couple of customers she recognized from the tasting room waved at her. And Jorge and Miguel, the guys who owned the new tequila tasting room next door to Banter & Brew, were just leaving. They fist-bumped her and told her to stop in before she left town. People in the industry were a tight-knit group wherever in the world you happened to be.

Sena was in her usual spot at the counter, talking to Knox—Lace's ex—while he dried glasses. When Sena saw Tessa, she jumped up and gave her a hug. Knox smiled broadly from behind the counter. "Would you two like a table? Might be easier to spread out."

Tessa didn't know Knox particularly well, but Sena absolutely loved him. He wasn't just everybody's favorite barista, he was the town's best real estate agent. He was helping Sena make the real estate deals she needed, at the pace she wanted, and helping her navigate all the politics. From the sound of it, that was no small feat. Sena liked him so much, they had gone into business together. They bought the building that housed Banter & Brew and planned to turn the whole block into an incubator for small, local businesses like the tequila room. What was there not to like?

But it was a little hard to imagine Knox and Lace together. He was, well, he was a *he*.

After they were seated, Knox asked, "What'll you have, Tessa? Can I get you something?"

"Any specials this morning that I don't want to miss?" Tessa hadn't taken time to eat breakfast.

Sena butted in before Knox even had a chance to respond. "Order the biscuits and gravy. Knox just got fresh sausage in from a ranch east of town. And have some eggs. They're local and he's getting them from the new co-op. I have no idea what those chickens are being fed, but their yolks make the inside of a Cadbury egg—did you have those in your Easter basket as a kid?—look pale in comparison."

Tessa just stared at her. Then both she and Knox started laughing.

"If this real estate business thing doesn't work out for you, Sena, you should have Knox hire you as his marketing director."

Tessa ordered it all, plus a chiltepin cold brew—something new on the menu. Knox was grinding the little red peppers himself. Sena confessed it was her influence, a recipe inspired by her family. She was creating all kinds of changes at Banter & Brew, and throughout Owen Station. Sena was the force behind bringing the Fertile Ground food co-op to town, and that was creating steady demand for local, organic products. She was encouraging Tessa to offer a few of her larger production wines at the co-op, as well. When Sena was involved, things happened.

"Okay, let's get to it. As you know, I've been working with a few new tech start-ups, young innovators who want to locate here in Owen Station, and the concepts are great. The problem is the business side of things."

"I get it. It's like those engineers I bought the vineyard from. They thought they could become the next Madame Clicquot just by wishing it."

"Exactly." Sena smiled. "Of course you would use the namesake of my favorite Mujer Fuerte wine as an example."

"The *Grand Dame of Champagne*—"

"—and one of the most famous French businesswomen of the nineteenth century." Sena finished Tessa's sentence—which was emblazoned on every bottle of Clicquot—with a flourish.

Tessa sat back in her chair. "I love how much of a cheerleader you are for local businesses in town, Sena. Including mine."

Sena tilted her head and furrowed her brows. "You sound so serious all of a sudden."

"I am serious. You're doing this amazing thing on the other side of town. Turning abandoned buildings into a tech park." Tessa spoke more softly so she wouldn't be overheard. "You have the resources to do anything you want here. You could line the streets with big name retail stores and famous franchises."

Sena shuddered. "I wouldn't even think of it."

"That's what I'm saying. Instead, you're helping build an infrastructure to support local business owners like Knox, and me, and others like us." Tessa paused. "Thank you."

Sena looked at a loss for words. That didn't happen often.

Tessa laughed. "So, alright then. How can I help?"

"Well, for starters, Hazel is launching a series of classes at the library right after the first of the year. I'd like to get one started to help first-time entrepreneurs learn the basics. How to navigate state agencies, get set up with the IRS, access funding. Things like that. You've been through all these things. You could teach it."

"Sounds simple enough, and mid-winter, when the vines are asleep, is a great time for me to start something like that. What else?" Knox dropped off Tessa's breakfast, and she dug in.

"A small business series, with progressively more complex topics bringing in guest speakers, experts on marketing, finance, operations, supply chain, all of it. You could organize and facilitate it."

"Okay, that's sounding a little more involved." Tessa smiled and took another bite of biscuit. Sena wasn't kidding—the food was mind-blowing. So was Sena. The ideas just kept rolling. Tessa missed half of them.

"Maybe we could partner with the community college to create a small business certificate. That way, these entrepreneurs would make connections beyond just you and me."

"This all sounds really powerful, Sena. Not just for newcomers, either. I bet there are people right here in town who have had dreams their whole lives, but never had the support to make it happen."

"Exactly! I knew you would get it."

Tessa wiped her plate clean while Sena dreamt out loud. Lace was texting dollar signs about every five minutes. Knox brought her another cold brew. And Ricki, another friend in the industry, stopped by. She looked fabulous in her well-worn cowboy boots, boot-cut jeans, and crisp white shirt. Back in the day, Ricki did the rodeo circuit as a barrel racer. Her great-grandfather was the first African American inducted into the Rodeo Hall of Fame, a fact she loved to share with anyone who would listen. He won the bar after he retired from the circuit. Ricki didn't compete anymore. Said she was too old for that nonsense. Instead, she spent mornings fueling up on Knox's coffee, and evenings behind the bar. The only person who knew more about what was happening in Owen Station was Delaney, although that depended on the time of day.

"Mornin', ladies! I just love seeing powerful women at work. It's about time we take over. Men have done nothing but make a big mess outta things." Ricki grinned and crossed her arms over her chest. "I said what I said."

Tessa thought about Spencer, those poor cows, his aquifer-killing wells, the balls hanging from the back of his truck. "You're not wrong, my friend."

"So, what mess are you ladies fixing today?"

Sena flexed her arms in front of her. "You know me. I'm working my ass off to make this town a place where people who look like *us* have a shot at success, and the opportunity to create real change. Technology could solve most of the biggest problems in the world. But the white guys in Silicon Valley are more interested in making a buck than making a difference."

Tessa sat up a little straighter and looked around to see who else might be hearing this. She felt more powerful just sitting at that table.

"I've got a dozen women-led tech start-ups pitching me on their ideas, looking for investors, thinking about locating here. Tessa is going to help them understand how to actually start and run their businesses, so their solutions see the light of day."

"Sis, I knew you were good trouble." Ricki slapped Sena on the back. "Carry on, you two!"

Tessa spent another hour making plans with Sena, and then headed over to Frisky Business to give Lace a hand with the orders that needed to be shipped out that day. As she drove back to her vineyard that evening, she realized she never did talk to Sena about her encounter with Spencer. It all seemed so insignificant in the context of everything that was happening in her friends' lives and her own. Anything and everything seemed possible. And her universe just kept expanding. Arizona really was starting to feel like home.

The sun was setting and dried grasses, sandy soil, and leafless mesquite trees whipped by as she flew down Route 88. The brown landscape made everything around her look dead. But, inside, she was feeling more alive than ever.

Her phone started quacking on the seat beside her, which made her laugh. Lace had a way of doing that to her.

She didn't plan to change that ridiculous ring tone anytime soon.

Chapter Five

G o get frisky!" Lace gave a little wave and a couple dozen smiling people on her laptop screen waved back. That's how she had been ending every workshop in the new year.

Most of Lace's educational programs had been online since the pandemic. But that "best of" award right before the holidays changed everything. It wasn't unusual to have as many as sixty people online with her now.

At the start of each workshop, Lace asked everyone to read the group agreements, a simple set of guidelines to make sure everyone felt welcome and safe. She invited people to be on or off video, whichever they preferred, and encouraged them to include preferred pronouns next to their name, if they were comfortable doing that.

At the end, she always stayed on until every last participant signed off, just in case someone had a question. After forty-four squares blinked off one-by-one, Bri (he/him) remained. His camera had been turned off during the workshop, but his face suddenly appeared.

"Hi, Bri. Thanks for coming to the workshop. Do you have a question?"

Bri smiled softly. "No, not exactly. I just wanted to thank you. I really appreciated the way you used trans inclusive language tonight."

Lace nodded and waited, giving Bri space to share.

"I've had so many bad experiences, where I've been in a shop looking for things that fit my body, but they're called *women's* products in most places. It's triggering, and painful."

Bri dropped his eyes and his pain shot right through Lace's heart. She had heard so many stories, from so many people, and seen so much hurt.

"I'm really sorry you've had that experience, Bri. The human sexuality space has a long history of both racism and harm to the queer community. This industry is changing, but it's a slow process. Too slow. I'm sorry for the pain that has caused you."

Bri looked back at Lace with a lopsided smile. "Well, it was really good to feel included tonight."

Lace took a deep breath as she clicked her laptop closed. It was such a privilege to be even a tiny part of helping people heal from whatever trauma they had experienced. Emphasis on *tiny*. Controversy swirled throughout the industry, as it had done for decades, as the journey to liberation for all bodies continued. She was painfully aware of her own privilege and, if there was anything she knew for certain, it was that she still had so much to learn. That was the main reason she started leading a workshop called *Sex Changes Everything*, on the interrelated history of sex education and social change movements. It was an opportunity for her to learn.

But her most popular workshop, by far, was the one she just finished. *Sex Toys 101* attracted the most age-diverse groups. Her oldest participant so far had been almost ninety. There were always so many newbies. And so many questions. Can you get addicted to your vibrator? What's the point of a cock ring? How can I feel less self-conscious when using toys? In these post-holiday workshops, inevitably someone held up a toy they'd been given as a gift and asked, "How in the hell am I supposed to use *this*?" There was always a lot of laughter.

Her phone buzzed just as she flipped off the main lights to close up the store for the night. Lace knew it was a text from Tessa even before she looked.

How'd it go, birthday girl?

Lace smiled as she responded. *It was so great. Fun group. And my birthday's not till tomorrow.*

I know! But I'm looking forward to celebrating with you tonight. Me too! See you at 8.

Tessa responded with a thumbs up, birthday cake, whiskey tumbler, and three ghosts.

When Tessa asked what she wanted for her birthday, Lace didn't even have to think about it. She was an Aquarius. When she wasn't working to make the world a better place, by helping people know and love their bodies, she wanted to be outdoors and, all the better if it was with a close friend. Lace had been trying to get Tessa to come with her to visit one of her favorite spots on the planet for months. How could Tessa say no?

Lace had to hustle to close the shop and get there early to set up before Tessa arrived. She packed up her Bronco and headed out of town on Old Route 88. The winding, two-lane road hugged the side of a mountain. It used to be the only way in and out of town until a tunnel was built on New Route 88 to go through the mountain. Some old-timers still preferred the mountain road. They said it was bad luck to blast through the mountain like that, that one day the mountain would have payback. Never mind that the tunnel had been working fine for sixty years. The whole debate was silly. But Lace actually did like driving the mountain road once in a while. The view of the town below, especially all lit up at night, was breathtaking. Plus, it was the only way to get to Mule Pass Cemetery, Owen Station's very own Boot Hill.

She pulled up right in front of the gate. Bud had left the padlock open, just like he said he would. He knew she'd lock up when she was done, like always. She left the Bronco lights on while she unloaded and got set up, but the soft solar lamps inside the gates and the full moon actually gave plenty of light.

The first couple of things she pulled out of the back of her Bronco were two camp chairs, which she slung over her shoulder, and a portable smokeless fire pit. It was a little warmer than a typical night in early February, but cool enough that a small campfire would help keep them toasty. She carried them through the gates of the old cemetery and set them down in her usual spot, a patch of dirt not far from the mesquite tree that guarded the graves of four Buffalo soldiers. They had been part of an African American regiment out of Fort Huachuca, who helped protect stagecoaches and the earliest

Owenites from attack. After she grabbed the rest of her stuff, she started working on the fire.

Tessa pulled up just as the blaze got going. She came through the gate carrying a small glass baking pan, wearing jeans, of course, midform, lace-up boots, and a gray sweater. Her mid-length puffy coat was unzipped. And instead of her usual Mujer Fuerte trucker cap, Tessa was wearing a knitted beanie with a ball on top. She looked ready for an outdoor adventure. And she was beaming.

"That drive is spectacular! Also, happy day-before-your birthday." She put the pan down on the little table Lace had set up between the chairs and gave Lace a quick hug.

The light from the fire gave Tessa a warm glow. That, and the birthday cake she had carried in, made Lace feel all warm inside, too. "Yes, it is spectacular. Also, thank you. Is this the whiskey-glazed sponge cake you've been telling me about?"

"It is." Tessa stood a little taller, clearly proud of her creation. "But, actually it's a chiffon cake, which is a type of sponge cake, except way better. It's basically the California state cake. We invented it."

"You invented it? Like, you and your family or something?"

Tessa shook her head. "I mean *Californians*."

"*All* Californians? Like, everyone in California pitched in and made the recipe?"

Tessa zipped up her coat, shoved her hands in the deep pockets, and shook her head, laughing. "Lace Reynolds. You are ridiculous. No, not *all* Californians. Some guy from California. I think he was an insurance salesman or something. I don't remember the details. Anyway, this is my mother's recipe, which she got from *her* mother. The whiskey glaze is something I added just for you."

Lace put her hands to her chest and gave a half-bow. "I am deeply honored."

Tessa punched her softly in the shoulder. "You should be. I don't bake very often. And I never mess with the recipe." Her voice dropped to a whisper. "Don't tell my mother."

Lace crossed her heart. "You have my word."

Tessa nodded and then looked around for the first time, her smile slowly fading. It was insane how quickly the silence of the old graveyard enveloped them, once they stopped talking. Tessa's eyes grew wider as they bounced from headstone to headstone, and she put her arms around herself, as if chasing off a chill. "I've been pumping myself up for this all day, but I'm still not sure I'm ready for it."

Lace grinned at her. "It's safe, I promise. There's not a living soul within fifteen miles of here."

Tessa turned her eyes back to Lace. "It's not the *living* souls I'm worried about." She shivered and held herself even tighter.

Lace put an arm around her shoulders and gave her a squeeze. "I've never seen any ghosts out here, either."

"Well, that's a little comforting, I guess." Tessa sounded skeptical.

Lace took her by the elbow. "Come on, let me give you the tour."

"The t-t-tour?" Tessa moved closer to Lace and leaned up against her shoulder. "You mean, you want me to walk around with you?"

Lace laughed. "You're killing me, Tess." But a shiver shook Tessa so hard Lace could feel it, and Lace took a step back so she could look her in the eyes. "Tessa, are you really scared? You're like the bravest person I know."

Tessa tilted her head and looked at Lace sideways. "Am I, though?"

"Yes. You are. You moved to Arizona with a sixteen-year-old kid and started Mujer Fuerte on your own. You live ninety minutes outside of town, in the middle of nowhere, in that Airstream, alone on that vineyard, with just Bleu for company and protection. You're fearless."

Tessa shrugged and started to say something, but Lace kept going.

"But out here, where nothing or nobody could hurt you—"Lace reached out and held Tessa's elbows. "You're *shaking*."

Tessa laughed nervously. "Well, it *is* cold."

"It's not that cold."

Tessa dropped her eyes. "And I'm not as fearless as you think."

Now, what was she supposed to do with that? Tessa never seemed afraid of anything. Hurt, yes. Like when Madison left. Angry, yes. Like every single time she had a run-in with Mr. STUD. A little insecure, yes. Which hardly ever happened and was always surprising when it did. But afraid? This was new. And unsettling.

Clearly, the last place on earth Tessa wanted to be was in an old graveyard, under a full moon, in the middle of the night. And yet, there she was. Because it was Lace's birthday weekend, and that's where Lace asked her to be.

Because Lace asked.

A lock of light brown hair, which had fallen out from under that silly hat, hung down onto Tessa's cheek. Instinctively, Lace reached up and brushed it back behind her ear. When Lace's fingers touched her cheek, Tessa's head snapped up, and suddenly Lace couldn't see anything except Tessa's eyes, which were a swirl of greens and blues. Hazel. That's probably what they were called. Hazel. Not like her friend, Hazel. Hazel, the color.

Lace lost track of where she was for a minute.

Tessa reached down for the hand that was holding her elbow—Lace's hand—and gave it back to her. That woke Lace up real quick. This was Tessa. Not a three-month girlfriend. Not a date. This was *Tessa,* her movie buddy, business brainstorm partner, the person who made her laugh at herself, the one who was always on the other end of the phone, who used way too many emojis.

Her best friend.

Whoa.

Tessa was her *best friend.*

That was a new thought.

When had that happened?

Lace took a step back, laughing uncertainly. Whatever it was she just experienced was, well, it was nothing.

Tessa was her friend.

And that was the something that mattered most of all.

"I'm going to get you a blanket."

She grabbed one from the pile she had brought from home and held it out for Tessa to take. "Put this around your shoulders. I want to show you something."

Tessa obediently wrapped the blanket around her and reached out to grab Lace's elbow. "Okay. I'm ready. But I'm not letting go."

Lace laughed and patted Tessa's hand. "I got you."

She led Tessa around the small graveyard, pointing out the different sections. Each had its own unique character. There was a Jewish section, a Chinese section, a Mormon section. A monument in the center of the yard honored the twelve miners who lost their lives in the 1912 explosion.

"How old is this place, anyway?" Tessa was still holding on tight.

"It dates back to 1873, same as Owen Station. It was the town's only cemetery for about forty years. They built a new one right in town in 1917, just before the flu epidemic that broke out the next year—and that's actually what I want to show you."

Lace pointed out two small stone monuments, each with a pile of rocks marking the burial sites. One said "Elizabeth Owen 1893–1918" and the other said "Madam Trouble ?–1918."

"Is this *your* Mrs. Owen?" Tessa whispered.

Lace nodded. "And look at the date!"

"She was buried here *after* the new cemetery opened?"

"Yes. Her husband died ten years later. He's buried in town."

Tessa crossed her arms. "What the hell?"

"It's weird, right? And who is 'Madam Trouble'? It's a big mystery!"

"This is not making this place less creepy."

"Okay, sorry! Let's go over here." Lace steered her toward the far back corner. "This is the oldest section—my personal favorite—and the reason they call this Boot Hill. Owen Station was the wild, wild West back then. Life was hard and, for the most part, short. Most people died quickly—with their boots on." She used a small flashlight to illuminate the old stone slabs and waited for Tessa's reaction.

"Are these for real?"

"Yes, they're for real."

"But they're so…silly."

"They're not silly. Some of them just say 'Unknown.' There were a lot of people coming and going back then, and it's not like people carried driver's licenses. The other ones are, well, they're just straightforward." Lace read, "Sam Brown. Shot dead in the center of town. 1852–1878."

Tessa laughed. "That is, too, silly. They're like morbid poems." She read another one. "Here lies Ernest Flake. He made a big mistake."

Lace sort of laugh-snorted. It did sound silly when Tessa read it. She kept going, too.

"Billy 'Cap' Light—Lost his last fight.

"Outlaw John Moore—Robbed his last store—Four slugs from a forty-four.

"Harry King couldn't sing—He weren't no angel. Legally hanged 1879."

"Oh my God, stop." Lace was laughing. "That's not even funny. It's horrible!"

But Tessa was on a roll.

"Poor Roger McGraw—Quick on the trigger, slow on the draw.

"It was a cough that carried her off—That was the end of Elizabeth Moss.

"Here lies Lucas Yeast—Pardon me for not rising."

Lace's stomach hurt and she had to wipe her eyes to see because she was laugh-crying so hard. "Stop! Please stop!"

Tessa turned to look at her. "What was *wrong* with these people?" She looked so confused, it just made Lace laugh harder.

Instead of answering the question, Lace took Tessa by the shoulder, turned her around, and led her back to the fire. She was still laughing as she put a blanket on Tessa's lap, put another piece of wood on, and took her seat in the other camp chair.

"Oh my God." She was still trying to catch her breath. "I haven't laughed that hard in a long time."

Tessa looked amused but still confused. "Seriously, Lace. What the hell? I've never seen anything like this before. Are those tombstones really for real?"

"A hundred percent." Lace had finally pulled herself together. "Some of them are the original stones. Others have been erected to replace wooden ones that had decayed. But they've all been historically verified. There's a group in town that oversees it all."

"Hazel—our friendly neighborhood librarian—is part of that, I'm sure."

"Of course." Lace smiled. Hazel was the town's informal historian, too. "And Caretaker Bud manages the grounds."

"I just don't understand the humor. Oh, and that's another thing. *Caretaker* Bud. What is that?"

"What do you mean?"

"Why don't you just call him Bud?"

"Because then we wouldn't know whether you were talking about him or Groundskeeper Bud, who takes care of the schools. It's like Plumber Joe and Electrician Joe. It's a way to keep them straight."

"What are you, Dildo Lace? When you need a new driveway, do you call Concrete Dick?"

A laugh shot up out of Lace's gut and she almost wet her pants. "Oh my God, Tessa. Stop it! No! First of all, I'm the *only* Lace in town. And the concrete guy is Harry."

Tessa lost it. And it took her a second to catch on, but then Lace did, too. They laughed until tears streamed down their faces.

Finally, when she caught her breath, Tessa shook her head. "This is all so weird, Lace. This town. This *cemetery*. I mean, who writes *jokes* on headstones?"

"It's gallows humor, I guess. It's what helped people back then deal with it all." Lace paused, trying to remember all the stories she'd been told. "You could get shot just for looking at the wrong person the wrong way, or because someone thought you were cheating at the poker table, or because you fell for somebody else's girl. And there weren't many consequences—not legal ones, anyway. You had to do something really terrible for the law to get involved."

"Something 'really' terrible? You mean more terrible than shooting somebody because they fell in love with the wrong girl?"

Lace shrugged. "Yeah, I guess. Like robbing a bank or a stagecoach."

Tessa clicked her tongue. "In other words, doing something that hurt the rich and powerful."

"Exactly."

Tessa shook her head and tucked the blanket tighter around her. "I mean, it's not like things are totally different now—people like Spencer still seem to get their way. But I am glad I wasn't around back then."

"I don't know." Lace grinned and shifted in her chair to look at Tessa. "I can see you as Calamity Jane. All rough-and-tumble, riding hard, fighting hard, holding your own." The firelight danced across Tessa's cheek, until Tessa turned to look at her, and then the light started dancing in those eyes, too.

"No, no, no. I think *you* would definitely be Calamity, Lace. You already have the costume for it, right?" Tessa's face was soft except for the little smile lines that started at her eyes. "I can just see you, tough but tender. Smarter than all the men in town, and funny as hell. Living life the way you want to live it. Swaggering through town, dazzling all the ladies."

Lace did not know what was happening. She quickly looked around to see if maybe Tessa was talking to somebody else, but when she glanced back, Tessa was still looking at her. Tessa looked fine. Normal. But Lace could hear her own heart beating. She had to say something before Tessa wondered what the hell was wrong with her. She managed to sniff out a laugh, and a jokey voice.

"Why, thank you kindly, ma'am. I bet you say that to all the—"

"Nope," Tessa inserted matter-of-factly. "Just you." She patted Lace on the arm and shot her a big smile. Then she shifted back toward the graveyard.

Lace exhaled. Then she slowly sat back in her chair, feeling like she just missed getting run over by a squadron of javelinas. Tessa seemed fine, so Lace could be fine, too.

"So what is it you like about coming up here, anyway? I mean, I get why you think this place is interesting."

"And funny," Lace added. "Now I think it's funny."

Tessa laughed. "You're welcome. But why do you come up here at night? It might be funny, but it's also spooky as hell."

Whatever it was that seemed to happen a minute ago, and Lace didn't really want to think about it, vanished. She was just hanging out with her frie—her *best* friend, again. Something that had become her very favorite thing to do.

"That's a fair question." Lace paused. "The easiest answer is—I need to show you." She stood up and reached for Tessa's hand, then she turned her back on the cemetery. Tessa followed. Out, beyond the gates, the lights of Owen Station twinkled below them. "This is the best view in the state," Lace said in a whisper. "Maybe in the world."

Tessa squeezed her hand and took in a deep breath. When she exhaled, Lace felt Tessa's whole body relax.

"Do that again."

Tessa took another deep breath, held it for a few seconds, and then let it go.

"Feel better?"

Tessa nodded. "I'm getting there."

"Okay, now turn around again."

Lace let go of Tessa's hand and they both turned. Now the cemetery was in front of them. Tessa tensed beside her. "No, don't look out. Look up." After a few seconds, Lace said, "Keep looking. Let your eyes adjust."

A minute later, Tessa moaned. "Oh my God."

The clear sky wasn't just sparkling with surface stars, the ones it was easy to see once you got out beyond the edge of town. There were layers of stars, endless layers, deep enough to get lost in, trillions of them, each one thousands of years old. The Milky Way was long and rich, and poured across the sky like a whiskey glaze.

"Those must be planets, right?" Tessa pointed to the two brightest points of light above them. "Jupiter—"

"And Venus. Yep. Give them a few weeks and they'll practically be touching each other. Mars is over there, on the horizon."

Lace sat down and Tessa lowered herself into her camp chair slowly, her head still tilted back. "I thought the night sky was incredible at the vineyard," she said softly. "But, wow. And there's a full moon, too!"

"Well, we're like three thousand feet higher than the vineyard. I think there's something about the air up here. And it's a *micro* moon," Lace explained.

"A *what* now?"

"A micro moon. There's always one right around my birthday, which is why I always come up here to celebrate it." She waved her arms out toward the graveyard. "There's enough light to see things, but not so much that you can't see the stars."

Tessa kept her head back but tilted it toward Lace, so she looked a little like an adorable bobblehead version of herself. "I still don't get it. What's a micro moon? It doesn't get smaller, does it?"

Lace laughed and flicked the ball dangling from Tessa's hat. "Of course not. It just looks small because it's as far away from the earth as it can get and still be within our orbit. Kind of like you."

Tessa sat up and shifted in her chair so she was looking at Lace, her head cocked sideways, a crooked smile on her face. "What does that mean?"

What *did* that mean? The words just sort of popped out.

A jumble of images and thoughts from their last year and a half together whirled through Lace's brain. But the one that stuck was that first day, when Tessa wandered into Frisky Business, so serious about finding the right gift for Madison. Loose, long brown hair. Jeans that hugged her mama hips. A flowy, white linen button-down highlighting a rugged tan. Layered silver necklaces. Well-worn boots. Smart. Composed. A good sense of humor. But no-nonsense. Layered, like those necklaces. Like the stars.

This wasn't the kind of woman Lace would ever, in a million years, have had a three-month relationship with, even if she hadn't been a customer. It never even occurred to her to *date* Tessa.

Okay, maybe she thought about it for a very hot minute that first September afternoon.

But then they started talking.

And they hadn't stopped since.

Lace knew what Tessa ate for breakfast, and that she loved thunderstorms, balloons, and bleu cheese. Well, that one was easy.

She knew that her ex-wife had an affair and broke her heart, but that Tessa never blamed her for it. She blamed herself for being such a workaholic and not paying enough attention to her family. Lace knew that Tessa called her mother and talked to her for thirty minutes on the tenth of every month, because her dad had died on the tenth of April, but that she hadn't been back to the farm, except for the funeral, since she married Olivia. Her family didn't understand. Her town didn't understand. Why put herself—or Madison—through that?

Lace knew things about Tessa she didn't know about Delaney or Hazel. Maybe even more than she knew about Knox.

And speaking of Knox, the last time she saw him, he pouted. Said she never called or texted him anymore. They still saw each other once in a while, of course. He was planning her big birthday dinner the next night, on her actual birthday, closing Banter & Brew early to get ready, and all their friends would be there. But it was different between them now. He was right about that, even though she told him he was imagining things. What was she supposed to say?

That Tessa was the new moon she looked to in her sky, to keep her oriented and grounded? Or maybe Tessa was the earth, that Lace was now orbiting around. Tessa was the first person she wanted to talk to when something good happened, the first one she called when she was in trouble, the one she planned her month around—nothing ever got in the way of movie night. She was the one Lace would drop everything to have a quick lunch with, whenever Tessa made a rare trip into town. She was the reason Lace kept her phone on all night, and looked at it as soon as her eyes popped open in the morning.

Well, no. Lace wasn't going to say that. First of all, she would never hurt Knox like that, not again. And second, it sounded absurd.

It sounded like a crush.

And Lace was definitely *not* crushing on Tessa.

What she had with Tessa was way more important than that. The thought of *not* having that anymore made it hard to breathe.

So, one hundred percent *not* crushing.

"Lace? What did you mean by that? That I'm as far away as I can be but still in your orbit."

Lace shook her head and tried to refocus. Tessa was still looking at her, but her brow was furrowed. She looked as confused as Lace felt.

Lace forced a laugh. "Sorry, I spaced out there for a minute. I was thinking about the three whiskeys I brought for us to do a tasting tonight. And about how that California cake is going to taste so good with it."

Tessa nodded. "It's going to be amazing, but seriously. What did you mean about me being in your orbit but so far away?"

Lace thought fast. "I just meant that you're, um, so much a part of everything, you know? You've got a lot of friends in Owen Station, you're working with Sena on starting up those classes, you come into town to do all your shopping and to see Delaney at Color Me Crazy, you've got *me*." Lace paused to choose her words carefully. "It's like you're in the Owen Station orbit, you know? But you're so far away. The vineyard, I mean. It's so far out there."

Tessa leaned in closer, like she was expecting something more, and nodded. "Ninety minutes outside of town, to be exact."

"Well, I was just thinking, um, have you ever thought about opening a tasting room in town?"

Tessa leaned back, looked up at the sky again, and took a deep breath. "Oh. That."

After a few minutes, she nodded her head slowly. "As a matter of fact, Lace, I have been thinking about it. I just need to figure out the right place and the right time."

Lace realized she had been sweating, even though she could see her breath. But it was getting colder by the minute, so she put another log on the fire. They tasted three spirits—a single barrel bourbon, one aged in Pinot Noir barrels, and a whiskey aged twelve years in a toasted oak barrel—from three different distilleries, all led by a woman master distiller. Tessa was trying hard to learn the nuances, and said Lace was a good teacher, and agreed that the cake went best with the whiskey.

After they packed up to head back down the mountain, they loaded the Bronco, and Lace walked Tessa to her truck. Tessa hesitated before opening the door to climb in. It was like she didn't want the night to end.

Lace didn't either.

"Thanks for meeting me up here, Tess. What a great way to spend the night before my birthday."

Tessa smiled softly and looked up at the sky. "You mean up here on this mountain? In this magical space, between an infinite universe where anything and everything seems possible—" She waved one hand back toward Boot Hill. "And this spooky-ass reminder that, because our lives are finite, we shouldn't waste a single moment of them?"

Actually, Lace meant no such thing. She just meant that she couldn't think of a better place to spend that night than with her best friend.

She didn't say that, though. That would mean talking about things she wasn't ready to talk about. Things she didn't even want to be thinking about.

So, instead, she did what she was best at. She flicked the ball on Tessa's hat again and laughed. "I might need a shovel to dig us out of here, Tess. That was deep."

Tessa laughed, too, and gave Lace a hug good-bye that lasted just a little longer than usual.

But all the way home Lace wondered, *was* she wasting time on things that didn't matter? Like dates that were never going to go anywhere?

And what would she do if anything really was possible?

What would Tessa do?

CHAPTER SIX

The sun was setting as Tessa looked out at the vineyard and took a deep breath. Midday temperatures had been in the seventies, with full sun, for a few weeks, and the leaves were beginning to unfold. Bud break was close. But the nights were scary. Temps that dropped too low with too much moisture rolling down from the mountains could mean frost. And this early in the season, that could mean disaster. Not for the first time, Tessa thought about how fragile it all was, especially this early in the season.

March seemed like such an absolutely crazy time to have a party.

At her vineyard in California, they celebrated with a hootenanny *after* harvest—a big party for all their wine club members and friends. But when they moved to Arizona, Madison suggested a bud break bash, right on the cusp of spring before the grapes even started growing. Madison said it would be a sign of how much they believed in their vines. And in themselves. And wasn't that what a couple of strong women would do? Tessa couldn't disagree.

Each year, the bash had gotten bigger. Each year, frost or no frost, the grapes came in. And each year the wine got better and better.

But that didn't mean it wasn't stressful as hell.

"Hey, Madison, where do you want the stage set up?"

Tessa turned back toward the wine barn at the sound of Lace's voice. Lace had driven in from Owen Station to help set up for the bash, and she must have come right from work because she was still wearing a Frisky Business camp shirt. That, plus jeans and a pair of Chucks were her usual workday uniform. But standing there, carrying a box full of something, with that cocky pompadour, Lace looked so strong. Solid. Ready for anything. As usual, she had jumped right in to help before she even said hello.

Sometimes Tessa wondered if she depended too much on Lace. But right at the moment, she didn't care. Because, as usual, whatever Tessa had been worrying about vanished at the sight of her.

"I was thinking right over there, in between the big barn doors and the fire pit," Tessa said loudly, walking down the short hill toward Lace. Madison gave a quick wave, knowing that Tessa was on it, and popped back into the barn.

"We can have the guys set the lights up out here and place heaters all around. That way we can have the big doors open all night, food inside, music outside, party everywhere. Also, hi."

Lace grinned back. "Hi. How are you feeling?"

"You know, it's only the night before the biggest event of the year. So, nervous."

"In other words, the usual?"

Tessa shrugged. "I see you're beginning to understand me."

"Oh, I understand you, all right," Lace laughed. "Award-winning wine maker. Successful business owner. Mother of the year. Queen of emojis. Bestest of friends."

"Insecure and not ashamed to say it."

Lace dropped the box she was carrying—which seemed to be full of extension cords and power strips—in the spot Tessa wanted the stage. "You should maybe see a therapist about that. Or my psychic."

Tessa laughed. Nobody else ever talked to her like that. Jeremy, her vineyard manager, wouldn't dare. Neither would Madison. Her family didn't really talk to her at all. The only other person she had ever let get close enough was Olivia. And Olivia had said things like that, but only at the end, when everything was falling apart, when Olivia got mean.

Somehow, though, Lace could tell her the truth and it felt good. Sometimes Tessa could even laugh about it.

"Yep. Maybe I should. See a therapist, I mean. Not your psychic."

"Don't knock it till you try it." Lace slapped her on the back. "Come inside and see what Jeremy and Madison have been up to."

All of the equipment had been shoved off to the sides. The center of the winery was completely clear, surrounded by oak barrels, and the floor sparkled. Twinkling lights had been strung from the rafters. It was magical.

Was all this really hers? How was that even possible?

"Hey, Mom! You just missed Jeremy. He was out in the vineyard so early this morning, he's exhausted. I sent him home."

Tessa nodded. Madison knew how to take charge. That was one good trait Tessa would take credit for. And she was in a zone.

"I just want to get the tables set up before I call it a night, and I figured Lace could help me with that. If that's okay with you, Lace?"

Lace smiled and shot off a quick salute. "You're the boss, kid."

Madison *was* a boss. And Lace not only saw that, she affirmed it. Just one more reason Lace had become such an important part of their lives.

With Olivia, there had ever only been room for one boss: Olivia. Leaving her was the hardest thing Tessa had ever done. But here on the other side of it, she was figuring out how to plow her own field. Madison was learning how to be her own person, too.

"I'm thinking this year we'll put the low-top tables in the center," Madison said. "The high-tops will go between the barrels along that wall. The couch and chairs can go in between the barrels on the other side, and we'll put candles everywhere to set the mood."

Lace got to work as Madison showed Tessa the punch list, with all the things that would need to be done in order to be ready for guests by four o'clock the next day. Tessa only made one edit—she wanted guests to get their wine glass at the check-in table, as soon as they arrived. Getting those glasses filled was the first priority.

Then Madison fired up a playlist, all women, all country. And the two of them got busy helping Lace set up tables. When they finished, Tessa offered to put together a cheese board. Lace jumped at the idea. She said she'd been in such a hurry to get out to the vineyard, she hadn't even stopped for dinner. But Madison was pooped.

"I'm going to head over to the Airstream, put on a movie, and try to get a good night's sleep. Tomorrow's going to be a long day. Plus, Bleu and I have been waiting all day for this sleepover."

Tessa gave her a hug. "Thanks for everything today, Maddie."

Madison smiled. "I love you, Mom. Thank you, Lace. I don't know what we'd do without you. Now, come on, Bleu. Let's go to bed!"

After she left the barn, Tessa turned to Lace. "I think Bleu misses having her live here more than I do."

"I doubt that."

Tessa punched Lace playfully in the shoulder. "You're right. Bleu couldn't possibly miss her more than I do." Actually, Tessa never imagined it would be so hard. "Don't get me wrong. I'm glad she's on her own. It's been good for her. You should see her at work! Wines rearranged. Drawers organized. Small but helpful changes in the POS system. She's blowing up our social media. We've had twice as many guests in the first quarter of this year as we did last. *Plus*, she's taking a full load this semester."

Lace nodded. "I got a little glimpse of Madison in action here tonight. She's a force of nature. Just like her mom."

"The weird thing is, I see her almost every day—and her mark is all over this place. But after the day is over, it's just so, I don't know? Quiet."

Lace shoved her hands in her pockets, like she was trying to stuff down whatever words wanted to come out of her mouth.

"What?" Tessa had spent years behind a bar. She knew when someone had something on their mind. Plus, Lace would be a terrible poker player. "Come on, what are you thinking?"

Lace shrugged, with a crooked smile. "Nothing. I'm not thinking anything."

"That's not true."

"Okay, fine. I am thinking something. I'm thinking about how much I hate the thought of you out here all by yourself. Of course it's lonely, because you're literally *alone*."

Tessa straightened her back. "I didn't say I was lonely. I said it was quiet."

Lace held her hands up in the air, like she was being robbed. "Okay, okay. I'm sorry. Sore subject." She cracked a tiny smile. "How 'bout that cheese board?"

Tessa left Lace in charge of placing candles on all the tables and went into the kitchen to pull a snack together. She was feeling a little annoyed, not with Lace but with herself. And she was annoyed that she was annoyed. She was so proud of her winery and everything she was accomplishing—on her own. California was feeling farther and farther away all the time. Arizona's high desert felt like home in a way no place else ever had. And she loved the feeling of doing life on her own.

But Lace was right.

It did feel lonely.

Most of the time she was too busy to notice. There had been seasons when she'd been too busy to pee. But now Madison was on her own, Jeremy had things in the vineyard under control, and the tasting room was running great. Suddenly Tessa had time to notice how much more fun it would be to share a meal with someone at the end of the day. And maybe a bed.

Thank God for Lace. Even when she poked too hard. She was a lifeline. The first person Tessa talked to every day, even if it was just a text. And the last person she talked to every night. Life without her had become unimaginable.

Tessa grabbed a couple of glasses and a bottle of Isabella's to go with the cheese board and went looking for Lace. She found her in the office, looking at the wall of awards—best in show, first, second, and third place ribbons from wine competitions all up and down the West Coast. Most of them were from her previous winery, but there were a growing number for Mujer Fuerte vintages, too. Why was it that, no matter how many accolades she got, it never felt like enough? *She* never felt like enough.

"You are impressive as hell, Tessa Williams."

"You're not bad yourself, Lace Reynolds," she said as she put down the goodies. "Or have you forgotten that you're famous?"

Lace laughed. "Notorious, maybe. I got a call this morning from the editor at *Pleasure Principle.* They want to put me on their fall cover."

"What? That's amazing!" Tessa threw up both hands for a double high five. "Lucky for you, I've got all the fixings for a celebration."

She had piled the cheese board with all of Lace's favorites, and Lace dove in like she hadn't eaten all day.

Building out such a nice office, complete with a comfy Murphy bed, had seemed a little extravagant, especially back when money was tight. But Tessa was glad she had done it. It got the most use at harvest, when club members who volunteered all day in the hot sun, and then enjoyed the fruits of their labor, had a place to crash for the night. Tonight, it was perfect for Lace. It meant she would be there to help get ready for the bash at the crack of dawn.

Tessa plopped down next to her on the leather couch. It was burgundy colored, to make it easier to cover wine spills. Then she poured two glasses.

"Thanks for being here, Lace." She held her glass up for a toast, and Lace did the same.

"It's my pleasure, Tess. That's what friends do." Lace held her glass in midair, without clinking it. Like there was more she wanted to say. Her closed smile and the little furrow between her brows made her look thoughtful, serious, but in a good way. And her deep brown eyes just stared, as if searching for something in Tessa's own. Finally, she sighed deeply, clinked Tessa's glass, and took a sip.

"What was all that?" Tessa said softly after she took a sip of her own. It was bad luck not to drink after you toast. "It looked like a thousand thoughts ran through your mind."

Lace glanced down, shook her head, and then looked back at Tessa. "I don't know?"

She glanced down again uncomfortably, but when her eyes met Tessa's, they were steady. Tessa could have been sucked right into them. "I guess I was just thinking about how thankful I am for this. For you."

Tessa closed her own eyes and took a deep breath. She could feel Lace looking at her.

"Did I say something wrong?" Lace's voice quivered a little. "I just meant…"

Tessa slowly exhaled and felt every muscle in her body begin to relax. Then she opened her eyes and smiled. "No, you didn't say anything wrong. Not at all."

How had she not noticed how tight her shoulders had been? Or how clenched her stomach muscles were? How long had she had that pain in her neck? Did her face look as taut as it felt? As she breathed, sitting there next to Lace, she allowed her forehead to relax, then her jaw, her shoulders, her belly. She let herself breathe.

"It's a lot, isn't it?" Lace's voice was tender. "Doing all of this on your own."

It was a little scary how well Lace knew her. Tessa was the expert on reading people. That's what years behind a bar would do to you. But she wasn't used to being read.

"It is a lot," Tessa said. "But it's not more than you deal with every day."

"Not true." Lace waggled her eyebrows. "I just play with toys."

"That is *not* all you do."

Lace smiled. "I know. I'm just saying I think your work is way more complicated. I mean, what you do is mind-blowing to me. Farming. Chemistry. Marketing. Hospitality. Finance. Managing a whole crew of people. And, I *know* you have help, but at the end of the day it's all on you. Plus, you're a mom. And you're a really good friend. I honestly don't know how you do it all."

Tessa gently slapped Lace's thigh. "Well, when you put it like that, all I can say is I'm thankful for this, too. For you."

She was, too. Somehow, with a few words, Lace managed to touch the most vulnerable, insecure places inside of her and make her feel strong. Tessa picked up her glass and settled back into the couch. Gratitude, like nutrients soaked up through the roots of a thirsty vine, coursed through her veins. It was a rare opportunity to hang out with Lace in person, and Tessa wasn't going to waste a second of it.

They stayed up way later than she had meant to. Tessa filled Lace in on all things Madison and gave a longer than Lace probably expected or wanted description of everything that happened from bud break to harvest. Lace told funny stories about the newest products she was seeing and the wackiest questions she had been asked by customers lately. It felt so good to just *be*, with no expectations and no agenda.

Unfortunately, there *was* a schedule. She left Lace pulling out the Murphy bed at about midnight and headed back to the Airstream to get some sleep.

She could have used a lot more of it.

The sun was peeking through the window when she heard Madison rustling in the kitchen.

"Good morning, sleepyhead. You were out late last night." Madison already had coffee going. "Did you and Lace have fun?"

Tessa sat up and rubbed the sleep out of her eyes. "We did. Do you have a cup of that for me?"

"Of course." Madison added a dollop of organic cream and handed her a cup. "What's up with you two, anyway?"

"Who?"

"You and Lace."

"What do you mean *what's up*?"

"You know what I mean." Madison grinned. "Do I have to give you another lesson on the birds and the bees?"

Tessa laughed. "Please, no." She took a first sip of coffee. She was going to need a gallon to get through the day. "Lace and I are friends." She paused and thought for a moment. "*Best* friends."

"Well, that sounds very second grade."

"It's a good thing I wasn't mid-sip because you would have made me snort coffee out my nose." Tessa laughed. "Sometimes it does feel kind of second grade, though. I mean, I haven't had a friend like this since then. It's—"

"Kind of weird." Madison raised an eyebrow at her.

"What's weird about it?"

"Seriously? I mean, Lace is great. Really great. You two clearly care about each other. You're constantly calling and texting each other. You're both single. You both like girls. What isn't weird about it? Why aren't you two, you know, dating?"

It was a fair question. Tessa remembered the first time they met. It seemed like a hundred years ago now. She wandered into Frisky Business looking for Madison's birthday present. And Lace was there behind the counter. Big grin. Big hair. Big everything. It didn't take long to realize that underneath it all was a big heart. Would Tessa have said yes if Lace asked her out? Maybe. But she really wasn't looking, at that point. She was still healing after Olivia. And, besides, she was so damn busy.

Later, when she found out about Lace's approach to dating, she was very glad Lace hadn't asked her.

"Lace has a three-month rule."

"A what?" Madison cocked her head and raised both eyebrows.

"She doesn't date anyone for more than three months. It gets too complicated after that."

Madison scoffed. "Okay, maybe *that* is the most second grade thing I've heard today."

Tessa laughed and got out of bed. "We better get moving. How about if you put that coffee in a thermos and bring it with us. Lace isn't used to getting up so early. She'll need it injected."

Surprisingly, Lace padded out of the office to meet them, wearing her flannel pj's. Her hair was sticking up in every direction. Madison cooked up a quick breakfast, and before long the three of them were hard at work. A steady parade of deliveries started coming before eight o'clock—dishes, glasses, linens, folding chairs, flowers, table centerpieces, sound equipment, the stage, porta-potties and didn't stop until after noon. Around three, the Fireballs, a new band made up of local first responders, pulled in with their truck.

Allison Jones, Owen Station's new assistant fire chief, Chief of Police Dana Garcia, and four women who looked like they could handle just about anything, jumped out.

Tessa was elated. "Chief Jones, Chief Garcia, I'm so glad you're all here! I still can't believe you said yes!"

"Please, Tessa. Call me Dana."

"And call me Al. Also, why wouldn't we say yes? A kick-ass woman, busting through stereotypes, to become the best winemaker in Arizona?"

"Who named her winery Mujer Fuerte," Dana added.

"I can't think of a better place to play." Al looked around at her bandmates. "Can you?"

They all jumped in with how much they were looking forward to the night. And they did look excited.

"Where do you want us?"

"We've got the stage all ready for you," Madison said. "Including heaters and mood lighting. Follow me."

About an hour later, Tessa was standing in the doorway to the wine barn, taking one last look to make sure everything was ready, when she heard "Check, check, one, two, three, check." Then the Fireballs kicked off with a tune that made Tessa want to hit the dance floor. But that would have to wait.

Lace stopped by carrying a case of glasses. "Everything looks beyond amazing, Tessa. I've got to get this to Madison at the check-in table, but I wanted you to hear that. Let yourself have fun tonight!" Then she gave Tessa a quick kiss on the cheek and hurried off.

Tessa touched her cheek, feeling just a little more confident, as she watched Lace go. Lace had a way of making her feel that way. But she didn't have time to think about it. Guests were already arriving.

Sena and Hazel were the first to make it through the line. Tessa leaned in for hugs. "You two look fabulous as always. Sena, someday you need to take me boot shopping." Sena's were brushed suede and caramel colored, with chocolate brown leather toes. Fabulous. And probably outrageously expensive.

Hazel rolled her eyes. "It's hard to keep up with Sena in the footwear department."

"Hey now, you hold your own just fine." Sena smiled and gave Hazel a kiss. "I can't be the only one who knows you have a thing for high-priced, classic shoe wear."

Hazel's red curls fell softly to her shoulders. She was wearing a pair of vintage leather cowboy boots.

"Sena's right. You do just fine. Also, I love the new haircut!"

"Thanks! I guess I am capable of change. It just takes me a minute." Hazel grinned.

"You have *me* to thank for that haircut, thank you very much!" Delaney, with a man attached, burst into the circle. "Tessa! The place looks beautiful! Also, this is Derrick. I don't think you two have met. He's a pastor in town. I'm crazy about him, anyway."

Derrick's cheeks turned bright pink. "It really does look great, Tessa." Speaking softly, he seemed the exact opposite of Delaney in almost every way. "I can't believe I haven't made it out here sooner. Delaney has me hooked on your red blend. I'm really looking forward to tonight."

"Well, let's get you all started!" Tessa directed them to the tasting table. "I recommend starting with the rosé. It will go great with the bacon-wrapped dates and tepary bean hummus, not to mention the jalapeño-marinated goat cheese. We brought Maia's Kitchen in for the party tonight. She makes magic happen with local ingredients."

"I can testify to that!" Knox joined the circle, holding a glass with the Mujer Fuerte logo etched on it.

Lace was right beside him. She nodded at Tessa with a crooked smile on her face. "How about if I take this gang off your hands, Tessa? I know you have a lot of people to talk to tonight."

Tessa folded her hands in a silent thank you and nodded. Somehow Lace knew exactly what Tessa needed, without her having to say a word.

"Have fun, everyone!" Tessa yelled over the music, as they all scrambled toward the tasting counter. "I'll come find you as soon as the crowd gets checked in."

The Fireballs were absolutely killing it on the main stage, and people had started lining up for food. There was still a long line at the check-in table, where Madison was working as fast as she could. Tessa fell in next to her, greeting people and handing each one a wine glass. After about an hour, Madison told her to go grab a plate because she had things under control.

Plate in hand, it didn't take long for Tessa to find Lace and her friends—*their* friends. Their laughter drew her in like a warm fire on a cold night. Lace pulled out a chair as Tessa balanced her plate and wine glass.

"I shouldn't have piled my plate so high," Tessa said. "I just couldn't decide what not to eat. I think I could eat these tostadas every day for the rest of my life, and the elote dip was calling my name. And these ribs!"

"Would you just eat already!" Lace butted in. "Are you even hearing the Fireballs? The faster you eat, the faster we can all get out on that dance floor."

As soon as Tessa took her first bite, everyone started talking at once.

"Your rosé is out of this world."

"The red is a perfect pairing with the ribs. What is in this blend?"

"This white is so crisp! Just what I needed for the heat in those tostadas."

"Oh my God! When did you start making bubbles? Everyone needs these in their life!"

Tessa paused in between bites. "I just love you all so much. And I am so thankful for you. How did I get so lucky?"

Sena's answer came quick and loud enough to be heard over the Fireballs' version of the Electric Slide. "Luck had nothing to do with it, Tessa. These wines, this place, you. It's all perfect. And it's all because of your hard work and sacrifice. It shows in every sip." She lifted her glass, and everyone followed her lead. "To Mujer Fuerte."

"To Mujer Fuerte!" Everyone shouted at the same time and clinked their glasses together.

"Tessa, are you *crying*?" Delaney said across the table.

Lace swung around, brows furrowed, worry etched across her face. She put her hand on Tessa's shoulder. "Are you okay?"

Tessa shook her head and smiled. Yes, she was crying. Not like tears flowing down her face, but definitely filling her eyes, making everything a little misty. "Yes, I'm okay. I guess it's just been such a long road. There have been times when it felt like too much. But tonight, sitting here with all of you, it really does seem like all dreams are possible."

"Well, you know what I'm dreaming about?" Delaney shouted. "I'm dreaming about a Mujer Fuerte tasting room in town. So I can eat and drink as much as I want and not have to worry about a ninety-minute drive back home! Also, close enough that I can come see you more often."

"Oh my God, yes!" Hazel said.

"And please serve all of this great food, so I won't have to cook anymore." Derrick was tunneling through a second helping.

Tessa laughed. "I did say all dreams are possible, didn't I? Honestly, this is something Madison and I have been talking seriously about. And I've been thinking about it for a while. I would love to open a tasting room in Owen Station, especially now with the work you're doing, Sena, to support local businesses and attract new entrepreneurs to town. I feel like Owen Station is on the cusp of something really exciting. I just need to find the time—I can't even imagine what it will take to actually make it happen—and the right space."

"Well, I know the right space." Knox said it in such a definitive way that everyone turned to look at him.

"Are you going to tell us?" Sena asked impatiently.

Knox nodded and looked right at Lace. "I think the carriage house next to Owen Mansion would be the perfect spot."

Everyone, except Tessa and Lace, started shouting at the same time.

"Yes!"

"That building is so beautiful!"

"Rustic. Classic. So much potential."

"And it's just sitting there empty!"

"The grounds are incredible. It's like a park almost."

"Perfect for outdoor events like this, weddings, concerts."

"Did someone say weddings?" Delaney grinned, pinching Derrick.

"Tessa." Sena's tone shut down the conversation. All eyes pivoted. "Tessa, what do you think about this idea?"

Tessa felt everyone staring at her. This was all moving so fast. She looked at Lace, who seemed a little shell-shocked herself. "Lace? What do you think?"

Knox stepped in when Lace didn't answer. "Lace, given how fast you're expanding, it might be helpful to have some rental income coming in. That building has just been sitting there. Make it work for you. Also, think about the visibility Frisky Business will have, with the millions of wine lovers Tessa will bring in."

Tessa cleared her throat and shifted on her seat. "Well, probably not millions."

Knox laughed. "I'm exaggerating. But the point stands. This could be a win-win for both businesses."

Lace started nodding slowly. "I think this makes sense."

You would have thought Lace just said she was picking up the tab for the whole group, for the whole year, the way their enthusiasm exploded around the table.

"Tessa." Sena's voice silenced them again. "We haven't heard from you."

Sena had that look in her eyes. Tessa had seen it before. It signaled big things were about to happen.

"Well...?" Delaney said.

Tessa looked around the table at the faces so eager to support her, and around at the huge crowd that was eating, drinking, dancing, and laughing. What would it be like to share this magical experience with more and more people?

And to do it all right beside Lace.

Maybe they could have lunch together more than once a month.

Tessa couldn't stop the big smile that erupted.

"Yes!" Everyone yelled at the same time.

"Okay," Sena said, moving into go-mode. "Knox Reynolds, this is the best idea you've had all year. First thing tomorrow I'll line up an architect. I'll put my best construction team on the renovations. We'll have Tessa up and running—"

"Before harvest," Tessa said. "It has to be up and running before harvest."

"How many months does that give us?" Sena asked.

"Four. Five at most."

"Done."

"Let's dance!" Delaney said, and the group leapt up to join the crowd on the dance floor.

Tessa looked at Lace. She was still sitting next to her, completely still, eyes wide-open, mouth slightly ajar.

"Lace?"

Lace turned and looked at her.

"We're going to be neighbors."

CHAPTER SEVEN

L ace was getting ready to pull dinner together in her kitchen with the windows open. It had been an absolutely perfect spring afternoon. When Tessa screamed her name. Lace dropped the frying pan she was carrying to the stove and everything in it. It all clattered to the floor as she tore out the back door to the carriage house, where Sena's best construction crew had been working nonstop for six weeks.

Her heart was racing as she skidded to a stop in front of Tessa.

The crew had one eye on Tessa, but they were carrying on, just like always.

Tessa wasn't bleeding.

All limbs where still attached.

"What the absolute hell, Tessa? You scared me half to death!"

Tessa shook her head, laughing. "I'm sorry, Lace! I didn't mean to scare you." She picked up the box and held it up for Lace to see. "But look what I just found!"

Lace needed a minute to catch her breath and try to reel her heart back in. It was still bouncing all over her chest.

Tessa finally stood up, carrying the box under her arm, and took Lace's hand. "Oh my God. Come on." She pulled Lace outside and led her to a picnic table in the side yard. They both sat down and Tessa, eyes sparkling, pushed the box in front of Lace. "Open it!"

Lace put a hand on each side of the box. It was about the size of an old PlayStation, but a whole hell of a lot older. The metal had tarnished with age, but the initials engraved into the top were still visible.

"E.O.," Tessa said reverently.

Lace inhaled sharply. "Elizabeth Owen."

Tessa nodded. "Who else could it be?"

Lace opened the box slowly and tried to make sense of what she was seeing. Most of the items looked like mementos from a childhood in the late 1800s or early 1900s. A handful of buttons made of wood capped with a layer of silver. A deck of playing cards. A small handmade doll. Some marbles. A set of tiny, blue enamel toy dishes. Underneath the toys was a linen hankie with the initials M.T. engraved in the corner, a leather coin purse. And a small diary.

Lace looked back up at Tessa. "Did you read it?"

Tessa shook her head. "I didn't touch anything. As soon as I realized who this box belonged to, I called you."

"You screamed for me, you mean. My heart still hasn't stopped racing."

Tessa threw her arms up in surrender. "I'm sorry!" Then she looked down at the box, back at Lace, and shrugged. "Do you blame me?"

Lace shook her head and smiled. "No. I can't say that I do."

"Well, open it."

"The diary?"

"Yes, silly. The diary!"

Lace took a deep breath, held it, and exhaled slowly. Tessa scooted closer on the bench, so they were shoulder to shoulder as Lace carefully picked the diary out of the box. It was small, bigger than a phone, but smaller than a tablet. Lace held it in her open palms, feeling the weight of the worn leather cover, and of history.

"I feel weird."

Tessa didn't respond. She just put her hand lightly on Lace's back.

"I feel like if I open this and start reading it, I'll be invading her privacy." She peeked over at Tessa. "Mrs. Owen, I mean."

Tessa tilted her head and squeezed her eyes shut, as if trying to see something that wasn't right in front of them. She nodded and then opened them. "I get it."

"You do?"

"I do."

Lace glanced up at the house, half-expecting to see Mrs. Owen looking back at her through a window, and lowered her voice. "I mean, I live with her."

Lace had kind of expected an argument. Tessa hadn't grown up in Owen Station. She had made it clear that she thought the way people in the Southwest were so spiritually aware was strange. A little spooky, even. Crystals and chakras and meditation were one thing. Tessa was from California, after all. But spirits? That wasn't something Tessa, the descendent of very practical farmers from the northern tip of the Central Valley, had much experience with. Or wanted to have. And she never liked it when Lace talked about Mrs. Owen. But for whatever reason, maybe being confronted with physical evidence and the reality of the woman who had lived in that house, Tessa seemed, for once, to finally get it.

Tessa folded her hands on the table and leaned in, examining but not touching the little book. "Maybe Mrs. Owen wanted us to find it. I mean, it's not like she's shy."

Lace pictured Mrs. Owen's favorite red dildo bouncing around in the middle of her shop every morning. "No, she certainly isn't." She laughed.

She looked at the house again. Still no sign of her. Then she looked back at the box.

"Okay, maybe I'll just take a peek."

Lace opened the little notebook slowly. The spine crinkled when it opened, like old bones. "Oh my God, I'm afraid I'm going to break it."

The pages were brittle and yellowed, each one filled with the tiniest, neatest handwriting.

At the top of page one, Mrs. Owen had written *January 1, 1910.*

"What does it say?" Tessa was leaning in, squinting. "The writing is so small and faded, I can't read it!"

"I arrived on the twelfth of December." Lace read the words reverently. "Sent by my mother to marry Mr. Owen, who was widowed one year ago. This morning we are to be wed and my new life will begin. I promised her I will try to be a good wife to him, but I fear that I will not know how.'"

Lace paused. "She couldn't have been more than sixteen or seventeen years old."

"Okay, wow. I have a much different picture of 'Mrs. Owen' in my head now." Tessa spoke quietly, as if not wanting Mrs. Owen to overhear.

Lace nodded. "Remember? You saw the gravestone. She was only twenty-five when she died."

"Twenty-five. I mean, I guess that was, like, middle-aged back then. But, still. Getting married off like that when she was just a girl. And to an older man."

"And then the bastard went and buried her on Boot Hill."

Tessa shivered, even though it wasn't at all cold, and put her arms around herself. "It seems like maybe she never figured out how to be a good wife. Whatever that meant back then."

Lace was already opening to another page, toward the middle. The date at the top said *December 17, 1915*. "There's only a few entries every year. It looks like young Mrs. Owen wasn't much of a diarist, either."

She flipped to the very back, where the last entry was dated *March 31, 1918*.

"That was the year she died." Tessa's eyes were apparently adjusting.

Lace snapped the book shut. "I can't do this, Tess. I feel like a Peeping Tom."

Tessa snorted a laugh and then covered her mouth, her eyes wide. "Oh my God, I'm so sorry, Lace. I'm not laughing at you. Or at young Mrs. Owen. I swear!" She shook her head, like she was trying to get control of herself. "When you said Peeping Tom, I thought, is that supposed to help us tell the difference between him and Blacksmith Tom or Farmer Tom?" She snorted again, then started giggling, and then burst out laughing until tears sprang from her eyes.

It was so silly, Lace started laughing, too.

"Um, Ms. Williams?" Jack McDonald was Sena's guy, and he was overseeing the build-out of Tessa's new tasting room. Lace had known him since kindergarten. It seemed strange to hear him call Tessa "Ms. Williams," but Jack was working for Sena now and, well, let's just say she set a high bar.

Tessa took a breath and got her laughter under control, but she still had a goofy grin on her face. "Yes, Jack?"

"We're done for the day. I just wanted to let you know we're headed out."

"Okey dokey, Jack," Tessa said in a singsong way that made it seem like she was still on the verge of cracking up. "See you tomorrow."

Tessa watched him walk away, and as soon as he was out of earshot, she waved at his back. "See you later, Builder Jack!" And then she started laugh-crying again.

Lace laughed, too. How could she not? But she was also a little worried. "Tessa, how much sleep did you get last night? And when's the last time you ate something?"

Tessa leaned into Lace, holding her stomach, which had to hurt after so much laughing. Lace put an arm around her. "Take a few deep breaths."

Tessa did as she was told and, after a few minutes, seemed to have calmed herself. But she didn't move. She just sat there with her head on Lace's shoulder.

"I'm tired."

Lace gave her a squeeze. "I bet you are."

The build-out schedule had been brutal. Sena wasn't kidding when she said she could work magic to get the tasting room open before harvest. They were on track to open in time for mid-summer tourists. Crews had been working six days a week, from sunup until sundown. Tessa came into town every day, after getting up before dawn and working five or six hours at the winery. There were fixtures, furniture, equipment to choose, and all kinds of details to manage. Jack had a list of decisions for her to make every day. And Tessa liked to be as hands-on as possible. When she moved to Arizona, she and Jeremy built the winery themselves. It went against her nature to hire guys to do this build-out. She knew it wouldn't happen any other way, but that didn't mean you could keep a paintbrush or a nail gun out of her hands.

"You've been working so hard, Tess. You must be exhausted."

Tessa didn't answer. She didn't move, either. Had she fallen asleep? It was entirely possible. But every once in a while she would take a deep breath and exhale slowly. Her head was heavy on Lace's shoulder and, the longer they sat there, the heavier her body felt.

When the idea of opening a tasting room in the carriage house first came up, Lace couldn't have imagined what it would be like to have Tessa working right next door. Frankly, there hadn't been time to think about it.

It all happened so fast.

Lace had popped the question first. In a panic, that night on Boot Hill, she asked Tessa if she had ever thought about opening a tasting room in town. Then, their friends ganged up on her at the bash, urging her to open a space closer to town, where they could hang out and have fun without having to worry about a long drive home. And then, Knox had the big idea to open it there, in the carriage house next to Frisky Business. Next to Lace's *home*.

And now it was happening. The minute Tessa said go, Sena snapped her fingers, pulled her best construction crew off another job, and put them to work. It had only been six weeks since the bash, but Tessa was already starting to move inventory in, and she was making plans for the grand opening next month.

It was dizzying.

But it did make sense. Owen Mansion sat on the most beautiful piece of property within the town limits. A half-acre covered with trees and plants that thrived in the mile-high, desert landscape. Desert willows, Arizona cypress and sycamore trees, and large cottonwoods created enough shade even in the heat of summer, to allow plumeria and even a few fruit trees to thrive. And so many birds! Lace kept a log of those she spotted. Canyon wrens, black-chinned sparrows, red crossbills, cedar waxwings. A large flock of turkey vultures roosted in the cottonwoods every evening. Then there was the carriage house itself. Tessa loved the rustic vibe, old wood and stone, just like Lace knew she would. She was going to keep the huge, heavy sliding door, big enough for a horse and a carriage to get through, and open it up on beautiful days to create an indoor-outdoor experience. It was everything Tessa could want. An idyllic setting, convenient to tourists, right on the edge of town.

It was all absolutely perfect.

And it was starting to make Lace twitch.

Tessa took another deep breath, let out a sigh too deep for words, shifted slightly under Lace's arm, and relaxed even more deeply. Like every inch of her was sinking into Lace, letting go.

Her best friend was leaning on her. That's all she should have been thinking about. That's what friends did for each other. Right? She and Tessa had been leaning on each other emotionally for going on two years. Celebrating each other's wins. Cheering each other on through the hard days.

But you couldn't smell sandalwood soap through the phone. And that's what Tessa smelled like right then, cradled in Lace's arms.

Lace shut her eyes and breathed it in.

"Lace?"

Lace kept her eyes closed and sat still, not wanting the moment to end. "Yes?"

"What are you going to do with Mrs. Owen's diary?"

Lace opened her eyes and looked down at the book. The brown leather was cracked and one of its corners had peeled or fallen off. The delicate little lock looked like it had been snapped off, but at some point, young Mrs. Owen—Elizabeth—had wanted her privacy. There was no reason to think that had changed. But she couldn't just put it back in the box and tuck it back inside the wall in the carriage house. Could she? It had been found. And, who knows, maybe Tessa was right. Maybe Mrs. Owen had wanted it found.

But Lace knew one thing for sure. She wasn't going to be the one to examine it.

She had enough drama of her own right at the moment.

For one thing, she wasn't sure what she was going to do about the fact that her mind was in the middle of packing its suitcases, because her body was getting ready to kick every rational thought to the street.

The tingling had started in her belly the moment Tessa scooted over to take a closer look at the diary, and the outside of Tessa's thigh grazed her leg. When Tessa leaned over and put her head on Lace's shoulder, the tingling shot upward and downward at the same time, hardening her nipples and awakening everything below her hips.

Lace could have stopped it. Probably.

Should have stopped it. Abso-fucking-lutely.

But, God help her. She didn't want to.

Tessa's right hand was tucked in between them, but her left one was sitting in Tessa's lap. Lace couldn't stop looking at the small tattoo on the inside of Tessa's wrist. Black ink. Two numbers: 01-26

Tessa's passcode.

Madison's birthday.

The day Tessa's body opened up and brought new life into the world *alone*.

The skin there looked so tender. Even though Tessa was one of the toughest people Lace had ever known, that tiny, naked, vulnerable spot was a reminder of all that Tessa had endured, all that she had survived. It was the mark of love, the kind of love that sacrifices everything.

Lace wanted to touch it. She wanted to—

"Lace?"

Tessa's voice was like a blast of ice-cold water. It put out the fire that had been building so fast, Lace didn't even know what happened.

"Oh, shit," she yelled, yanking her arm back, jumping at least a foot away from Tessa.

Startled, Tessa leapt up off the bench. "What? What happened?" Her eyes searched Lace's face, arms, hands, and then scrambled down her own body, where she was already frantically brushing off her own shirt and pants. "What *happened*? *Lace!* Say something! Did something sting you?"

"What? No!" Lace was confused and a little panicky. She looked down at her own pants and flicked her hands up and down, chasing off whatever might be there, forgetting for a second that *she* was the threat, not some poor creature. "No! I'm fine! I'm okay."

What the hell did just happen? One minute she was just Tessa's friend, her *best* friend, offering support and comfort in the midst of a crazy, freaking time. Giving her a shoulder to lean on, literally. The next minute she was on the verge of…oh God!

It was like waking up in a cold sweat from a forbidden dream, one that you want to keep having, but you know will end in disaster.

"I thought maybe a scorpion got you." Tessa was breathing fast and her cheeks were bright red. "They come out at dusk, right? I hate scorpions."

"No, no, no. Not a scorpion. I've never even seen one out here." Lace's heart was racing, but Tessa looked even more freaked out. Lace put a hand on Tessa's arm. "It's okay, Tess. Everything is okay."

But Lace was lying. It was *not* okay. She was not okay. Nothing felt solid anymore. Even the earth felt too soft to hold her. Squishy. Like quicksand. Maybe if she was lucky it would swallow her up, so she would never come so close to doing something so stupid ever again.

Tessa was her friend. That relationship had become one of the most important things in her life. Now they were neighbors. Essentially in business together. So much was at stake. How could she even think about screwing that up?

Tessa was still brushing off her clothes, looking at the ground nervously. "So, um, I guess I better get back to work. I have a lot to do before I head home tonight. But I do have a thought about the diary."

Lace was afraid to make eye contact but, when she finally did, Tessa's hazel eyes looked gray. It could have been the fading light. The sun had set almost an hour earlier. Or it could have been the close encounter with the scorpion that wasn't. Or it could have been…

No, it couldn't be that.

Tessa couldn't possibly know how close Lace came to ruining everything.

"Do you want to hear it?" Tessa was frowning again. "Are you sure you're okay? You're acting weird."

Lace nodded. "I'm fine. I'm sorry. I guess I just have a lot on my mind. This whole thing with Mrs. Owen has me pretty shaken up." That was true, at least.

Tessa's face relaxed a little. "Of course."

"So, what do you think I should do with it, with the diary?"

Tessa smiled like she had a secret Lace should already know. "I think you should give it to Hazel. She'll know what to do with it and how to make sure it is preserved."

"Oh my God, Tess. That is perfect. That is exactly what I'm going to do."

The screech owl who prowled the neighborhood trilled from somewhere nearby.

"Somebody's hungry," Tessa said, squinting up into the trees.

"Speaking of, I was just about to make dinner when you called me out here. Can I bring you a plate?"

"You're cooking dinner?"

"Don't sound so surprised."

"I'm just teasing."

Lace was starting to breathe normally again. "I'm actually a very good cook, my friend. And now that I've got Sophie working the counter for me three afternoons a week—thank you very much for nagging me until I did that—I've started doing it more often. I'm making a pot of Nana Maria's spaghetti sauce tonight. You'd be amazed at what this Italian girl can do with some fresh oregano and a few heads of garlic."

Tessa laughed and gave Lace a quick kiss on the cheek. "Can I have a rain check? That sounds amazing. But tonight I think I'm going to just close up and head home, after all. Builder Jack's list is going to have to wait till tomorrow. I need a night off."

As Lace watched Tessa head back into the carriage house, she was both disappointed and relieved.

She put everything back into Mrs. Owen's box and scooted through her back door into the kitchen. When she flipped on the lights, she saw the frying pan, wooden spoon, two heads of garlic, a large container of tomato paste—which had popped open when it hit the floor—and four very fresh, now very bruised, tomatoes everywhere. One great big mess of a metaphor. She would literally drop everything to be there for Tessa. And she knew Tessa would do the same for her.

It just took a few minutes to clean things up, but her stomach wasn't in it anymore. She pulled out the popcorn—which used to be dinner a lot of nights, before she had Sophie working in the shop, when she was doing everything on her own. Before Tessa intervened.

Before Tessa.

She could hardly remember what that was like.

Through the window, she could see the light in Tessa's office. The guys had renovated that space first, up in what used to be the hay loft, so Tessa would have a place to work when she was in town. It was totally her, somehow both rustic and refined. She had asked her brother to pull their great-grandmother's desk out of storage and ship it to her. Lace helped move it upstairs, swearing all the way. Tessa rewarded her with a bottle of Cliquot and the story. Tessa's great-grandmother grew up in a family of performers. She was a trapeze artist. And she had Hollywood dreams. But when the circus came to Yuba City, she was swept off her feet by a young farmer. She married him, but she never let anyone forget she was a star. The desk was a gift she made him buy for her. It was wood, adorned with colorful, whimsical designs in the Monterey-style that was popular with all the Hollywood types back then. And it was unlike anything anyone in California farm country had ever seen before. Kind of like the woman herself, who never quite figured out how to be a farmer's wife. Tessa loved everything about this story. And she loved that desk, which had been stored out in the barn for as long as she could remember. As soon as she had a place of her own, she claimed it. Tessa said she knew what it was like to feel like you never quite fit in, and never measured up.

Lace watched the window, hoping to get a glimpse of Tessa and, as if on cue, Tessa appeared and waved. Which freaked Lace the fuck out. So, without thinking, she dove out of sight, down behind the kitchen sink. Then she really felt stupid. Now she didn't just look like a peeping Tom, she looked guilty.

She was guilty.

What a disaster.

Still crouched down, Lace reached frantically inside the cabinet under the sink and pulled out a bottle of dish soap. Then she jumped up and waved back, with the soap bottle in her hand, like *there's nothing to see here!* Not weird at all.

Super fucking weird.

What the hell was she going to do about this? She paced back and forth across her kitchen, running her hands through her hair, trying to make a plan.

Thank God, Tessa left not long after the window incident.

Lace tried to relax, made popcorn, opened a bottle of locally made kombucha from the new co-op, and pulled out her phone. Then she scrolled through her contact list. She needed a date. And she needed it bad.

In fact, maybe that was what was wrong with her. Life had gotten too serious. It all started with that damn Best Of list, when business went from good to Oh My God. The holidays had been just a prelude to the big toy event of the year, Valentine's Day. And business hadn't slowed down since. Her new assistant Sophie was a big help, as much as Lace hated to admit it, and maybe she needed to be full-time. But it wasn't just her own business that had Lace wound around the axle. She was Tessa's main sounding board. Tessa didn't really need her help. She just seemed to like having Lace help her.

The texts were endless.

Do you think I should be open five days a week? Or just on the weekends?

How many tables do you think I should order for the outdoor area?

Should I use granite or wood on top of the tasting counter?

There were multiple phone calls every day, too.

Plus they spent hours together on site every week.

Plus virtual movie nights.

It didn't leave a lot of time for dating.

Honestly, Lace hadn't even thought about dating for months.

And, clearly, that was a mistake.

She looked down at her phone. Date-related contacts were in three groups. The DF group were the people who had gone from Dates to Friends. That was a very long list. The DD group was short but important. That was the Don't Date again list. She skipped past those two lists and opened up the FD group, Future Dates. These were people she met here, there, and everywhere, who were clearly interested and interesting but, for whatever reason, Lace hadn't dated yet. Maybe when they met, Lace was dating someone else. Or they were. Or whatever.

Well, she was ready.

Hey there, Angela. It's me, Lace.

Little dots appeared immediately on Lace's screen.

Lace! What's up, girlfriend?

Lace smiled. *TBH you are…been thinking about you.*

I'm blushing.

Lace paused, waiting for the little dots to turn into whatever Angela had to say next.

I hope you've been thinking frisky thoughts.

Lace let out a long breath. She was back in the saddle.

And that's what she needed to get Tessa off her mind.

CHAPTER EIGHT

Construction went faster than anyone thought possible. Just six weeks after Tessa found Mrs. Owen's diary in the carriage house, the space had been completely transformed.

Tessa checked her phone again for the tenth time in the past fifteen minutes. Still no morning text from Lace. Given that the sun was still coming up over the mountain, as she pulled out onto Route 88, she wasn't surprised. But she was impatient.

The grand opening was tomorrow and there were a million last-minute details.

Not that she *needed* Lace to help her decide whether to put cocktail or dinner napkins on the food table, or what kind of gift she could give Sena to thank her for everything she had done to make this happen.

Tessa laughed at herself.

She was perfectly capable of making all these decisions by herself. She'd been doing life on her own for a long time, and was very successful at it, thanks very much.

Lace often *did* have great suggestions. But mainly, it just felt good to have her on the other end of the phone.

Tessa looked again. Still no text.

Tessa had lost the ability to sleep in long ago. Madison was a fussy baby. For the first two years of her life, Tessa hadn't gotten more than three hours of sleep at a time. It turned out to be good training for everything that would come. The vines, the wine, the tasting room, all the demands of parenthood. Now Tessa rarely missed a sunrise.

She was glad Lace could sleep in, and she wouldn't even think of sending a text or calling before she knew Lace was up. But she did wish that, one of these days, Lace could see what she saw. Sunsets were fine. But there was nothing like watching the sun chase away the darkness.

Maybe one morning Lace would be convinced to meet up at that cemetery she loved so much for a view of the city, bathed in pink and orange, as the sun rose over the mountain. Mugs of fresh coffee, her favorite blanket spread out on the ground, fresh pastries and fruit.

Tessa laugh-snorted. That'd be the day.

Bleu had been curled up on the passenger seat for most of the drive into town, but she hopped up to stick her head out the window as they neared the tunnel. Bleu loved coming to town. There were treats waiting for her at Banter & Brew. Knox couldn't resist those sad puppy eyes. He was always ready with a pup cup filled with whipped cream. And she was having fun exploring the grounds at Owen Mansion.

Most of all, Bleu loved Lace. She spent more time inside Frisky Business, following Lace around, than she did in the new tasting room. Of course, that might change now that construction was done, once the place was full of guests. But a strong bond had developed between the two of them during the past few months. Bleu was even protective in a way that Tessa had never seen before, with anyone besides her and Madison. One afternoon, when Angela, Lace's current girlfriend, popped into the shop, Bleu started growling. Lace sent a text, asking Tessa to come get her. It was unusual behavior, but Tessa couldn't be too upset. Angela wasn't her favorite person, either.

The town was just starting to stir as Tessa pulled onto Main Street. She waved at Walt, who was walking to work. After she parked, he stopped so she could catch up with him, and confirmed that he was still running ads on the radio for her grand opening. They would run right up until noon tomorrow. His sister station in Tucson was running them, too.

Walt could have talked all day, if she let him, but she was in serious need of a cup of Knox's strongest roast after the long drive. She excused herself and popped into Banter & Brew. Jorge, from the tequila tasting room next door, was already at the counter.

"Morning, Tessa! Morning, Bleu!" Knox called from behind the counter. "Two of my favorite people. It's going to be a great day!"

It had taken a minute to get used to places allowing dogs inside. That never would have flown in California. Now Tessa couldn't imagine living in a place where that wasn't the case.

Knox came around the counter with a pup cup and scratched Bleu behind the ears as she gobbled it up.

"You're here even earlier than usual, Tessa," Knox said, standing up and wiping his hands on his apron. "Everything okay?"

"The grand opening is tomorrow, so, no, everything is not okay."

Jorge and Knox laughed.

"Tell us how you really feel, Tess," Jorge said. "I get it, though. I remember when Miguel and I were opening up next door. I didn't sleep for weeks, worrying about every little thing."

"Same." Knox was back behind the counter. "But you have so much support, Tessa. Everyone in town is talking about the grand opening tomorrow. I know Lace has been all-hands-on-deck for you. I hardly ever see or hear from her anymore. Sena is making it rain in every direction in this town, and you have her on your side."

Tessa nodded. One of the most surprising things about opening up a business right in town was how good it felt to be more a part of the community. At her core, she was a farmer. She felt more comfortable on a tractor, on her own, in a field under the open sky, than anywhere else in the world. But she had been so warmly welcomed, especially by the close-knit group of entrepreneurs. She knew Sena and Knox had a lot to do with that. They were like the town's unofficial co-mayors. And, of course, Lace.

"You're right. I'm thankful for all of it. And I am feeling so at home in that carriage house. You were right, Knox. It's perfect. I can't wait for it to be filled with people, hanging out, enjoying each other, learning about the great wine scene here in Southern Arizona."

"Enjoying *your* wines. Miguel and I are big fans, as you know." Tessa kissed Jorge on the cheek.

"All right, m'lady. What will it be this morning? How about a cup of my home-brewed chai tea, instead of your usual coffee?" Knox raised his eyebrows and looked down his nose at her, teasing. "You look wound up enough, maybe you don't need a blast of caffeine?"

"Thank you for your concern, sir." Tessa teased back. "But I have quite the day ahead. I'll take your famous B&B roast pour over please, and a wet cappuccino for Lace. I don't dare come empty-handed at this hour of the morning. The guys will already be banging away, which usually makes for a hairy start with my landlord."

"I feel you." Knox laughed, turning toward the coffee bar to put her order together. "Lace has never been a fan of mornings."

A shot of heat hit Tessa low in her stomach, sending a web of tingles across her midsection. She squinted, trying to see Knox more clearly.

He had been married to *Lace*.

She was the first person he saw every morning, for years.

She slept with him.

Tessa did her best to block the images that flashed before her. She did not need to picture Knox naked. She did not need to picture Lace that way. And she definitely did *not* need to picture them that way together. Her stomach dropped, the way it did when Madison would get injured or was threatened in some way. On high alert. Protective. And nauseous, all at the same time.

She closed her eyes and took a deep breath.

"Anything else I can get you?" Knox was back. His eyes were twinkling. He was a good guy. He loved Lace still. She loved him.

There was no reason to be so weird about it all.

Tessa cleared her throat and tried to get back on track. "Yep. Let's see, I'll take a breakfast croissant with your thick cut ham, scrambled egg, and that local jalapeño goat cheese you've got, on top. That's for me. And I'll take a chocolate croissant to go with Lace's cappuccino." She smiled at him, letting him know everything was fine. Even though he had no reason to think otherwise.

"Coming right up!"

He headed off to the kitchen for the sandwich, and that should have been it, but Knox's dessert case was calling to her. "Throw in a couple slices of your world-famous rhubarb pie, too, please," she called out. "I think I'm going to need a prize after I get all my work done this afternoon."

He peeked out of the kitchen and gave her a thumbs up.

Jorge wished her good luck, said he and Miguel would be there with bells on tomorrow, and headed out to start his day. Tessa took a seat at the counter, where the latest issue of the *Owen Station Caller* was open to the police blotter. Stray cats were creating havoc on Hill Street again, dumpster diving, and spreading garbage everywhere. A town meeting was being called to address the problem. A fight broke out last weekend in front of the Miners Hole. It could have ended badly since both of the out-of-town idiots were open-carrying, like they were extras in an old B-movie. But Ricki had grabbed her granddad's rifle off the wall and already had them both face down on the ground, with their hands behind their heads, when Chief Garcia arrived. The annual adults-only soap-box derby was coming up and everyone was being reminded not to park on Main Street after seven p.m. on Friday.

Just another week's worth of news in Owen Station. Tessa laughed and folded up the twenty-page paper, just as Knox brought her order.

Ten minutes later, she was pulling up to the carriage house with goodies in hand, and the first thing she saw was the new Mujer Fuerte sign hanging above the door. After all the hard work, all the worry, all the money—this was *real*. She sat in the truck, letting herself enjoy the moment, as construction workers scurried in and out of the carriage house, probably as anxious as she was to wrap up every loose end before tomorrow. Sena really had been a godsend. And Lace, well, she couldn't even begin to imagine what she would have done without Lace.

Just then her phone started quacking.

"Coffee. I need coffee." Lace moaned as soon as Tessa said hello.

"Well, you're in luck. I'm right outside."

Tessa let herself in through Lace's back door, just as Lace was padding her way slowly into the kitchen in a pair of plaid flannel joggers and a well-worn Lilith Fair T-shirt. Her usually coifed pompadour was sticking out in almost every direction.

"Oh my God. What *time* is it?" Lace's eyes were still semi-closed and her mouth hardly moved.

"Oh my God, is right. You are adorable. It's almost seven. And I know better than to come empty-handed this early. I brought you a wet cappuccino, and a still warm chocolate croissant. Knox sends his love."

"Okay, you can stay."

Tessa shot her an air-kiss and dropped the goodies on the table. Then she grabbed small plates and two juice glasses out of a cabinet, a couple of napkins out of a drawer, and the OJ from the fridge. This had become a routine during construction. They started the day with a quick breakfast together, then they'd split up to do their own thing, coming together for lunch, or whenever Tessa needed a brainstorm session. Lace's kitchen table was ground zero for all their plotting and planning.

"Why do you look so perky?" Lace croaked, as she plopped down at the table. "This is such an inhumane hour of the day. And don't think this coffee and croissant is making up for it."

"Everything about you is making me smile this morning." Tessa grinned. "Plus, I'm happy. My new sign is up!"

That got Lace's attention. Her mouth slowly cracked into a smile. "That is the bomb." She jumped up from the table. "Let's *go!*"

Tessa gathered up their coffee and half-eaten breakfast and followed Lace out the door. A few steps ahead of her, Lace was already standing beneath the sign, staring at it.

"Tessa." Her voice was thick. "This is—" She turned to look at Tessa. "I am so happy and excited for you. You deserve this. "

Looking deep into Lace's eyes, Tessa felt every anxiety she had been carrying fall away.

Everything she had ever done, all the time, all the hard work, every mistake she had ever made and everything she had learned from them, all of it, over all these years, had led to this moment. She *had* this.

And she had Lace.

It was all going to be okay.

The sound of cars on the gravel road behind them made them both turn around. Sena's sport car was first and, behind it, an old hybrid sedan belonging to Elena Murphy, the artist whose photographs would be hung in the new tasting room for opening night.

"Sena!" Tessa waved as they pulled into the parking area. "Elena!"

"Um, I'm going to go make myself presentable," Lace said. "I'll pop over in a bit. Sophie is covering for me in the shop today, so I'm all yours."

Tessa grabbed her hand. "You don't have to go. You look fabulous."

"Fabulously ridiculous, you mean."

"Okay fine. Maybe a little. Go do you." Then she leaned over, kissed Lace on the cheek, and gave her a pat on the bum as she headed back toward the house.

Elena came up the drive first, carrying packages of what Tessa assumed were photos for the show. Tessa air-kissed her and sent her inside the tasting room.

When Sena reached her, her eyebrows were plastered to the top of her forehead. "Well, well, well."

"Well, well, *what*?" Tessa asked, confused.

"Well, well, what do we have here?"

"What are you talking about?" Tessa laughed. "It's too early for riddles, even from my guardian angel."

"I saw all of that. You. And Lace."

Tessa looked at Sena, then at the door through which Lace had disappeared, then back at Sena, trying to imagine what Sena was talking about. "You saw what exactly*?*"

"Lace out here with you, looking like she just climbed out of bed, the close talking, the kiss, the way you grabbed her ass."

"Sena!" Tessa was horrified. "I did no such thing!"

Sena's eyebrows still hadn't dropped back into normal territory. "Come on, Tessa. We all knew it was just a matter of time." Then her face relaxed into a smile. "I'm happy for you."

"Sena," Tessa said in the most serious voice she could muster, like she was scolding Madison for missing curfew. "I appreciate your enthusiasm, but it is misplaced. There is nothing—*nothing*—going on between Lace and me. I mean, other than the fact that Lace is a really good friend. And that is more than enough."

Sena cocked her head and squinted at her, as if weighing whether or not to believe her. Like, seriously? Why would she lie about something like that?

Finally, Sena said, "Listen. I'm sorry. I didn't mean to offend you. And I'm sorry I jumped to conclusions." Sena paused and then grinned. "I guess I just saw what I wanted to see."

Tessa sighed heavily, relief flowing through her. The last thing she needed on the eve of the grand opening was a bunch of drama, caused by gossip, based on a misunderstanding creating any kind of weirdness for her and Lace.

"Apology accepted. But wait, what do you mean *everyone thinks it's just a matter of time*?"

Sena shrugged. "You and Lace would be great together. Everyone thinks so."

Tessa's heart started beating hard again. "Oh my God, Sena. Can't two people just be friends without, without—"

Sena just stood there listening.

"Lace and I are essentially in business together now. So we don't need any drama. Besides, she is dating what's her name?"

"Angela."

"Right. Angela."

"That won't last long." Sena sniffed.

"Exactly. Because Lace isn't interested in a long-term relationship with anyone. Just fun."

"And sex," Sena said. "Yes, I know."

"Well?" Tessa realized her voice was getting higher and louder.

"Well what?"

"Well, why would I want to mess up my friendship with Lace, and all of *this,*" she waved her arms around to mean the new tasting room, the outdoor event space, and everything it meant for Mujer Fuerte, "just for a few months of fun."

"And sex."

"Oh, for God's sake! Are you listening to me?" Tessa's heart was racing. "It is not going to happen, okay? I don't even *want* it to happen."

She stared at Sena for a long minute, willing the conversation to end. Finally, Sena put her hand on Tessa's arm. "Hey, I'm sorry. Really. I guess I'm not as good at having these little talks as you are."

Tessa took a breath and let herself smile. "You can say that again."

"Forget I said anything."

"Done."

Tessa led Sena into the tasting room for a look at what her ace construction crew had managed to pull off in just a few months. And she did try to forget what Sena had said.

Her own words, though, were still bouncing around in her head. I don't even want it to happen.

Tessa wasn't sure those words were true.

But they damn sure needed to be.

"Tessa, this is spectacular." Sena was standing in the middle of the carriage house, now transformed.

Sena's architect had worked with the construction crew to preserve the exposed wooden beams and the worn brick walls. The floor had to be replaced, but Sena connected her with a woman-owned company out of Tucson that specialized in reclaimed building materials. They were able to come by enough reclaimed Douglas fir flooring to make the floor look like it had been there for a hundred years. Brand-new cement counters had been poured the day before. Lace had suggested light gray, because that would make glasses filled with red wine really pop. She also turned Tessa on to a local ceramics company that had created creamy white, square plates with the Mujere Fuerte logo in the corner.

"You are right, Sena. It is spectacular. And I could not have done it without you. Not just making sure I had the best architect and crew. I know you fast-tracked the permitting processes. I don't know how you did it, except by some kind of magic."

Sena's laugh ricocheted off the brick walls. "Magic? Me? Have you tasted your wine?"

"Speaking of wine!" Elena yelled across the room. "Is it too early?"

Tessa looked at her phone. "Um, it's only eight-thirty."

Elena laughed, coming closer. "I'm kidding. I'm just feeling a little overwhelmed."

Tessa met Elena at the grand reopening of the library earlier in the year. The Murphy Funeral Home and Mortuary, Elena's family's business, had been the chief sponsor of the event. It was one way for them to make amends after the tragedy her grandfather accidentally caused. Elena had just come home, after many years away, to take over the front of the house. The rumor was that when her brothers had taken over, things had gone sideways. Elena got the empathy chip in her family. Her brothers had none. And it was starting to hurt the business. She had answered her family's call. But her passion was art. Her medium was photography.

"I am also so nervous to be doing this here, in my hometown," she said.

Sena jumped in. "Well, I can't wait to see this show, Elena. I've had a peek at just a few of your pieces, and I know you've done shows in L.A. and the Pacific Northwest. This is the perfect place to have your first show in Arizona. I know for a fact there are people coming to the grand opening tomorrow just to see your work." She shot a look at Tessa. "Sorry. No offense."

"None taken. I'm thrilled to have you here, Elena. I never could have imagined having an artist of your caliber hanging a show here. Thanks to you, I already have artists from three states away contacting me about showing their work here at some point."

"What's the first piece you're going to hang?" Sena asked.

Elena picked up one of the largest pieces and began to unwrap it. "Well, I was just thinking that I want this piece hung directly across from the entry."

She propped it against the wall and Tessa's breath caught in her throat.

A crisp, full moon was at the top of a black-and-white photo. Owen Station lay below it. Tessa recognized the view. It had been taken from Boot Hill. But unlike the clear night she experienced with Lace, a long, thick bank of clouds lay just above the town. So, instead of being ablaze in the full moonlight, the town was in the shadows, its color muted. It looked like it was literally floating.

Tessa shivered. "I know this spot," she whispered.

"You do?" Sena sounded surprised.

"You took that from Boot Hill."

Elena nodded. "About twelve years ago. Before I had much more than instinct to work with. I shot it one night while I was home from college on break."

"It's breathtaking," Tessa said softly.

"I forgot," Sena said, turning toward Tessa. "You were up there with Lace. On Boot Hill. For her birthday."

Tessa didn't respond to that. Instead, she turned to the artist. "Elena, this is perfect. It is dramatic and thought-provoking and beautiful. It is haunting. I love it."

Plus, it was a perfect way to honor the friendship that had made all this possible. But Tessa wasn't going there. Not with Sena. Not at that point. Not after their exchange about Lace in her pajamas. No way.

"Well, there you have it!" Sena said. "Carry on, you two. I have a meeting with Knox this morning. Let me know if you need anything. Otherwise, I will see you for the big event tomorrow."

Tessa air-kissed Sena good-bye, but she didn't move from her spot in front of the photo.

Elena shifted beside her. "Um, are you sure you like it?"

"What?" Tessa laughed, a little embarrassed to realize she had let herself wander off. "Yes, yes, I do. Sorry."

"Don't be sorry."

"I guess I was just thinking about everything it's taken to get to this point. And everyone who has helped make it happen."

"Like Lace."

Tessa raised her eyebrows. Not Elena, too.

Elena held her hands up. "Sorry, I don't mean to pry."

She started unwrapping the other pieces and laying them out on the floor in front of them. "You know, it's been a while since I've looked at some of these. They've been in storage during the move. They look different in here." She stood up and took a good look at them. "I'm feeling a little vulnerable."

"I get that," Tessa said. "I mean, I'm excited to share this space with everyone tomorrow. At the same time, it has been such a personal project. It's such a reflection of who I am. It's scary."

Elena took a breath. "I actually can't believe I'm back here. This was never part of my plan."

"Why *did* you come back, if you don't mind my asking?" Tessa knew what it was like to feel like you were moving backward, even as you tried to put one foot in front of the other.

"Hmmm, that's a good question. The simple answer is, I was ready for a change. L.A. was a lonely place to be after everything shut down. When my family called and said they needed me, it was hard to say no."

"And the complicated answer?"

"I finally admitted that I was never going to be able to escape the things I was trying to run from when I left."

Tessa had heard a lot of stories from a lot of people, during all her years behind the counter. But this level of self-awareness and honesty was rare.

"I was always a little different. I can see and hear the things others can't. And let me tell you, when you have a gift like that, growing up in a mortuary is *very* noisy. Most people in town didn't know what to make of me. My family didn't really know, either. Finally, my high school art teacher put a camera in my hands, and that helped me survive. It turned out that my gift also helped me capture things with my camera that others couldn't see. As soon as I was old enough, I left town, went to school, poured everything into my art, and hoped the noise would go away. Or at least quiet down." Elena paused. "It didn't."

Tessa was trying to adjust to life in the Southwest. Lace was trying to teach her. But she had never had a conversation like this. She couldn't even imagine what her very down-to-earth brothers would say if they were standing there listening to someone talk about how they could see ghosts. Hell, *she* wasn't sure what to say.

"Anyway, when my dad called and asked me to come home, to help make sure my brothers didn't ruin our one-hundred-year-old family business, I didn't have a good reason to say no."

"Well, I'm glad you're here, Elena. And if your gift helps you take photographs like this, I'm glad you have it."

Elena bent over to pick up a couple of photos, and took a look around the room, as if sizing up where to hang them. Tessa started to turn away. There were glasses and dishes to unpack, wine to stock, a party to get ready for.

But that photo, the one taken from Boot Hill under a full moon, drew her back.

"Yes." she said. "Like Lace."

Elena looked up. "Excuse me?"

"Before, when you asked if I was thinking about Lace. I was. I *am*. The last time I launched something like this, I was married to Olivia, my ex. After we divorced, I never thought I'd do anything like that again. It was too much, even with the two of us. But here I am. Doing it alone. Except I'm not alone. I have Lace. And I'm really thankful for that."

Elena was very still.

"It's been a wild few months. But now that it's almost over, I'm going to miss it. My daughter, Madison, is going to run this tasting room. It makes sense. She lives here in town. And I'll go back to the vineyard."

Tessa was talking to herself. That photo had surfaced thoughts she hadn't let herself think before. Now those thoughts were coming out of her mouth before she even knew what they were.

"I'm going to miss the banter, and the creativity it creates. The way she looks in the morning before coffee, her crazy hair sticking up in every direction, her face all scrunched up from being smashed into her pillow. And how grumpy she is before coffee. The way she surprises me with dinner before I even know I'm hungry and how she always has time to listen to whatever impossible idea pops into my head. The way she makes me feel like I can do anything."

Tessa paused, and looked at Elena, who was looking at her. And her cheeks got fiery hot. "Oh my God. You must think I'm crazy."

Elena smiled gently. "Not at all, Tessa. I think you're just at a crossroads. In a liminal space. In the *in-betweens,* I call it. I've been seeing people who are in that space since I was a toddler. Some of them are in between here and there. But they helped me understand there are lots of in-between spaces. Right at the moment, you're in between the *now* and the *not yet.*"

"Ms. Williams?"

Thank God for Builder Jack.

"I think we're done here."

Tessa turned to see him holding out his hand. She took it and they shook.

"My wife and I are planning to come to the opening tomorrow. We're really excited to have this place in town, and I'm proud to have been a small part of it."

"Jack, you've been a *huge* part of it. And I'm thankful. Please tell your crew they're all welcome tomorrow. I'd like to send each one of you home with a gift, so make sure they tell whoever is at the counter that they're part of the crew that did this renovation."

"You got it, Ms. Williams."

"Tessa, Jack. Please, call me Tessa."

And just like that, this phase was over. If Elena was right, that she had been in an in-between space, then the *not yet* was right around the corner.

Tessa couldn't even begin to imagine what that might look like.

CHAPTER NINE

A ngela was not happy about not being invited to the grand opening.

"It's open to the public, you know. I can just go, if I want to. You can't stop me."

Lace rolled her eyes. They had been dating for six weeks. She really needed to rethink that three-month rule. Three months was way too long.

"Yes, of course you can go, if you want to. All I'm saying is I'm gonna be too busy tonight to spend time with you. That's why I didn't ask you to come with me. I told Tessa I'd help."

"Tessa, Tessa, Tessa! What *is* it with you, two? You're constantly on your phone with her, even when I'm with you!"

"She has been building a new tasting room, Angela. At an impossible pace. Everything she has built for herself is on the line." Lace bit every one of those last three words. She was up to her eyeballs with Angela's dramatics. "This is a very big deal. So, when she asks for my help, I give it, because I'm her friend."

"Yeah, that's what you keep saying. Except you hardly have time for me because you're always helping her. And now everyone in town is going to this thing tonight."

"Not everyone will be there." Lace shook her head, wishing she had just let Angela's call go to voice mail. "Besides, you don't even live in town."

"They've been running ads for it all week in Tucson. It's all I've been hearing about!"

And that was why Lace had the no-locals rule. Just imagine if Angela lived in Owen Station, rather than ninety minutes away. She was definitely keeping *that* rule.

And she was going to break it off with Angela.

But she was not going to do it the right way, not in the midst of an argument, while frustrated.

"Listen, Ang. I'm sorry. I'd really like to talk about this. But can we do it tomorrow, please?"

"What is there to talk about, Lace? The way Tessa is the most important person in our relationship?"

Lace closed her eyes and tried not to react. How many times did Lace have to remind her they agreed, from the beginning, that they weren't having a relationship. They were just having a bit of fun.

At least, it was fun in the beginning. Sort of.

"Angela, really. Let's talk tomorrow. I'll call you first thing in the morning."

Angela didn't respond because she had already hung up.

Three hours later, Lace had forgotten all about it. Like the rest of her friends, she had pulled on a Mujer Fuerte T-shirt and hat, and reported for duty. Tessa had asked all the volunteers to show up an hour early, to get final instructions and be at their stations when guests started to arrive.

At first, the idea that people would volunteer to help a business, any business, was so foreign. Lace would have done whatever Tessa asked, of course. But why would other people show up on a Saturday to spend their day parking cars, serving food, clearing tables, cleaning bathrooms, and all the other things that needed to be done when throwing a party for two hundred people? That's what happened whenever Tessa hosted an event. Members of her wine club jumped at the opportunity to get on the volunteer list. It was weird, right? But only until Lace saw Tessa in action. She made every single person feel like they were a VIP. Like they were part of something that mattered. The volunteer pool was getting even bigger as Tessa's friend network expanded.

Lace had volunteered to park cars for the grand opening. She knew the property best, and had actually created the parking plan for the day. But Tessa vetoed that idea. She wanted Lace nearby and in the tasting room, in case she needed her. So she put Lace on bussing duty. It wasn't the sexiest job—clearing tables, bringing glasses back to be washed, making sure the place always looked ready for company—but Lace was looking forward to it.

After the volunteer orientation, and team cheer led by Delaney, of course, Madison took Lace by the elbow and led her to a quiet corner. She looked so much like Tessa. And Tessa had been so young when she was born. It wasn't surprising people often assumed they were sisters.

"What's up, Madison? Is everything okay?"

Madison nodded. "I just wanted to thank you for everything you've done to help make this all happen."

Lace exhaled. "You looked so serious! I thought maybe something was wrong."

"No, nothing's wrong." Madison smiled. "But I am serious. The last five years have been amazing in a lot of ways. I have so much respect for my mom and everything she's done." She glanced over at Tessa, who was across the room helping Elena, who was nervously making a last-minute change to the show, and then back at Lace. "But *this* is dope. This new tasting room is taking everything to the next level. And it would never have happened without you."

Lace felt her cheeks grow warm and she looked away. As happy as she was for Tessa, and as proud as she was of what Tessa had accomplished, the weeks leading up to the opening had not been fun. Waking up every morning to the sound of construction next door. The tight timeline. Having Tessa right next door, in her physical space. And, every day, taking up more and more space in her brain.

Jumping back on the dating bus had not been the antidote Lace thought it would be. In a lot of ways, it had made things worse. What used to be fun—breezy conversations, chilling together with no past to fret over and no future to worry about, consensual, casual, playful sex—now felt like hard work.

Angela wasn't wrong. Tessa was always in the room, even when she was ninety minutes away.

Tessa had become the measure of a good conversation. Nothing helped Lace chill out more than her quiet, steady presence. And sex? Well. It took way too much work to constantly push down the thoughts and images that swirled up from her unconsciousness, unwelcome and unbidden. It was like playing Whac-A-Mole, except it wasn't a cute little creature that kept popping up every time Lace dropped her guard. It was Tessa.

Every day for the past several months, Lace felt like she was living on the side of a mountain. And every day, she could feel the rocks beneath her feet slip away one by one. Afraid to make a wrong move, say the wrong thing, touch her in the wrong way, feel something she did not want to feel.

Lace was exhausted from living on the edge of disaster. And she certainly did not feel like she had contributed to Tessa's success. She was just relieved that she had managed to get through the past few months without blowing it all up.

She slowly looked back up at Madison. "You're giving me way too much credit. Your mom is a force of nature. This"—she waved her hands toward the tasting room—"is all her."

"Wait a minute." Madison laughed. "Have you *met* my mom? She is the fiercest person I know." She cocked her head sideways. "But she doesn't always *feel* that way. Know what I mean?"

That night at the Triple D popped into Lace's mind. Tessa in those shorts and boots, dancing her buns off. Then sitting in the parking lot, under the stars. Confessing that she'd always felt incompetent. It didn't make any sense to Lace then. Now that she knew Tessa even better, it made less. But she nodded.

"I'm not blaming my *stepmother*." Madison spit out the word like a sour grape. "But she didn't help. Olivia is older than Mom. She comes from a rich family. She has so many connections. Everybody loves her. And because she's got such a big personality, everybody thought she was the one making the winery work. But my mom did everything. And never got the credit."

Madison paused, scowling, as if remembering it all. Kids always saw and knew more than their parents thought they did.

"That must have been hard to watch."

Madison nodded. "It was fucking terrible." Her head snapped back. "Oh, sorry!"

Lace smiled and covered her mouth with her hand, pretending to be shocked. "Madison, what would your mother say?"

"She wouldn't say that, that's for sure. Mom never blames anyone else for anything, and hardly ever loses her temper. She's so chill about everything. If something goes wrong, the first thing she thinks is, 'What did I do to cause this? What could I have done differently?'"

"That doesn't sound so bad," Lace said carefully. "It sounds mature."

"Maybe. But sometimes bad things happen because somebody does a bad thing." Madison clenched her jaw and her eyes darkened. "And sometimes the right response is to get pissed off. Not blame yourself."

Tessa hadn't shared many details of her breakup, but Lace knew the marriage ended after her ex had an affair. Given her own history with Knox, it wasn't a subject Lace wanted to probe too deeply. It infuriated her to think about someone betraying Tessa that way. Like, really. It made her want to hurt someone.

But it also made her feel guilty. Lace had inflicted that exact kind of pain on someone else once. *She* had done a bad thing. Lace didn't like the person she was back then. Or the one she could be again. She didn't like to think about it. And she sure as hell didn't trust herself.

Reason number one not to let anyone get too close or go too deep.

But she was really glad Tessa had Madison.

She put her hand on Madison's shoulder. "You know, your mom is really lucky to have you in her life."

Madison laughed. "That's what I'm trying to say to *you*. You bring out the best in her. Help her feel more confident." She looked down at the floor for a second and, when she looked back up, Lace noticed—not for the first time—that her eyes were the exact same color as Tessa's. "I'm glad you're in her life, Lace. In *our* lives."

Lace's stomach dropped through the floor. It was so loud in Lace's ears, it was shocking that no one turned around to see what in the hell was going on back in the corner. Also, the hole in the floor that her stomach made had sucked all the air out of the room. Which was why Lace was having trouble breathing.

This was not supposed to happen.

She had rules.

Three months.

No locals.

Nothing serious.

She was not someone anyone should be serious with.

She didn't want serious.

She didn't want the responsibility. She couldn't handle the responsibility.

That's why she wasn't a mother, wasn't it?

Even the universe knew she wasn't up for the job.

And that's why she would never, ever—not in a million years or a million lifetimes—ever let herself hope for anything more than a little fun.

She could be happy.

But a happy ever after?

No.

She just didn't have it in her.

So how in the hell did she end up here, looking into the eyes of a kid who was looking at her like she was *part of her life*?

Lace needed air.

"You're the best, Madison," she managed to mumble, with what she hoped was a smile on her face. "I need to grab something from the house quick before things get going."

Madison reached out before Lace could turn away and hugged her. "No, *you* are, Lace. Have fun today!"

She was what? *The best?* Not even close.

Lace broke away gently and hurried toward the door, pretending not to hear Tessa calling from behind, and didn't stop until she was in her own kitchen. She leaned on the counter with both hands, dropped her head, closed her eyes, and tried to breathe. In and out. In and out.

The first guests were starting to arrive. Lace could hear car doors opening and closing, happy voices, music. But she was on another planet. Looking up at an alien sky.

She tried telling herself that this could all go back to normal— that it *would* go back to normal. Once the tasting room was opened, Tessa would go back to the vineyard. And they could go back to the way they were. Funny texts. Lunch once in a while. Movie night once a month.

And she would be more careful.

Way more careful.

She wouldn't get close enough to smell sandalwood soap. They wouldn't sit up until late at night, sometimes talking and sometimes not, just enjoying being in each other's company. She wouldn't drop everything every time Tessa needed something. She would spend more time at Banter & Brew, hanging with Knox. With Madison running the tasting room, she wouldn't feel like she would want to pop over there all the time. She would mind her own business. Literally. Spend more time in her own shop. She would make her own coffee in the morning, instead of waiting for Tessa to appear, looking all awake and happy and soft and strong. She would date more. There were at least a dozen women on her FD list. Twice that many, probably. Smart, interesting, sexy women who would be thrilled to spend a few months with Lace, having fun, experimenting with the latest toys, and *not* being serious.

She could do this.

She had to do this.

Because she could not imagine life without Tessa.

And this was the only way.

Lace was finally able to take a deep breath. She exhaled and took two more. Then she stood up, straightened her shoulders, and looked out the window. A crowd had gathered. Tessa's grand opening was going to be a huge success. Lace was happy about that. Tessa deserved this. Lace was going to go out there and pitch in and help make it happen.

She was going to be a good friend.

Nothing more.

She opened her kitchen door to head back to the tasting room, and nearly tripped over Bleu, who was standing there waiting. Of course Bleu had followed her. Somehow, without realizing it, Lace had let even Bleu think she was part of the family.

"I am not part of your herd, Bleu."

Bleu just stared at her.

"You are not responsible for me."

Bleu cocked her head, one ear standing straight up like usual. She looked skeptical.

"Oh, for God's sake. Come on. Let's go see how we can be helpful."

Bleu fell in beside her as she headed back into the tasting room.

Fortunately, Tessa was swamped by guests. She had underestimated the number of people who would show up. Volunteers flew around the tasting room, delivering orders, clearing tables, getting people signed up for the Mujer Fuerte newsletter. Every table, inside and out, was already filled, and a line of cars was still making its way up the driveway. Tessa waved at her from across the room, a bright smile on her face. Lace gave a quick wave back and went to work.

She would have given anything to not have to talk to anyone. To just put her head down and not look up until the sun was setting. But people wanted to talk to her. And she was a pro.

"I can't believe this is the same carriage house!" Delaney bounced past her, following an older white couple Lace hadn't seen before, with Derrick following close behind. He was carrying a case of wine. "Are you happy with how it turned out? You must be, right? I mean, it's *gorgeous*!" Lace nodded with a tight smile, and the foursome kept moving to deposit that wine in the couple's car.

"I told you this was a good idea," Knox said from behind her. He put his arm around her shoulders. "Just imagine how many people have seen Frisky Business for the first time today. Have you talked to Sophie? Have people been stopping in?"

Lace shrugged. "I'm not sure. I've been too busy here to find out."

"I think I'll pop over and see how she's doing," Knox said.

"Great."

Knox stopped and turned to look at her. "Are you okay? You seem, I don't know, kind of off."

She nodded. "Yep. Just trying to keep up."

He patted her on the shoulder and smiled. "It has been a crazy few months, hasn't it? Hang in there. I'll see you in a bit."

A table full of first responders, all women, waved her over. Most of them were part of the Fireballs. "Lace! We have an idea and we want your opinion." Al patted the bench next to her. "Sit down."

"I'm good standing. I'm on the job today," Lace said. "What's your idea?"

"Well, Sam here was just telling us about the fire department she came from. In Michigan, right, Sam?"

A woman in her mid-twenties wearing a tight tank top, with a fresh-looking scorpion tattoo perched on her very buff right shoulder, nodded. She must have been new to the department because Lace hadn't met her yet.

"Sam says the guys in her department all posed for a sexy calendar. You know, wearing helmets or strategically placed hoses or whatever—" The women at the table all snickered. "And they used it to raise money for charity."

Lace waited. And then Sam jumped in. "We're thinking maybe we'd do the same thing, except we'd feature the *female* first responders of Owen Station. There are a lot of us between our department and the police force."

"And we'd use the money to support the new women's shelter," Al added.

"I think that's a great idea," Lace said, smiling for real for the first time all afternoon. "I know just the photographer, too. She specializes in photographing women's bodies. All shapes and sizes. They are breathtaking. I think she would have a lot of fun with this."

Al said she would be in touch and Lace left the group plotting creative poses and settings over another bottle of wine.

Every once in a while, Tessa would catch Lace's eye across the room and grin, but every time she started to make her way toward Lace, someone would intercept her. Lace couldn't have been more thankful for that.

"Hey there." Elena was holding a glass of wine, standing alone along the wall next to a table Lace was clearing. "How are you doing?"

"Me? I'm fine. How are you? Are you happy with the show?"

"I don't know. I always feel so weird when I show my work. It's like standing around in my underwear."

"Is that why you're hiding back here in a corner?"

Elena laughed. "Exactly." She paused and looked over at the main piece, which was hanging right across from the entrance. "What do you think of it?"

Lace looked, too, more carefully than she had before. "You took that from Boot Hill, didn't you?"

Elena nodded.

"That's one of my favorite places in the world."

"That's what Tessa said." Elena looked back at Lace. Her eyes were so piercing, it was almost uncomfortable.

"What else did she tell you?"

Lace wasn't sure why she asked that. And she wasn't sure she wanted to know. But Elena didn't answer because Hazel and Sena elbowed their way in.

"Just the person I wanted to see here today." Hazel had a grin on her face. "Elena!"

Sena jumped in. "First of all, Elena, let me just say the show is fabulous."

Elena smiled shyly. "Thank you."

"Second," Hazel's eyes were popping out of her head. "Any sign of her yet?"

"Who?" Elena looked confused.

"Mrs. Owen, of course!"

"Ah." Elena took a breath and her shoulders relaxed. "Elizabeth, you mean."

Lace snapped her head toward Elena. "How do you know her name?"

Hazel gave Lace a little push. "I told her, silly. The diary, remember? I've been researching her life, as much as possible, and I thought maybe Elena could gather some intel on her today."

"Nope. No sign of her today." Elena shrugged.

Sena sipped her wine. "Maybe she doesn't like crowds?"

Elena nodded. "I'm not a big fan myself. Do you think anyone would notice if I slipped away early?"

Lace wished like hell she could get out of there, too. But she stuck it out. It was Tessa's day, and Lace wasn't going to ruin it by acting like a selfish asshole. No matter how much she wanted to sneak off and lose herself in a movie. Alone.

Madison yelled last call at five thirty, and by seven o'clock most of the volunteers had cleaned up, put the place back together, and headed home with a thank-you bottle and a hug from Tessa. Lace was in the kitchen, washing the last dishes, when she heard Angela's voice.

"What do you mean you're closed?" Angela was loud. And she sounded drunk. "Let me talk to *Lay-sh*! Right now! I'm her *gesht*."

Lace couldn't make out exactly what Madison said in response, but whatever it was made Angela get even louder.

"I demand to see *Lay-sh*. I know she's in here *shom-where*. She's ALWAYS here, hanging around *Tesha* like a lovesick—"

"That's enough, Angela," Lace barked as she pushed through the kitchen door.

A young woman Lace hadn't seen before was leaning on the counter, checking out her own fingernails. Angela was face-to-face with Madison in the middle of the room. If anyone else had been there moments before, they had cleared out.

When Madison saw Lace, she held her hands out and shrugged, her mouth puckered in disgust.

"I got this, Madison. I'm sorry."

"What are you shaying shary for, Lace? Don't you dare apologize for me. You should be apologizing *to* me."

That was a surprisingly sober thought. But Lace wasn't getting her hopes up. She took Angela by the elbow and steered her outside. She smelled like cheap whiskey. If Lace had to guess, she would say the woman had spent the day barhopping through Owen Station.

"Angela, you need to go home."

"I don't want to go home, Lace. I drove all the way from *Tushon* to *shee y*ou."

"You're drunk. I'm calling a car to take you home."

"Mitzi *ish* here. She can drive, but I don't want to go home. We need to talk."

Lace took a breath. "Yes, we do. But not now. I told you. I will call you first thing tomorrow."

Mitzi strolled out of the tasting room. "Are you coming, Angela? I told you it was a bad idea to come here. We've been here all day and I am done with this ugly little town. Let's go."

Mitzi sounded sober, at least.

"Are you okay to drive?" Lace turned to Mitzi. "I can call a car. Or find you a place to stay for the night."

"I want to *shtay* with YOU tonight, *Lay-sh*."

Mitzi ignored her. "Yes, I'm fine. I haven't had anything but water for hours. While this one," she said, gesturing toward Angela, "just got more and more wasted." She scrunched her nose and shook her head. "Nasty."

Angela threw her arms around Lace, knocking her off balance, yelling, "Lay-sh! Please let me *shtay*!" They both almost ended up on the ground.

Lace pushed her off and steadied both herself and Angela. "Angela, I wouldn't let you stay here tonight even if you weren't drunk. This is over, okay? I'm done."

Lace hadn't meant to say that, not in that way, anyway, and not under these circumstances. But there it was. She was exhausted. Emotionally raw. And she was. Done.

Lace took Angela by the arm again and turned toward the car, where Mitzi was already waiting, holding the passenger door open.

Angela started to cry. "*Thish* is all *becaush* of *Tesha*, isn't it?"

"Tessa doesn't have anything to do with this, Angela."

"You're lying!" Angela yelled. "Everything you do is about *Tesha. Tesha, Tesha, Tesha!* I don't know why you don't just marry her already!"

"Angela, I wouldn't even *think* of marrying Tessa. Not if she were the last woman on earth."

Lace tucked Angela into the car, pulled the seat belt tight across her, and closed the door.

When she turned back toward the tasting room, she saw Tessa standing in the doorway, with Madison and Bleu beside her.

CHAPTER TEN

Tessa crossed her arms tightly across her chest, fists clenched, her right eye twitching. She could only feel thankful that all of her guests had been gone and there were no witnesses to Angela's messy display or the words Lace hurled like a grenade, exploding shrapnel in every direction.

Except for Madison, of course, who had been drawn right into the middle of it all.

It wasn't like Madison hadn't dealt before with tasting room guests who had been over-served by some other winery. That was just part of the job and, as young as she was, Madison was a pro. But she did not deserve this, not from Angela. And certainly not from Lace. Especially not after such an exhilarating, and exhausting, day.

Tessa had been up in the office when she heard it all start. By the time she got downstairs, Lace had been leading Angela outside. Tessa and Madison followed and watched the whole ugly scene unfold.

Tessa put her arm around Madison. Her daughter was shaking.

"I'm sorry you had to deal with this, Madison." Tessa spoke without taking her eyes off what was happening in her parking lot. "Thanks for everything you did to make today happen. It was amazing. Go home and get some rest. I will talk to you in the morning."

"Mom, I am not leaving you here. Not like this. Not after what just happened. What Lace said." Her voice trembled.

Of course Madison would feel protective, especially after everything they had been through together. Tessa turned and looked at her. Those hazel eyes, which usually sparkled, were cloudy and gray. Deep furrows had formed between her eyebrows, and she was frowning hard. Tessa couldn't tell if she was angry or sad. Probably both.

Tessa was.

"Why don't you come spend the night at my place." Madison begged her. "I'll help you close up, then we can grab some food on the way. It'll be like old times. Besides, you know Bleu would love a sleepover."

"Madison, really." Tessa worked to keep her voice even and strong. "Go home. I got this."

Madison hesitated, as if weighing how hard to push. Finally, she nodded, gave Tessa a tight squeeze, and headed to her car. She said a muted good-bye to Lace, barely glancing at her, as she passed her in the lot.

Tessa spun around and headed back into the tasting room, slamming the front door behind her, where the first thing she saw was the view from Boot Hill.

Tessa did not cry easily and never in front of other people. The saying "there's no crying in baseball?" Tessa was damn sure some farmer who just lost his crop in a hailstorm said it first. So, the second she felt her face get wet, she wiped it dry with the back of her hand.

Not if she were the last woman on earth.

The words stung more than Tessa would have thought possible.

But it was all her fault.

Lace never lied about who she was or the kind of life she wanted for herself.

Tessa let her in, anyway. She opened the door to her family, to her heart. She ignored every sign—every Angela, every Jennifer, every Maria, every lead singer in a peace-sign-covered van—every bit of evidence that Lace was only out for fun. And that as soon as the fun was over, Lace was out.

Tessa's big mistake was thinking those rules only applied to dates—not to best friends.

But now it was clear.

And it wasn't just Tessa who felt the sting. Madison felt it, too.

They meant nothing to Lace. *She* meant nothing.

Tessa didn't turn around when the door opened. She should have locked it behind her. Her mistake. Another one. Now, she had to deal with Lace.

"I'm sorry about all that, Tessa. She's gone."

Her face was wet again, and she didn't trust her own voice.

"Tessa. Say something."

Lace came closer when Tessa didn't answer.

"Oh my God, you're crying."

Tessa steadied her voice, steeled herself, and wiped one cheek. "No, I'm not."

When Lace reached out to wipe the other, Tessa flinched away. "Don't. Just…don't."

"Tessa, please. Believe me when I say how sorry I am. I didn't know Angela was going to show up here tonight. She wasn't even invited. I mean, she wanted to come but I told her not to because I'd be too busy working to hang out. I knew she wasn't happy, but I never imagined she would come anyway. Especially like that. I'm so sorry Madison had to deal with it. I will apologize to her, first thing tomorrow—tonight, even. I'll call her. I'll make it right. There is just no excuse for that kind of—"

Tessa spun around so she was facing her. "This isn't about *Angela's* behavior, Lace."

Lace's head snapped back and her eyes opened wide. "I know I should have handled that differently." She was choosing her words carefully. "It was not my finest moment. It was disrespectful and inexcusable. I'm going to call Angela tomorrow, too. Or go see her and apologize. I never end things like that, in a moment of anger or frustration. Ever. It's one of my cardinal rules—"

"Oh right. You and your *rules*."

"Yes. My rules. And one of them is always be respectful. I told Angela I would call her tomorrow and we would talk. I told her that *this morning,* before the opening. I knew things were not going well between the two of us. I knew it was time to end it. When she showed up like that tonight, and I saw her there, in Madison's face, I just sort of lost it. It was wrong to break up with her that way. I was—"

"Lace, just stop. I don't need these details. And I don't want to listen to your explanations. This is none of my business. Your life, your rules, your women. None of my business!"

"Of course it's your business. My life just splattered all over your grand opening. That is the last thing I wanted. I wanted this evening—the whole day—to be perfect. You deserve the best, Tessa, the absolute—"

"*Really*?!" Tessa knew she sounded shrill. She didn't care. "*REALLY*?"

"Yes, really. I don't understand why you're so—"

"Angry? Hurt? I don't know, Lace. How am supposed to feel?" Tessa swung her hand out toward the large black-and-white photo. "When Elena unwrapped this picture, I recognized it immediately. And I wanted it hung right here, right across from the front door, because I wanted it to be the first thing I'd see every time I came in. I wanted it to be the first thing *you* would see. A reminder of the night you asked me to celebrate your birthday, in your most favorite place in the world. The night I realized how important this friendship is. How important *you* are to me. I thought you felt the same way."

Lace's mouth was half open, but no words were coming out.

"How in the hell did I get it all so wrong?" Tessa's head hurt. "You know what, never mind. It doesn't matter. Go home, Lace. I'm going to close up. Then I'm going to head back to the vineyard. To my life. And we're just going to pretend that none of this ever happened."

"Tessa, I don't understand any of this. You didn't get anything wrong. I *do* feel the same way." Lace gestured toward the photo. "That night was one of the best nights of my life. Because I was there with *you*."

"Because you were there with *me*." Tessa mimicked Lace's voice. "Really? You mean the woman you wouldn't marry even if I was the last person on earth? That's precious, Lace. It really is."

Lace's eyes opened wide and she looked around, as if trying to understand where she was and what was happening. Her mouth opened and closed a few times, as if she was struggling to find words. Or to breathe.

Tessa shook her head, turned, and headed toward her office. She needed to get as far away from Lace as she could. And she was not going to fall apart. Lace was not going to take this day away from her. She had worked too hard. It had all felt so good. Over two hundred people. Elena had sold most of her work. Wine had flown off the shelves. Madison signed a dozen new members. All their friends had been there, some volunteering and others lending support—*their* friends. That's how she had been thinking about things. They had done this together—she and Lace. What had she been thinking? *They* weren't together. *They* weren't a thing.

"Please, Tessa. I didn't know you heard me say that. Oh my God. Please, let me explain." Lace was right behind her, following up the stairs to the loft.

"What is there to explain?" Tessa spun around to face her. "I get it. You don't do serious. You have a three-month rule. You just want to have a good time. I just never saw it up close and personal—how ugly and childish that can be. And I had *nooo* idea it included friendships. You forgot to tell me that part. I'm a big girl. I could have handled it. You could have just said, '*Sorry, Tess, we're over. Move along. I've got a whole line of people in my contact list just waiting to be my friend. So, it's been fun. See ya.*'"

Lace's head jutted forward and her mouth fell open as her eyebrows shot to the top of her forehead. But Tessa didn't care how shocked, hurt, angry, insulted, or whatever the hell Lace was feeling right then. She just wanted to close up the tasting room and get out of there. Alone. Back to the life she had gotten used to, the life she had worked so hard to build, with Bleu by her side. Life without morning coffees and Lace's hair sticking up every which way, without seeing Lace's goofy grin in the middle of the afternoon when she'd pop into the tasting room during construction with an unexpected snack, without the constant stream of texts with some funny story or words of encouragement right when she needed it most, without movie nights and late night phone calls and always, always knowing someone had her back. Correction: *Thinking* someone had her back.

"God *damn* it, Lace." Tessa's face was wet again.

This was not okay. Why was she even having this conversation? Why did this all hurt so much? Tessa's head was spinning. She leaned on her grandmother's desk and looked around her office, an office she built for herself because, even though she knew she would have to refocus her efforts at the vineyard once construction was finished, she also hoped, wanted, planned to spend a lot of time here. Because *Lace* was here. And, God help her, Tessa couldn't imagine not seeing her every day anymore. She couldn't imagine being without her. Thank goodness she had never said these things out loud. It wasn't anything she was going to have to walk back. Except to herself.

"Tessa, please. Oh my God. Please don't cry."

"I am *not* crying. I'm just angry. Angry at myself for letting this happen. Because, believe me, I know how dangerous and stupid it is to mix business and your personal life. I was married to Olivia. We had a business together. When the marriage ended, I lost everything. Now, look. I'm stuck with *you*. I've invested everything in launching this tasting room. It was stupid to let myself get too close to you, stupid to let you into my family. Madison thinks—thought—the world of you. My dog loves you. I don't know how I could have been such a moron. You never tried to hide who you really are from me. I just didn't see it. I didn't think it would apply to me. What an idiot I've been! So, thank you. Thank you for reminding me of that. Thank you for helping me see all of this so clearly. Now, please, Lace. Just go. Go! I can't do this anymore."

Then Tessa really did cry. She couldn't stop it. And she didn't even care who saw it. Every stupid decision she had ever made came crashing in on her. Billy. Failing her freshmen year. Dropping out. Letting herself get swept away by Olivia. Letting Olivia take all the credit for everything. Not seeing Olivia for who she was until it was too late. Losing everything. Trusting Lace, even when Lace herself told her she couldn't be trusted.

She dropped her head into her hands and let the shame and grief wash over her.

After a long few minutes, Lace hadn't said a word. Tessa thought maybe she had even left.

She shook her head, as if she could shake some sense into it, forced herself to stop crying, took a deep breath, and stood up as straight and tall as she could. Then she turned back around. And that's when she saw Lace on the floor.

She was in a tight kneeling position, her hands clasped over the back of her head, which was tucked into her chest. She was rocking slightly, forward to back.

"Get up, Lace." Tessa was not in the mood for whatever this was. She had misread the situation, put too much of herself into this friendship. Then, Lace spoke her truth, out there in the parking lot. Now, Tessa knew it, too. Fine. Whatever. There was no reason for all this drama. It was just time to move on.

But Lace didn't move and she didn't look up.

"Lace, get *up*."

Lace shook her head. "I can't." She was speaking into her chest, so her voice was muffled.

"What do you mean you *can't?*"

"I mean, I don't want to. I can't stand to see you looking so sad. Knowing that I'm the one who hurt you."

Tessa leaned down and grabbed Lace's arm. "Oh, for God's sake, Lace. Get up."

Lace sat back on her heels, balanced her elbows on her knees, folded her hands as if in prayer, and looked up. The skin between her eyebrows was pinched so tight, Tessa was sure she'd have a massive headache later. Lace started to say something, then stopped. Then started again. Then stopped.

Then she stood up, folded her arms across the top of her head, and squinted at Tessa. Her mouth was clamped shut, like she was afraid of what might come out of it.

She should have done that about an hour earlier.

"Do you have something to say?" Tessa didn't care if she sounded cold. She wished she was literally made of ice. Then maybe none of this would hurt so much.

Lace dropped her hands to her side, squared her shoulders, and took a deep breath. "I have been trying so hard to keep it together, Tessa. For weeks. Longer. Ever since you started building out this tasting room. Ever since you—I—since we started seeing each other every day."

Tessa shifted her weight from one foot to the other. The back of her neck started tingling. She held up a hand. "Stop. Don't say anymore." Tessa had no idea what Lace was going to say next. But whatever it was felt like something that, once said, could never be *un*said.

Lace shook her head. "I'm sorry, Tess. I am in completely uncharted territory here. Please listen." Lace looked away and took a deep breath. When she looked back at Tessa, her gaze was steady. "Angela was angry because she said you were the most important person in our relationship."

Tessa started to interrupt but Lace held up her hand. "She was not wrong."

Lace paused, but her eyes didn't stray.

"If I wasn't texting with you or talking to you on the phone, I was *thinking* about the text I wanted to send you or the thing I wanted to tell you. If you needed me, I'd drop everything to be there, no matter what Angela and I had planned. If we were watching a movie together or out having dinner or on a hike, all I could think about was how much more fun it would be to be doing it with you."

Tessa closed her eyes and tried to understand what Lace was saying. Half the time, they finished each other's sentences. But right in that moment, Tessa could not comprehend what Lace was trying to say. "I don't know if it's just been a really long day, or if you are making no sense, but I don't understand what you're telling me, Lace. Not even a little."

Lace ran her hands through her coiffed hair, which was now an absolute mess, and started pacing. Tessa had seen this before. It's what Lace did when she was overwhelmed.

"I know I am making a huge mess of things," Lace stammered. "I don't trust myself. I don't think anyone else should trust me, either. That's why I keep things short and sweet. Fun and run. It makes life breezy and easy."

"What the hell with the rhyming, Lace? Honest to God. It's like a terrible country song. If you have something to say just *say* it."

"I'm sorry, I'm sorry! I don't know what I'm doing." Lace's eyebrows met in an arch above her nose, and she looked terrified. She licked her lips, swallowed a gallon of air, and opened her mouth to speak.

"Okay. Here goes—"

"Out with it, already!"

"Tessa WIlliams. You are the last person in the world I would marry."

Tessa blinked hard. She wanted to rewind the last ten seconds and listen to them again. Because what she heard was—

"Oh my God, Lace! I heard that the *first* time, when you screamed it at Angela. Madison heard it. I think the whole fucking town heard it!" The vein in Tessa's neck was throbbing. Her heart was beating five million times a minute. "Do you really think I needed to hear it *again?* I get it. You don't do long-term relationships, and apparently that includes *friendships*. We're over. Done. Fine! Can we be finished with this conversation now?"

Tessa turned, shoved her laptop into the bag, and started wildly clearing her desk. She was leaving and didn't know when she would be coming back.

Suddenly, Lace came up behind her, reached around, and pulled her into her arms. She buried her face in Tessa's shoulder and breathed so deeply, Tessa felt every part of her body expand and then release. Tessa should have pulled away. But she didn't want to.

She didn't understand anything that was happening, and Lace was making zero sense. But feeling Lace's arms around her settled her heart. She closed her eyes and let her body relax against Lace's.

Part of her hoped Lace would never talk again because, every time she talked, Tessa got more confused and more upset. But she needed to understand.

"Lace, what the hell is happening? Why do you keep saying you would never marry me? No one ever said anything about getting married. That is the last thing I'm thinking about."

Lace lifted her head off Tessa's shoulder. "I will never marry *anyone*, Tessa. Ever again." Her voice was soft next to Tessa's ear. "And for sure. I would never marry *you*. Because I care about you too much. You deserve someone you can count on not to screw it up, someone who will never betray you, never leave you. Someone who will always, always be there for you. Not someone like *me*."

If Tessa was confused before, this made it worse. She gently pushed Lace's arms away so she could turn around and look at her. Taking Lace's hands into her own, she leaned back and sat on the edge of her grandmother's desk.

"Lace, you have been the best friend I have ever had in my life. You've been up at the crack of dawn over the past few months more times than you have in your entire life, all put together. For me. Because I needed you. You've been on the other end of that phone night and day for the past two *years*. It doesn't matter what I need, what I ask, you're there for it. You listen to me ramble on and on about rare varietals and soil types and organic farming options and what an asshole my neighbor is. You hold me up when being a mom is hard and make me laugh every day. You even watch Clint Eastwood movies with me, and I know how much you hate him. For God's sake, you bussed tables all day today, instead of minding your own counter, in your own shop, when you had the opportunity to make a hundred new sales because of all the people that were here on your property. And, oh yeah, this is *your* property, *your* house, and you are sharing it with *me*. You love my kid. You love my dog. And it's not just us. I see how you are with Hazel and Delaney, the way you still love on Knox. My God, all your *exes* still like you."

Lace's mouth drooped. "Not Angela."

"*Fuck*, Angela," Tessa snapped. Then paused and cracked a smile. "Umm, let me rephrase that."

And then Tessa laughed. They both did. And just like that, the *now* that Tessa had been living in faded into the past, and the *not yet* became the new now. And Tessa was pulling Lace toward her.

When their lips met, it was like slipping into her favorite down jacket on a crisp morning in the vineyard. Like lying in the bed of her truck on a warm night, staring up at a starlit sky. Like letting go of the rope swing at Clear Lake and soaring through the air before splashing into the water on a perfect summer day. It was effortless. The most natural thing in the world. Something she had done a thousand times before—and could do ten-hundred-thousand times more without ever getting tired or bored. Because having Lace's lips on hers, Lace's tongue entwined with her own, she felt completely and totally safe, and exhilarated, all at the same time. Alive.

"What is *happening*?" Lace croaked as she pushed herself away, blinking, and taking quick, shallow breaths.

"I don't know," Tessa managed to squeak out. "But I don't want it to stop. Do you?"

Lace shook her head and started to speak, but Tessa put a finger on her lips. "Shh. Don't talk."

Lace stumbled for words.

"I mean it, Lace."

Lace's forehead got all scrunched up again. "Tessa," she said quickly before she could be shushed again, "I don't know how to do this."

"Do *what*? Aren't you actually an *expert* at this?" Tessa laughed.

"I don't know how to do *this* with someone I really care about. Someone I don't want to disappear in three months." Her eyes dropped to the floor. "I like things short and sweet," she said quietly.

Tessa grinned. "I think I can do short and sweet."

She stood up, took Lace by the hand again, and led her to the couch.

"I want to see you," Tessa said softly. "Can I take your shirt off?"

"I'll show you mine if you'll show me yours." Lace smiled impishly.

Tessa quickly pulled her own blouse over her head, snapped off her bra, and dropped them both to the floor. Then she undid each button on Lace's camp shirt slowly, until it fell open, exposing a snugly fitting sports bra. She pulled the shirt off, and then ran her hands across Lace's shoulders and down her breastbone. She stopped at the front clasp, which she flicked open, and then helped Lace shrug off the bra.

"Somehow I didn't expect you to be the take-charge type." Lace smiled. "I like it."

Tessa smiled back, but she wasn't interested in a conversation. A fire was raging between her legs. Every part of her wanted to feel every part of Lace, who was magnificent. Flawless, olive skin. And her shape—nearly a straight line from her shoulders to her waist to her hips. No curves. No dips. Just solid. Square. Tessa ran her hands down Lace's sides, stopping to squeeze her waist. Lace smelled of citrus and jasmine, like a walk in the evening as spring turns to summer, just as the sun dips below the horizon. Tessa breathed her in, and then tucked her thumbs into the waistband of Lace's jeans.

Tessa looked into her eyes. "May I?"

Lace nodded. Tessa quickly unbuttoned and unzipped her pants. Lace gave a sharp wiggle and the pants dropped to the floor.

Lace grinned. "No hips."

"You're quite the comedian."

Lace shrugged. "You're next."

Tessa was out of her own pants in a second.

"Hey, I recognize those." Lace waggled her eyebrows.

Tessa had bought the Merlot-colored panties from Frisky Business last season. Of course, she never imagined in a bazillion years that Lace would see her wearing them.

"Do you always wear panties to match your wines, or is this just a special occasion?"

"Do you always do stand-up before having sex, or is this just a special occasion?"

"You're pretty funny yourself."

Tessa put her finger on Lace's lips again. "More kissing. Less talking." Then she pushed Lace down onto the soft leather couch and lowered herself on top of her.

She traced the edges of Lace's face, circled her ear, and then dragged a finger across her lips. Lace reached up and grabbed Tessa's hand to hold it still so that she could pull Tessa's finger into her mouth. As Lace sucked, pulling Tessa's finger in and out of her mouth, Tessa thought she might come flying apart. It had been way too long since she had felt this way. Sex with Olivia had gotten more and more infrequent over the last few years, and since she left Olivia? Well. She had been very busy.

Lace shifted her attention to Tessa's mouth, which she covered with wet, passionate kisses.

When Lace reached down and grabbed Tessa's nipple, Tessa's pussy tightened and then shot wide open, sending waves of heat down through her legs and up through her torso. Lace shifted just slightly beneath her, in order to press her thigh up between Tessa's legs, and Tessa did not need further instructions. She rubbed herself against Lace's leg, harder and harder, faster and faster, with Lace holding her ass, urging her on, pulling her closer, opening her pussy, pressing against her swollen clit, until she exploded. Wetness oozed through her panties and she rode Lace through wave after wave of ecstasy.

"I guess I *am* an expert." Lace laughed.

"You're *something*, alright," Tessa said, smiling, once she caught her breath.

But she didn't need words to say the rest of what she was thinking, which was that she had never wanted anything or anyone more than she wanted Lace right now. She scooted down Lace's body, stopping to kiss her heart, and then farther down, licking and kissing her belly. She grabbed the waistband of Lace's black silk boxers and yanked them off.

"Wait!" Lace reached for her pants on the floor. "I have a dental dam in my pocket."

"You keep a dental dam in your pocket?"

"Actually, I have three."

"You have *three* dental dams in your pocket?"

"Some people carry business cards. I carry dental dams with my logo on it. You never know when someone might need one."

Kneeling between Lace's legs, Tessa explored her face. "Do you always use a dental dam when you have sex?"

"Of course. And condoms and gloves." Lace shrugged. "I'm a big fan of latex."

"And how often do you get tested?"

"I had my annual exam last month."

Tessa looked into Lace's eyes. "I haven't had sex with anyone since my last exam."

Then Tessa let her gaze scroll slowly down Lace's body to the dark bush between Lace's legs. She wanted what lie between it. She needed to know what Lace tasted like. She was desperate to find her way in. But she looked back up and into Lace's eyes.

"If you would be more comfortable, grab the dental dam."

Lace stared at her. She opened her mouth, but nothing came out. Finally, she took Tessa's arms, pulled her close enough to reach her shoulders, and then pushed her gently into place, so that Tessa's head was between her legs.

Tessa could have come again right there. Instead, she made her way to Lace's warm wet folds, and teased the swollen clit hidden within them. A sigh escaped her lips as she tasted the sweet saltiness and Lace moaned as Tessa thrust her tongue inside of her, sucking and drinking in the wetness. When she had her fill, she withdrew her tongue and replaced it with her fingers, turning her full attention to Lace's clit. She was a patient explorer, thrilled to be discovering a new land. A curious chemist, experimenting with new exothermic reactions. She tested different angles, applying different amounts of pressure at each point, trying different speeds, until she found the spot and the rhythm that made Lace arch her back, made her breath quicken, and that, finally, had her begging Tessa to make her come.

And then, Tessa didn't stop until Lace's pussy was contracting so hard Tessa thought her fingers might break. She pulled back for a second to watch the rhythmic twitch of Lace's clit and felt herself begin to contract all over again. She pressed her mouth against

Lace's clit, knowing the gentle pressure would deepen and lengthen Lace's climax, and Lace reached down to grab the back of her head, holding her in place. As if anything could have made Tessa move away from that moment.

When Lace was finished, Tessa lay down between Lace's legs, with her face on Lace's belly. It was warm. And it felt right. They had both come so quickly. Effortlessly. As if their bodies were meant for each other. As if they both knew exactly what would make the other happy.

"I told you I could make it short and sweet." Tessa smiled.

Lace sighed. "Yes, you did."

CHAPTER ELEVEN

*D*on't think—don't think—don't think.
  That's all Lace would allow herself to think.

Tessa hadn't moved since she laid her head on Lace's belly. She was thankful Tessa was still there, seemingly immovable, because the weight of her, pressing down on Lace's hips and torso, was all that was keeping Lace from leaping off that couch, flying down the stairs, and running as far away as she could go.

What had she done?

Tessa hadn't said another word. She was just lying there. Every once in a while, she would take a deep breath and let out a long sigh.

Don't think. Don't think. Don't think.

Tessa picked up her head to look at Lace. Her hazel eyes were bright green, and her expression soft, but her head was cocked ever so slightly, as if she wasn't quite sure what she was seeing, like she was asking a question Lace couldn't hear.

"What?" Lace asked, smiling nervously, not at all sure if she wanted a response.

Tessa didn't answer, but a satisfied smile slowly stretched across her face, and then she inched her way up the couch to lie beside Lace. Lace tingled everywhere Tessa's body touched her. The tingling made the thinking easier to ignore.

Tessa propped herself on one elbow and looked down into Lace's eyes.

Her hair, the color of caramel or a cool glass of chocolate milk, with bright sun-kissed highlights, cascaded across her tanned face, over her bare shoulder—which looked like it maybe hadn't seen the sun since the early 2000s.

Lovely Tessa had a farmer's tan.

"Why are you smiling like that?" Tessa asked, studying Lace's face.

"I'm just thinking about how beautiful you are."

Tessa playfully raised an eyebrow and gave her head a little shake. "I don't believe you."

Lace shrugged. "Don't believe that you're beautiful or don't believe that I *think* you're beautiful?"

Tessa laughed, and then reached out a finger to touch a spot above Lace's right eyebrow. "How come I never noticed this before? How'd you get it?"

"That little scar? That's the day I was attacked by a slide on the playground during recess. Third grade."

"You were attacked by a slide?"

"That's the story I told my dad when he came to get me. *He* believed me. Took me to the ER. It took a stitch to stop the bleeding."

"A stitch. You had *one* stitch?"

Lace nodded.

"I've never heard of such a thing. Why didn't they just put a Band-Aid on it?"

"Don't dismiss my pain and suffering. You're adding to the emotional scars right now."

Tessa laughed and tussled Lace's hair. "What were you like? When you were in third grade?"

Lace tipped her head back and closed her eyes, trying to remember. She opened one eye and looked at Tessa. "Adorable."

"Before you became scarface, you mean."

Lace snorted a laugh. "Obviously. After the attack and the near fatal wound, I was very badass. In a sexy way."

"You were a sexy third grader?"

"Weren't you?"

Tessa's laughter warmed Laces insides, better than even the spiciest, ten-year, single pot still Irish whiskey could ever do. She reached up and guided Tessa's head toward her, until their lips met, and then used her other hand, tucked underneath Tessa, to pull her body closer. When Tessa swung her leg up on top of Lace, it sent a wave of heat coursing through her body. Suddenly, Lace needed to be on top. She needed to feel Tessa beneath her, giving way, opening.

Still kissing, Lace attempted to roll toward her, intending to pull Tessa underneath. But the leather, sticking to her naked body, made that very challenging. And then, when she finally managed to break free of it, the noise it made sounded a lot like—

"Did you just fart?!" Tessa's shoulders started shaking and she burst out laughing.

"No! I did not fart!" Lace's cheeks felt like they had been lit on fire. "It's this couch!"

"The couch?"

"Yes! The couch. It's sticky."

"Well, who's fault is that?"

"Not like that kind of sticky. It's the leather. It just makes it hard to move."

Tessa arched an eyebrow. "Where are you trying to go?"

"I'm not going anywhere." Lace rolled her eyes. "I just want to be on top of you. Although I feel like maybe the moment has passed. You know, like when you have to explain the punch line."

Tessa put her hand on Lace's warm cheek and looked into her eyes. The longer she held Lace's gaze, the easier it was for Lace to breathe. After Lace settled, Tessa tipped her head in the direction of the wall on the other side of her grandmother's desk. "Would you like me to pull down the bed?"

Lace's breath caught in her throat. She couldn't think of a single thing she had ever wanted more.

Tessa led the way to the Murphy bed. She had installed it, anticipating there would be nights when she would have to work late and wouldn't want to have to drive home. Padding along behind her, Lace admired her curves. Tessa was lithe, her arms and legs muscled, her belly toned, from a lifetime of work in the fields. But you could have built a city on those hips.

Their bodies could not have been more different.

Lace came up behind her and put her hands on Tessa's hips. She leaned back, allowing Lace to explore every inch of her. She ran her hands along Tessa's shoulders, and then down the full length of her arms to Tessa's hands, where their fingers danced. Then she reached around to explore Tessa's belly, the tightness of her muscles and the suppleness of her skin, before tracing the distance up to Tessa's breasts. D-cup, she guessed—she *was* in the business. A previous pregnancy and pushing forty had relaxed them, and their weight filled Lace's hands. She gently squeezed a nipple and Tessa inhaled sharply, pressing back harder against Lace's body. Then Lace ran her hands down along Tessa's sides to those glorious hips. Although Tessa was much thinner than Lace, her hips were several inches wider. Lace used them to pull Tessa closer, until her ass was jammed hard against Lace's throbbing pussy.

"I want you," Lace whispered roughly in Tessa's ear.

"Well," Tessa whispered back. "What are you waiting for?"

Lace spun Tessa around and gently but firmly pushed her onto the bed. Tessa's panties were the only piece of clothing separating them from each other.

"These need to go." Lace reached under Tessa's ass and pulled them off. Then she held them against her cheek, to feel their silky smoothness. "They're wet."

Tessa smiled back. "So am I."

Lying on her back, Tessa used her index finger to signal Lace forward.

Lace did not need another invitation.

She climbed in between Tessa's legs and braced herself, in push-up position, as she slowly lowered her ass, bringing her pussy within an inch of Tessa's.

And then Lace froze. As in, couldn't move. Couldn't speak.

"Lace, what is it? What's wrong?"

Looking into Tessa's eyes, Lace knew that what she was feeling was dumb. But it was real.

"Um, I feel naked."

Tessa laughed, softly at first, looking puzzled, and then so hard it shook the bed. Every time it seemed like she was going to stop,

Lace tried to explain. But then Tessa would start all over again. Lace rolled her eyes as Tessa struggled to stop laughing. It was a good thing she had been working on her upper body strength.

Finally, Tessa took a deep breath and seemed to have gotten it under control. "Um, you feel naked because," she snorted a laugh, "you *are* naked."

Then she started up again, laughing so hard her eyes were watering.

Looking down at her, Lace raised an eyebrow. "I think you're delirious."

"I am. Deliriously happy, that is." Then Tessa breathed in and exhaled slowly. "Okay. Sorry. I'm alright."

Lace shook her head. "Obviously, we don't have any clothes on. That's not what I mean."

"Okay. Tell me. What do you mean?"

Lace rolled off and lay next to her, propped up on an elbow. "I'm in the toy business, remember?"

Tessa nodded.

"Well, I have quite a nice collection."

"I'm sure you do."

Lace squinted one eye shut and looked at Tessa with the other. "It's been a very long time since I did this without them."

"Ahhh." Tessa scrunched her mouth sideways, as if pondering that. "Do you want to go get them?"

"Do you *want* me to go get them?"

Tessa thought for a moment. "No. I don't. For one thing, I don't want you putting clothes back on, and I don't want you to leave this bed. And, for another, I kind of like the idea of this—of *us*—being different. At least for now."

"I'm afraid you'll be bored."

Tessa grinned. "If you're not careful, I'm going to start laughing again."

"Please, don't."

"Lace, I can't even imagine what boring would look like with you."

Tessa propped herself up and rolled over, pushing Lace onto her back. Her kisses started out soft, and Lace returned them, but then something seemed to ignite in Tessa. Her tongue darted around, searching for Lace's, finding it, attacking it, as if fencing, as if wanting to win it, to own it. She bit Lace's lower lip and chin, then pushed Lace's face to the side, so that she could kiss and nibble on her neck. Her hands slid down Lace's body, from her neck to her breasts, where she pinched Lace's nipple hard enough that it shot a heat missile right to her pussy and made her yelp. Then Tessa's hand dipped lower, crawling down Lace's belly, teasing just below her hips, gently pulling her hair, dragging her fingers along her slit.

Lace couldn't have had a thought in her head if she tried. Every cell in her body was screaming for more.

She flipped Tessa over onto her back and got on her knees between Tessa's legs. "Open wider."

Lace didn't mean to sound so gruff, but her voice no longer belonged to her. It belonged to someone with no list of exes in her phone, no business to worry about, no history of betraying the ones she loved, no home except that bed, no future beyond that single moment.

Tessa spread her legs wider.

"Now, open yourself up."

Tessa reached down and spread her lips apart, exposing a huge, swollen, clit.

"Oh my God, Tess. You are beautiful."

"I am on fucking *fire*, Lace. Honest to God, if you don't do something about this, I am going to do it myself."

Lace grinned. "Oh, I'm going to do something, alright."

She leaned forward so that she was hovering above Tessa, bracing herself with one hand. With her other, she opened her own lips, and lowered herself until her throbbing clit was pressed hard against Tessa's wet pussy.

Tessa grabbed Lace's ass and drove herself up into Lace with a moan.

Lace moved faster and harder against Tessa, and Tessa's eyes widened. Lace could have come. *Wanted* to come. Tessa was there for it.

But *Tessa* wasn't ready. Lace could see that. So, right before she reached the point of no return, Lace let out a loud groan and flipped over onto her back, pulling Tessa on top of her.

"Why did you stop?!" Tessa's eyes were wild.

"Because. *This*." Lace pulled Tessa up by the waist, until Tessa was straddling her.

Tessa's face and neckline, in the shape of a vee, mirrored the color of her hair. Everything below was ten shades paler, reminding Lace of how hard Tessa worked. Lace smiled imagining her out walking the vineyard—talking on the phone with her. Or racing around her property on that little ATV of hers. Long pants. Long sleeves. Boots. She was sexy as fuck. And although Tessa may or may not have been a badass in third grade, she sure as hell was one now.

Lace grabbed her by the waist.

"You are magnificent, Tessa."

"And you are a tease, my friend."

Lace ran her hands up and down Tessa's torso, ending at her hips, which she gave a tight squeeze.

"I find these irresistible."

Tessa tilted her head. "Really? Why? Not exactly my finest feature."

"What are you *talking* about? These hips are *epic.*"

Tess laughed. "Epic, huh? You mean *huge.*"

Lace rubbed her hands back and forth across her hips. "They are not small, that's true." She smiled. "But look."

She traced the deep lines on either side with her fingers. "These are incredible." She looked up into Tessa's eyes. "They're stretch marks, right? This is from Madison?"

Tessa got very still and put her own hands on her hips, rubbing the spots where her body had expanded to make room for another human. She nodded. "I didn't carry her in front. Everything happened here. In my hips. I used to be thin as a bean pole. And I know. We grow beans on my family's farm. Then came Madison. My body has never been the same since."

Lace continued caressing her hips, but her eyes were on Tessa's face, her bright, inquisitive eyes, the smile lines that framed her

mouth, lines that Lace had helped deepen, the chin that jutted out
when she heard something she didn't believe or didn't approve of,
or when she talked about the latest horrible thing STUD had done.

How had she gone so long without looking this closely? Or
seeing so clearly? Tessa was the strongest, most beautiful, most
compassionate, most courageous woman she had ever known.

"Are you ready for me?" Lace grinned.

"I'm ready if you are." Tessa grinned back.

Lace gave her hips one last, hard squeeze, and then grabbed her
ass, urging her higher and higher until Tessa's pussy was right where
Lace wanted it.

Tessa put her hands against the wall for support and lowered
herself over Lace's face. When Lace drove her tongue up inside
of her, Tessa threw back her head and moaned. Lace drank her in,
sucking and licking, until Tessa's grinding let Lace know she was
dying for release. Lace wanted that, too. But she also wanted this
to last. She took a breath, grabbed Tessa's ass, and tried to regain
control of the tempo and the timing.

Tessa groaned. "Oh my God, Lace, please. I want to come.
Make me *come*."

Lace pulled her tongue out of Tessa's pussy. "Has anyone ever
told you that you are very bossy, boss lady?"

Tessa moaned. "Yes. No. I don't know. What are you *doing*?"

"Stand-up?"

"Not now, Lace. Please!"

"Tessa?"

"What?"

"You taste good."

Tessa let out a sound that would have frightened a pack of
coyotes.

And then Lace went back to work. For the past two years, Lace
had done anything Tessa asked—supporting her, listening to her,
cheering her on, helping her out of tough spots, mundane things and
important ones. Nothing was more important than whatever it was
Tessa wanted and needed. Tessa had become the center of Lace's
world, the sun she orbited around. When Tessa needed her, she was

there. So, making Tessa feel alive, like this, felt like the most natural thing Lace had ever done. And right now, in this moment, nothing could have given Lace more joy.

Lace licked the inside of Tessa's inner lips and then down along her opening, while she entered her with a finger. When she realized how wet Tessa was, she slid in a second, and then a third. With her free hand, Lace explored the rest of Tessa, playing with her nipples, squeezing her ass. Tessa groaned and then came down hard, riding Lace's fingers, while Lace licked and sucked her clit.

"There! Right *there*." Tessa stopped moving. "Do it."

Tessa's pussy tightened around Lace's fingers, and it was clear they were reaching the point of no return, so Lace reached up with her other hand and slid two fingers into Tessa's mouth. Tessa sucked and licked them until Lace withdrew and reached down to find her own clit.

As she licked Tessa, she stroked herself, until they were in sync, rocking toward orgasm, together.

Tessa exploded first, smashing her pussy into Lace's lace, head thrown back, Lace's name in her mouth. Lace came five seconds later, back arched, ass in the air, screaming into Tessa's sopping wet pussy.

Tessa stayed on top of her, leaning hard against the wall, as wave after orgasmic wave shook them both. When Tessa was done, she slid back down and lay on top of Lace, her head on Lace's shoulder.

The old building was silent. It had settled decades ago, and even the stir of two hundred people earlier in the day had not changed its character. Somewhere off in the distance, a car alarm was going off. And Lace thought she heard the screech owl, probably out hunting for his dinner. But mostly the world was still.

Lace's spirit was, too. Tessa's body had exorcised the rambling, troubling thoughts that had tortured Lace for months. It seemed stupid now to have fought so hard not to feel or see or think what was now so impossible to ignore.

She and Tessa had stopped being just friends long ago.

Tessa twitched. She had fallen asleep, lying on top of Lace. Her hair tickled Lace's cheek, so Lace gently tucked it behind her ear. Then Lace stroked her cheek, which was soft and warm.

It didn't surprise Lace that Tessa had been able to fall asleep so quickly. She had come to count on Tessa's calm, steady presence. Especially when business or life seemed overwhelming.

Lace had never seen Tessa really rattled, until earlier that evening.

It wasn't that Tessa didn't see or acknowledge hard things. It's just that she *expected* things to be hard once in a while, but she also knew, down in her soul, that things wouldn't stay hard.

Everything has a season, she would say.

Storms come.

Storms pass.

Well, they were in a season, alright. Lace didn't know exactly what kind or what was going to happen next. But Tessa felt good, lying on her, making sweet little sleep noises.

In fact, it felt so good that Lace didn't realize she had fallen asleep until Bleu was licking her face, hours later, and the sun was peeking through the windows. She leapt up off the bed. Tessa was gone.

Don't think. Don't think. Don't think.

"Dammit, Bleu. What did I do?"

The pup just stood there in the middle of the loft wagging her tail.

"This is a disaster."

Bleu couldn't even begin to understand. Lace *had sex with Tessa.* That changed everything.

Or did it?

Maybe Tessa would see it for what it was—a terrible mistake. Maybe they could just sort of pretend it hadn't happened, and they could go back to being friends. Texting, talking, movie-watching friends. Maybe this didn't have to ruin everything.

Because having a relationship with Tessa—as in a dating relationship—was impossible. And if that was what their friendship had become, because Lace had totally screwed up and fucked her best friend, then their *friendship* was impossible.

And Lace couldn't live that way. She couldn't imagine a way forward without Tessa as her best friend.

Lace quickly picked her clothes up off the floor and was pulling them on when she heard the door to the tasting room open and close downstairs. Tessa came up the stairs with a tray of coffee and a tin of cookies.

"I found these in your kitchen. There's not much to choose from. I tasted them, though. They're not moldy." Tessa was beaming.

Lace laughed nervously. "Why would I have moldy cookies in my kitchen?"

Tessa just lifted an eyebrow and laughed. "Want to have coffee in bed?"

Lace glanced at the bed and her stomach fell. "Umm, how about over on the couch?"

"As long as it's not too sticky," Tessa said with a chuckle.

Lace shook her head. "It wasn't actually sticky, it was just—"

"I know. It was just *sticking* to your bare ass. I got it."

Lace tried to remind herself that Tessa was a morning person. She was always happy when the sun came up. It didn't mean anything. It certainly didn't mean that Tessa expected anything, anything that a friend couldn't provide. Because Lace knew from experience, she could not be trusted to give anything more than that.

Lace ran her fingers through her hair. "I'm a mess."

"Yep," Tessa chirped. "You are. It's cute."

Lace didn't mean her hair. She meant that, literally, she was a *mess*. A disaster waiting to happen. A *calamity* of historic proportions.

The last time Lace slept with her best friend, she crushed his heart.

What the hell was wrong with her?

It was happening all over again.

Tessa sat down, poured the coffee, and patted the seat next to her. Lace looked around the loft, as if there were options. There were not. So she sat down and took the mug Tessa handed to her. Bleu scampered over and lay down at Lace's feet.

Don't think.

"It is absolutely gorgeous outside," Tessa said happily. "I think it's going to be a perfect day."

Lace tucked her head down and took a sip of coffee.

"Hey!" Tessa's smile could have lit up the whole county on a moonless night. "I have an idea. Is Sophie working today? Or do you need to be in the shop? The tasting rooms—I have two of them now!—are both closed on Mondays. So, I could take today off, if I wanted to. Maybe you and I could drive up to Boot Hill with a picnic. I would love to spend some time up there during the day."

Lace's heart was beating faster and faster, and the air seemed to be getting thinner and thinner. It was getting hard to breathe.

Lace nodded.

Tessa tilted her head. "Yes, Sophie is on today? Or, yes, you need to be in the shop today?"

Lace nodded again. "Sophie's off. I have to be in the shop. And I have a meeting right after work."

"Okay. We can do that another time. But, Lace? Are you all right? You seem, I don't know, kind of distracted."

"Um, yeah, sure. I was just thinking."

"Thinking about what?" Tessa took a sip of coffee.

"Oh, I don't know, thinking about how last night was—"

Tessa sighed and her face softened. "I know, right? Last night was life changing."

"It was?" Lace's heart was revving. Like it was getting ready to fly out the door.

Tessa put down her mug, scooted over right next to Lace, and leaned against her, putting her head on Lace's shoulder. "It was."

"Um, how?"

Why did she ask that question? She did not want to hear the answer. She knew that whatever Tessa said next was never going to be able to be unsaid.

Tessa took a deep breath and melted into Lace's side. "Well, this is probably going to sound ridiculous coming from me. I mean, you're the one who sees ghosts."

"I don't see ghosts."

"Okay, you just see the vibrators they leave behind." Tessa laughed. "But you believe in them. You have a psychic. You're, you know, a little woo-woo."

"Is this going somewhere?" Lace was suddenly feeling itchy all over.

Tessa snuggled closer. "Yes. What I'm trying to say is that, even this non-woo-woo girl can see it. I think," her voice dropped to a whisper, "I mean, I've never believed in this before, but I think that, if soulmates are real, you must be mine."

Bleu hopped up and started licking Lace's hand.

But Lace wanted to sink into the couch, melt through the floor beneath them, and disappear into the earth below, vanishing into history, erased from memory, forever.

"Oh my God. I just remembered." Lace jumped up. "I told Sophie I'd put this week's order in before eight."

She gave Bleu a quick pat on the head, grabbed her mug, and flew toward the stairs.

"I'll call ya later," she said over her shoulder.

The last thing she saw was Tessa glued to her seat, eyes wide, her mouth opening and closing like a fish in a polluted lake, struggling for air.

CHAPTER TWELVE

Tessa stared at the spot where Lace had vanished, as if expecting her to pop back up the stairs to say something funny. Bleu was standing there, too, looking down the stairs, wagging her tail. As if that little disappearing act was all just part of yet another stand-up routine.

Because this couldn't be happening for real, could it?

But Lace did not reappear. She was gone.

She said she had work to do.

She said she would call later.

Apparently, Lace did not expect to *see* Tessa anytime soon.

Bleu turned to look at her. She was a working dog. A herder. What should she do now? Go get her? Her eyes begged the question.

"I don't know, Bleu. Your guess is as good as mine."

Tessa looked around and made a mental list of chores she would need to get to. She had work to do, too. Order more glasses. Call Plumber Joe about the leak under the bathroom sink. Update the POS system to distinguish in-town sales from out at the vineyard.

Strip the bed.

Strip. The. Fucking. Bed.

She strode to the bed and grabbed a corner of the blanket so hard, the pillows flew into the air and landed on the floor. She ripped the sheets off and twisted them into a tight ball, to take home and wash. Then she slammed the bed back into the wall.

"Let's go, pup."

She left the coffee cups and dry-as-dust cookies on the table—
let them mold—grabbed her things and got out of there as quickly
as she could.

The drive back to the vineyard had never felt so long, especially
because every fifteen minutes, in between sets, Walt was reading the
news. And apparently the only news in Owen Station that day was
about how many people had come to town for the grand opening,
and how many photos Elena Murphy had sold, and what a coup
it was for tiny Owen Station to have two such award-winning,
locally-owned, innovative businesses—Frisky Business and Mujer
Fuerte—collaborating to bring so many new dollars to town. Walt
had even scored an interview with Sena, and he played the same
sound bite over and over again.

"The future of Owen Station is high-tech, but at the heart of
every community are small, locally-owned businesses. I could not
be more excited for Tessa and Lace…"

The third time she heard Sena say, "Tessa and Lace," she
snapped the radio off so hard, she could have broken it.

She was thankful she had already given her team the day off.
It was Monday and neither tasting room was open, anyway. Plus,
everyone had worked so hard to get through the opening. She knew
there was nothing that couldn't wait until Tuesday. She hoped they
were all planning to get some rest.

Now, though, she had a different reason to be glad no one was
going to be at the vineyard. Because there was nothing she wanted
more than to go home, and maybe go for a good, long, centering
walk with Bleu through the vines. Then she was going to crawl into
bed to spend the rest of the day watching sad movies. Scratch that.
Watching *Clint Eastwood* movies. Lace hated them.

Lace.

Her hair sticking up everywhere.

That silly grin.

That tender heart under all that swagger.

"What the *hell,* Lace?"

Bleu pulled her head inside the window and looked at her from
the passenger seat, one ear sticking up.

Tessa reached over and scratched it.

"I'm sorry, pup. I know you must be worried." Bleu was better at reading Tessa than any human had ever been. "You probably should be. Because I have no idea what I'm going to do."

How could she have been such an idiot? She heard what Lace said to Angela. She knew all about Lace's stupid rules. She even *told* Lace to get lost, threatened to go back to her vineyard, back to her life. She could live without their friendship. Fine. It was over. Whatever. Then something happened.

What the hell was it?

How did Tessa go from *Lace, get out* to climbing in bed with her?

She replayed the night. Angela. Boot Hill. Arguing. Crying. Lace crying. More arguing. Then Lace came up behind her. And *held* her.

Warmth crept from Tessa's stomach down to between her legs. She shifted on her seat to make it stop.

God dammit. Why would she *do* that?

Clearly, Lace had a problem. Maybe she just didn't know what she wanted. Maybe she was a sex addict and couldn't help herself. Maybe she was a twisted psychopath who got off on making otherwise stable people—

"Lose their fucking minds!"

At the sound of Tessa's voice, Bleu dove off the seat onto the floor and put her paws over her head.

"Oh God, Bleu. I'm sorry." She patted the seat next to her. "Come on, get back up here. It's alright. Everything is okay."

Bleu looked skeptical but jumped up, anyway. She lay down on the passenger seat and pretended to go to sleep but kept one eye on Tessa all the way home.

Back at the vineyard, in spite of her dark mood, Tessa could appreciate what a beautiful day it had turned out to be. Bleu traipsed along beside her as she walked the vines. They were her first love— except for Madison, of course. This was where she felt most at home. And, thankfully, the grapes were looking good. Daytime temperatures had been comfortable—the extreme heat was still at least a month away—and evenings had been cool. The soil was healthy, replenished by winter precipitation, and the vines looked like their root system was happy. The leaves had already furrowed out, creating a magnificent canopy that would protect the grapes and provide enough relief to let them ripen and thrive, even through the coming heat. Plus, the bright green of the leaves, against the red soil, was breathtaking.

It was turning out to be a perfect season. For the grapes, anyway. She was in her own season of stupidity.

A cloud of dust kicked up on the road coming down from the barn. Jeremy was in the vineyard's RTV. He pulled over when he saw her and hopped out.

"What are you doing here? You're supposed to have a day off."

Jeremy grinned. "I'm doing the same thing you are—checking on our babies."

Tessa shook her head. She had no idea how she had ended up with such a loyal team, but she was thankful for it. She grinned back at him. "Well, as long as we're both here, how do you think things are looking?"

"I think everything is doing great, Tess!" Jeremy didn't grow up farming. He came to it late, drawn in by a love of wine and in search of a life outdoors. Most people probably couldn't tell he was a first-generation farmer, but Tessa could. His exuberance gave him away.

"The Brix are continuing to climb. And the ph levels are looking really good. It won't be long before there will be enough sugar in these babies to harvest. And I'm feeling good about it! I predict this is the year that puts this vineyard—and your winemaking skills—on the map!"

It turned out that Jeremy was just the medicine she needed. Usually, Tessa would wave off this kind of praise. Today, she needed it.

"Do you really think so?"

"I absolutely do. You know I was very skeptical when you suggested planting these varietals. No one had done it here before. But it turns out, they are perfect for this terrain. And everyone is talking about your approach to soil remediation—growing native plants in between each row. Not only are the tepary beans selling surprisingly well at the farmers market, we're capturing more precipitation and nutrients than I ever could have imagined. No wonder the university loves you! Doc Winston said he's never seen anything like what is happening here. Every season his researchers are tracking bugs, butterflies, and birds here on this property that they haven't seen in these parts for decades. The last time he was here, he asked if he could get you to come do a guest lecture for the faculty next semester. I told him I'd see what I could do." Jeremy winked at her.

He knew damn well she would be freaked out just by the idea of being back on a college campus. But, you know what, maybe she wasn't as stupid as she thought she was.

"I am really proud of what we're doing here, Jeremy. Honestly, I thought maybe I was a little nuts, too, when we got started, bringing practices we were pioneering in California here, to the desert. But the natural, organic choices we're making are impacting the whole ecosystem."

A wind kicked up, and they both covered the lower half of their faces to try to block the noxious odor that came with it. "Oh my God," Jeremy said through his hands. "If only *Studly* over there would take a lesson. I think it gets worse every day."

Thankfully, the wind settled quickly. Jeremy took off. And Tessa started heading back up to the barn through the block of Sangiovese she planted her first year. That varietal, and the Tannat she planted in year two, were her favorites. They were both reds, but on opposite ends of the spectrum. One was bold, deep, rich—the other light, playful. As different from each other as they could be.

As different from each other as she was from Lace.

That's why they were so good together. Yes, they loved so many of the same things. But their differences were just as important. They balanced each other. Lace helped Tessa lighten up. Tessa helped Lace stay grounded.

Tessa stopped mid-stride and looked up at the bright blue sky. Why couldn't Lace let herself see that?

Then she dropped her head and closed her eyes. Maybe Lace couldn't see it because it wasn't true.

Maybe it had all been a figment of Tessa's imagination.

Or maybe Lace just played her.

Whatever it was, one thing was clear. Tessa had created a glorious mess. She let herself trust someone who *told* her she couldn't be trusted to stick around long term. She let herself fall in love with someone who—

Tessa dropped to her knees and covered her face with her hands.

She had let herself fall in love.

What a complete and total fool.

Grief washed over her and the sobs shook her, until Bleu, whining and barking, finally nudged her hard enough to make her stop, get up, and dust off her jeans.

"You're right, girl," Tessa said angrily. "The canopy looks beautiful. But it makes this a great place for snakes, too. That's all I need is to get bitten—*again*—today. Thanks for reminding me to get up and stand on my own two feet. I won't be making a mistake like Lace ever again."

She took long strides up the hill toward the barn, anger holding her up and moving her forward.

Madison's car pulled up just as she and Bleu reached the top.

"So much for giving everyone a day off," she muttered to Bleu. But Bleu wasn't listening. She had already taken off so fast, she was licking Madison's hand before she could even get out of the car.

"Hey, Mom!" Madison yelled.

"Hi, Madison." Tessa knew she was using her mom voice. She didn't care. "I wasn't expecting to see you here today."

"I know! I'm not here to work. Can't a daughter come see her mom on her day off?"

Tessa could always tell when Madison wasn't being honest. "Yes, of course. But you're not just here for a visit, are you?"

"What do you mean?" Madison laughed nervously. "It's a beautiful day! I love the high desert at this time of year—thank *God* you didn't move us to Phoenix—it's so much cooler here. I keep reminding my friends back home of that. Whenever they send me memes of scary weather reports. I'm, like, it might be a hundred and twenty in Phoenix, but Phoenix is hell, anyway, and we don't live in hell." She put her arms out to embrace the vineyard and the vista. "We live in paradise!"

"You're overselling it, Mads. Why are you really here?"

"Okay, fine." Madison dropped the charade and let her brow furrow. "I was worried about you. I haven't heard from you since last night after—you know."

"After Lace was an ass?"

"Yes, that."

"You do know you're the daughter and I'm the mother, right?"

Madison sort of smiled. "Yes, of course. But that doesn't mean I don't worry about you. When I drove past the tasting room and didn't see your truck, I figured you'd be here."

"Pretty much. Where else would I be?" And right then, Tessa really wanted to be there, in her vineyard, alone. Doing physical labor to get her mind off of it all. Or wallowing. Probably just wallowing.

"So, how are you?" Madison's brows couldn't have been closer together if she were Big Foot.

"I'm fine."

"You don't sound fine."

"Madison, I really don't want to talk about it."

"Okay," Madison said slowly. "Well, I drove all the way out here to see you. What *do* you want to talk about?"

For God's sake.

She couldn't just send Madison back home, could she?

"Okay. As long as you're here. Tell me how you think things went yesterday. We never got a chance to debrief."

Madison's face lit up. She loved the winery almost as much as Tessa did. And yesterday was as much her victory as Tessa's. Tessa felt bad that she had let the drama with Angela and Lace get in the way of being able to celebrate that. One more idiotic move.

"Really? That's what you want to talk about?" If Madison was a puppy, her tail would be wagging.

Tessa made herself smile. "I do."

"Well, I was in Banter & Brew this morning and, let me tell you, the new tasting room is all anyone could talk about. Everyone was, like, what do you mean you're not going to be open today? You're only open Thursday through Sunday? They want us to be open every day! I expected the opening to go well—but, Mom, it was epic!"

Tessa tried to jump in, but Madison wasn't ready to stop. "I've been thinking. We should talk to Maia about opening up a permanent space in the tasting room. Everyone absolutely loved her food at the Bud Break Bash this spring—I know I did. I had three plates of it. We may not be ready to actually hire a chef, but she could share our space. I know she's been thinking about finding a place of her own. Having access to our kitchen would make it easier for her to do catering. And, if we offered food, it would justify being open every day. People could come for lunch. Have meetings there during the day. If it worked, we could have extended hours on Friday and Saturday and do dinner. Also, selling food would make it easier for us to get a license that would allow us to serve local beer on tap. I have a friend who is dying to expand her kombucha business. We could add that to the menu for people who want a non-alcoholic alternative. And think about how much easier it would be to make event pitches, if people didn't have to go find their own caterer—"

"Slow down! Madison, you are making my head spin." It was great to see Madison excited. She deserved that. But opening that tasting room so fast had been exhausting. The opening yesterday was exhausting. The whole situation with Lace was exhausting.

Tessa was exhausted.

And she wasn't exactly feeling up to another challenge.

Madison took a step back. "I'm sorry, Mom. I wasn't thinking. You look so—"

The rest of Madison's words disappeared under the roar of Spencer's truck barreling up the drive.

Bleu got between Tessa and Madison and the oncoming truck and started barking wildly. Tessa dropped her head. This was the last thing she needed. Today of all days.

When Spencer got to the top of the parking lot, he snapped his wheel hard to the right and did a full donut, spraying gravel in every direction. Three guys who were riding in the truck bed thought this was hysterical. As soon as the truck stopped, they leapt out, beer cans in hand, and started slapping each other on the back. Then Spencer flung his own door open and jumped out—awkwardly, because the truck was jacked up so high.

When Tessa didn't say anything, Madison stepped in. "Bleu, that's enough." Bleu circled around and stood between Madison and Tessa. She finally stopped barking, but her ears were flat and she kept a low growl in her throat.

"What can we do for you boys?" The grimace on Madison's face made it clear they were not welcome.

Spencer sauntered toward them like he owned the place. "I just thought I'd stop by with my buddies here—they all work at the county, you know—and let you ladies know that you're about to be shut down."

The three men standing behind Spencer like members of some grotesque boy band, elbowed each other with nasty grins on their faces.

"The list of violations is three pages long. That wedding you had out here last weekend hit a decibel level that definitely broke the county's noise ordinance. You continue to serve people outdoors without the correct license. That *barn* does not have a restaurant permit—plus, it is regularly over-capacity. It's a fire hazard. You are putting people at risk. Ya'll should be ashamed of yourselves. And then there is the matter of my cows. They are delicate creatures, you know. The sound level over here is impacting my dairy production to such an extent that you're not just going to face the county. I'm coming after you for damages." He pulled himself up as tall as he could. "I'm going to *bury* you with lawsuits."

The men nodded and laughed, swigging their beers, slapping Spencer on the back. He laughed with them, high-fiving them, a smug, self-satisfied grin on his face, standing in front of his three-hundred-thousand-dollar truck like he owned the world.

And something broke in Tessa. She didn't have it in her to fight this. What was the point? She could never afford the lawyers it would take to defend herself. Who did she think she was, anyway? A farm girl who couldn't finish college. A single mom who couldn't keep her wife happy. A self-taught winemaker pretending to play in the big leagues. The water beneath her property was being drained away, anyway, and no one was stopping it. The air she breathed was toxic. She lived in a trailer. She drove a fifteen-year-old truck. She just lost the best friend she had ever had.

Madison looked at her, her eyes pleading with her to do something, to say something, anything. But Tessa had nothing. She just didn't have what it would take to make it all work. She wasn't enough. She had never been enough. She was done.

Madison stared at Tessa for a minute and then swung back to Spencer. "Why are you doing this?" Her voice was plenty loud enough to be heard over the laughing thugs. "You're not doing this to your neighbors on the other side of you. That winery is even bigger than ours. Their parties are louder. They have more traffic every weekend than we have in a month."

"That's true, little lady. But that winemaker has *balls*."

The guffaws from the goons grew louder. But Madison wouldn't be intimidated. She stepped forward, her hands in tight fists.

"Show us what you got, Spencer. Where's the paperwork, huh? Where are the decibel level readings? What codes are we supposedly violating? Where is your evidence of *anything* you are accusing us of?"

Madison took another step closer, and this time Spencer took one step back. "And let's talk about violations. Between the horrible sounds we hear from those cows you are torturing, and the toxic smells that blow onto our property every day, my guess is you've got a serious problem with waste management, and who knows what else. Aren't you supposed to have a hospital barn on site, to house sick animals? I can only imagine the kinds of diseases that are moving through those poor cows. And don't even get me started about how you treat your workers. We've all heard the rumors."

The three men had stopped laughing, and Spencer looked like he had shrunk two inches.

"You're right. My mom *doesn't* have balls, but she has a set of ovaries that will crush yours if you set foot back on this property. Have you heard of a little thing called a restraining order? We're filing one tomorrow." Madison turned to glare at the three county employees. "And I bet your boss would be very interested to know that you showed up here, riding in the back of this asshole's pickup on a state highway, drinking beer, and harassing taxpayers. You might want to rethink who you're hanging out with on your days off."

One of the guys hid his beer can behind his back and another one punched Spencer in the shoulder. "Come on, let's get out of here."

They all scrambled back to the truck—into the cab this time, not into the bed.

"You haven't heard the last of me, Tessa." Spencer yelled as he pointed his truck toward the road. "And you should teach that daughter of yours some manners."

Madison turned and looked at Tessa. Her eyes were wild, like she had just survived a tornado. And she was shaking. "What the hell was that, Mom?" she yelled. "Why did you let those guys come out here and intimidate you like that? Why didn't you say anything?"

Tessa didn't have an answer. "I'm sorry you had to deal with that, Madison. And I'm sorry to disappoint you. I guess maybe it's about time you came face to face with who your mother really is." Then she turned and stormed away. She was angry with everyone. But mostly with herself. She went out to the edge of the tasting area, overlooking the vineyard and sat in an Adirondack chair. She needed to be alone.

Which was all she had been wanting all day.

But Madison wouldn't leave it alone. Five minutes later, she came and sat in the chair next to her.

"I'm sorry I yelled at you, Mom. I was, I don't know, hyped up on adrenaline. Those guys—"

"I know, Mads. It's fine. You had every right to be angry. I shouldn't have just stood there and made you have to deal with it."

Madison put her hand on Tessa's arm. "Mom. What is going on? This isn't like you. Talk to me."

Tessa pulled her hand away, leaned forward, and dropped her head into her hands.

"Mom, are you crying? You never cry."

That was true. Not even when Billy told her to get rid of the baby. Or when her parents told her they would only help if she came back home and lived on the farm. Or when she filed her papers to withdraw from school. Or when she saw the texts on Olivia's phone, confirming what she had suspected. Or when she had to pack up all their things and move out of the only home Madison remembered.

"Mom, I don't know what is going on. But I promise you, we can get through it together. We always do."

"I slept with Lace."

Madison froze for a minute and then sat back in her chair with a heavy sigh.

"I take it that is not a good thing, for some reason?"

Tessa shook her head.

"When did this happen?"

"Last night."

"You slept with Lace after you heard her scream that you are the last woman on earth she would marry?"

Tessa nodded.

"Okaaaay. Well, I have definitely heard better pickup lines."

"*Madison.*"

"Sorry. JK. I'm just not sure what to say here. So what happened afterward?"

"I don't know. I brought breakfast up to the loft—"

"You slept with Lace in the loft?"

Tessa nodded.

"Gross. But, okay. Continue."

"I brought breakfast up, and we were talking, and it was great. It felt like a huge relief. For both of us. I mean, I think this has been building for a long time."

Madison nodded. "I could see that. We all could."

"Who is *we all*? Who could see it?"

"Everyone. Me. Jeremy. The crew. All your friends. Sophie. Bleu."

"*Bleu* saw it?" Tessa raised an eyebrow.

"Well, yeah. I mean, kind of. You know how she's adopted Lace, right? Like she's part of the family."

Tessa rubbed her forehead. This was such a mess.

"Anyway, you said it was a huge relief."

Tessa nodded. "The past few months, working so closely together. Being so close to each other while the tasting room was being built. It brought us closer together emotionally, too, I guess. I've been so busy, I just didn't notice. Or I didn't want to notice. And, then, last night...boom."

"Boom?"

"Well, I'm not going to give you the details."

"Thank you. But wait a minute. Why aren't you happy? What am I missing?"

Tessa looked at her. "It was a huge mistake, Madison. The biggest. Lace freaked out, ran off, and now she's ghosted me. No texts. No calls. Nothing."

Madison put her hand on Tessa's arm again. "I'm sorry, Mom."

"That's alright. It's not the first mistake. It won't be the last. It's kind of the story of my life, in fact." Tessa rolled her head back and closed her eyes. "Getting pregnant too young. Dropping out of school. Marrying somebody who was the most important person in her own universe. And now, falling in love with someone who can't be in a relationship for longer than three months. I don't know what I was thinking, Mads. I should have known better. Lace was totally honest about who she is. I have no one but myself to blame."

Madison didn't answer, which gave Tessa a minute to wallow in just how stupid she was. But after a few minutes of silence, she tilted her head to the side to look at Madison. Through one eye, she could see that Madison was silently crying.

Tessa bolted upright. "Maddie, what's wrong?"

Madison rubbed her nose and wiped her cheeks, but she just shook her head, unable to say anything. Tessa waited, stroking her arm. After a few deep breaths, Madison turned to Tessa.

"There are so many insane things in what you just said, Mom. So many. Let's start with you blaming yourself for all the fucked up things that have happened in your life and feeling inadequate because life hasn't gone as planned. Also, we need to circle back to the fact that you said you are *in love* with Lace. But—" Madison's voice caught in her throat and it looked like the tears were going to start again. She shook it off and kept going. "I really want to hear more about how you think having *me* was a big mistake."

"Oh, Madison, no! That's not what I said."

"It is exactly what you said."

"Well, that's not what I *mean*, Madison. I love you more than anything on this earth. It's just...I was so young when you were born. I had no idea what I was doing. I was on my own. I didn't—"

"Stop right there, Mom. You know, you act like there is some picture-perfect life out there that other people have figured out and you haven't. So you don't deserve a prize. But you're wrong. There's just *life*. And from where I'm sitting, you're doing a pretty damn good job at it. I mean look at me! Look at this place and everything you have accomplished."

Tessa dropped her head and took a deep breath. "I don't know how you turned out so great, Madison. I feel so lucky."

"It's not luck, Mom. You raised me to be a mujer fuerte. And you were able to do that because you are one. You are the strongest, most resilient, smartest woman I know. And I don't know what the hell is wrong with Lace. But if she is ghosting you, that is not your fault. That's on her. If she can't figure out how to be in a relationship for longer than three months, that is not your fault. That is on her. And if she can't see how lucky she would be to spend the rest of her life with you, then she is a complete idiot."

Madison took Tessa's hand and looked into her eyes. "You didn't make a mistake by falling in love with Lace, Mom. It will be her mistake if she doesn't let herself love you back."

Tessa sat back and let those words sink in. She wasn't perfect. But she had raised a nearly perfect daughter. And she'd done a lot of other things almost no one thought she could. Maybe that's why this hurt so bad. Because the one person who believed in her more than anyone else ever had and was always there to cheer her on and support her in every way possible, was willing to walk away from her because of some stupid three-month rule.

Tessa invited Madison to spend the night, not because she was unwilling to be alone, but because she just wanted to chill with her daughter. They made popcorn and watched a rom-com, Madison's favorite genre. They both cried at the end when it was clear there would be a happy-ever-after.

Tessa still hadn't heard from Lace by the time she was ready for bed, and she didn't trust herself to send a text. Not yet. But she would reach out in the morning, with a clear head. Madison was right, Tessa hadn't made the mistake here. The mistake would be ignoring the truth and letting the one person on this earth that she was meant to be with—her soulmate—walk away without a fight.

CHAPTER THIRTEEN

L ace leaned on the counter inside Frisky Business, holding her head in her hands. It had been a little more than thirty hours since Delaney's cheer kicked off the grand opening. Twenty-two or so since she tucked Angela into her friend's car and sent her home.

And exactly nine hours, forty-three minutes, and twenty-one seconds since she left Tessa in the loft, looking like someone had just ripped her heart out of her chest.

Which is exactly what had happened.

And that someone was Lace.

Not long after Lace flew down the stairs, past the Doot Hill photo, out the door of the tasting room, across the driveway, and into her own kitchen, where she slammed the door behind her, and collapsed on the floor in a heap, she heard Tessa's truck peel out of the parking lot.

Tessa hadn't stopped to say good-bye. Who could blame her?

And Lace didn't chase her. What would she say?

The last thing in the world she wanted was to hurt Tessa, but she couldn't let Tessa think they could be anything more than friends. After the divorce, Lace promised herself she would never do it again. Three months and no more. That was the limit. It was for the best, for everyone. And it turned out that Lace couldn't even get that right. Angela made that perfectly clear on the phone earlier when Lace called to apologize.

This was the bottom line. If she allowed herself to be anything more than a friend to Tessa, it would only be a matter of time before Lace screwed it up. And the pain that would cause would be so much more than the pain Tessa was feeling now.

Also, Lace—Lace was in pain, too.

She had never felt more at home than she did lying in Tessa's bed, with Tessa in her arms, as she slipped off to sleep last night. No one, not even Knox, had ever made her feel so safe. So loved.

But that was all beside the point.

It didn't matter what Lace felt or wanted.

All that mattered was Tessa.

And Lace would be damned if she would put her own needs and wants ahead of hers. Tessa was everything. And she deserved better than someone who would do to her what Olivia had done—or what Lace had done to Knox.

She looked at the time on her phone. Fifteen minutes to closing.

And nothing from Tessa.

No texts.

No missed calls.

Lace shoved her fingers through her hair and started pacing. She had been doing that all day, mostly with the dust mop in her hand. The floor had never been so clean.

She knew she had to do something, text something, call or go see her and *say* something. But she had no idea what that something might be.

At six o'clock, Lace shut down the POS system, flipped over the open sign, and counted the drawer. It had been a very slow day. Ordinarily, that would have created anxiety. She would have been constantly checking online orders, filling up social media with content and promotions, dreaming up new workshop offerings, searching for new products. Anything to drive sales.

But today, she had been thankful for the limited amount of human interaction. Her whole job was about helping people find happiness. That would have been hard to do when she felt like she was literally an agent of sorrow.

She closed up the shop and headed into the back of the house to the kitchen, where she popped a frozen burrito into the microwave and snarfed it down so that she would be ready when Hazel arrived. This meeting could not be worse timing. But yesterday, when Hazel grabbed her during the opening and invited herself over, Lace couldn't have known. Hazel said she had finished her research on Mrs. Owen and was excited to share her findings. Yesterday, today seemed perfect.

Today, not so much.

Lace was checking her phone—still nothing from Tessa—when Hazel knocked on the kitchen door and waved through the window with a giant grin. She wasn't alone.

Elena Murphy, the photographer slash funeral home manager, was with Hazel. Elena had been a few years behind Lace and her friends in school. Honestly, she had been kind of a weirdo. She and her family lived in the apartment above the funeral home, which was enough to make her an oddball to other kids, but there were also all kinds of rumors about how she could talk to ghosts. It didn't help that she dressed in full goth from the time she was about ten years old. She didn't look anything like the strange kid who left town ten years ago now. Her show at the opening had been amazing. And she seemed normal enough. But seeing her on the back porch sent a little shiver up Lace's spine.

What was Hazel up to?

On the other hand, maybe having Elena in the room would be a good thing. Hazel had known Lace a long time. She would probably be able to sense immediately that something was wrong. Maybe, with Elena in the mix, Lace wouldn't feel like she had to spill her guts. And, right at the moment, Lace wasn't ready to do that.

She opened the door to let them in. Hazel was carrying a small storage box, and Elena had a bottle of Pommery, Tessa's bubbly rosé. Lace felt sick at the sight of the Mujer Fuerte label but took the bottle with a smile.

"Tessa gave this to me as a gift yesterday. I thought it would be fun to pop it open tonight, in honor of Mrs. Owen!" Elena said, opening the cabinet where Lace kept her wine glasses. Since Elena had never been in Lace's kitchen before, it was a little weird that she knew right where to go. Maybe Elena really did have a gift for knowing things. Or maybe it was just coincidence.

Hazel sat at the head of the table with the storage box in front of her, like she was leading a graduate seminar. Or about to conduct a seance. Lace and Elena took a seat on either side of her.

"Before we begin, I propose a toast." Hazel paused dramatically and lifted her glass. "To complicated lives and the people who live them!"

Lace raised her glass and took a sip, as if Hazel hadn't just freaked her the hell out. Had she been eavesdropping or somehow spying on Lace's life for the past twenty-four hours? Complicated lives? Really? That was an understatement.

But Lace was not in the mood to talk about it. She folded her hands on the table, straightened her shoulders, and did her best to make her face say everything was fine. "Alright, Hazel, thanks for coming over. What have you found out about our dear Mrs. Owen?" Lace glanced across the table at Elena. She still wasn't sure why Hazel had brought her along.

A knowing smile stretched across Hazel's face. She extracted a pair of white gloves from her purse. As their town librarian and resident historian, Hazel knew exactly how to handle precious artifacts. She slowly pulled on the gloves, and then reached into the storage crate. Very carefully, she lifted the box Tessa had discovered during the carriage house renovations and put it on the table.

"You've seen this," Hazel said soberly.

Lace nodded and resisted rolling her eyes. The theatrics were a little much.

"This box is filled with the personal effects of Elizabeth Owen, born Elizabeth Smith in Kansas City, Missouri, to Robert and Anna Smith, on April 12, 1893. She died in Owen Station, Arizona, on April 12, 1918."

"She died on her birthday?"

Hazel pressed her lips together and nodded. Then she opened the box. She carefully lifted the diary and put it on the table. Then she placed her hand gently on top of it.

"This is one of the most exciting discoveries that has been made here in Owen Station to help us understand what life was like at the turn of the last century. It is raw history, a primary source, history unfiltered. But not just that. It is history from *below*, from the perspective of a *woman* who, by virtue of being a woman, had limited freedoms and limited options. This diary will challenge, confirm, and help shape our understanding of the history of this town."

This was all very impressive. Tessa had been smart to suggest having Hazel examine it all. But what did any of this have to do with Lace? Why the need for this big dramatic unveiling?

"Tell her what else you found, Hazel." Elena was really enjoying the bubbles. And the drama.

Hazel nodded at Elena, pulled a large white envelope out of the storage box, and cleared her throat. "There were entries in Elizabeth's diary of a personal nature that made me curious about one of the individuals she mentions. She never used anything but the initials MT to refer to this individual, unlike other people she wrote about, but it was clear from her use of pronouns, that this individual was a woman."

Lace glanced down at the envelope. "What's in there?"

"These are photocopies of newspaper articles from the *Owen Station Caller*, dated from 1915 to 1918. They are all in our library's archives." Hazel paused.

"And?"

"Through these articles, and the story Elizabeth herself tells in her diary, I was able to piece together the identity of the mysterious MT. Her initials are embroidered on this hankie."

Hazel gingerly lifted it out of Mrs. Owen's box. Lace remembered seeing it the day Tessa found it.

"This," Hazel said, "most likely belonged to a woman named Margaret Tarrants. In Owen Station, she was more commonly known by her professional name—Madame Trouble."

"Madame Trouble! The woman buried next to Mrs. Owen on Boot Hill."

"One and the same."

"Wait. Are you telling me that…" Lace was trying to wrap her head around the story Hazel was weaving.

"Margaret and Elizabeth were lovers," Hazel said.

Elena nodded, grinning, and drained the last of her glass, which she quickly refilled.

"Do you know anything else?" Lace leaned forward, so caught up in the story that everything else going on in her life faded into the background for a moment.

"Based on entries in Elizabeth's diaries, from November 1917 to February 1918, it seems she and Margaret were planning to leave Owen Station together."

"While she was still married to Mr. Owen?" Lace asked, knowing the answer.

Hazel nodded. "It was an unhappy marriage."

"He was much older than she was," Elena added. "It seems like he basically just wanted a housekeeper, and someone to keep his bed warm."

What a sad story. No wonder Mrs. Owen loved that vibrator so much.

"What happened to them? To Elizabeth and Margaret, I mean. Why weren't they able to get away?" Lace knew where they had ended up, of course. Buried next to gunslingers and outlaws.

"They were so close to making it, Lace. Margaret ran a small brothel in the gulch. As you know, it was one of the few ways women back then could make a living and be financially independent. Her establishment was renowned for being clean, professionally managed, and good to the women who worked there. According to the *Caller*, she was a sponsor of the arts and supported many good causes in town. She wasn't exactly what you would call a respectable woman. But she was respected. And she had been saving her money for years."

"But where did they think they would go—Margaret and Elizabeth—back then?" Lace couldn't even imagine.

"She and Elizabeth were making plans to go to Paris. They had heard there were others like them there—women who loved women—and that they could be free to live their own lives there together."

Hazel stopped and exchanged a look with Elena, before continuing. "Here's the thing, Lace. In late March 1918, the Great Influenza, also known as the Spanish flu, hit Owen Station. Elizabeth wasn't the first to be diagnosed. But she *was* the first Owenite to die. Margaret, who may have contracted it due to her close contact with Elizabeth, was not far behind."

Lace put the pieces together and felt her blood pressure begin to rise. "And somehow *Mr.* Owen found out what had been going on and—"

"Maybe." Hazel interrupted, holding her hand up to stop Lace before she could get too wound up. "That piece of the puzzle is harder to figure out. Elizabeth's last entry, obviously, was before her death. And an affair between two women, especially when one of them was a respected businesswoman and the other was the young wife of Mr. Owen himself, wasn't exactly going to make it into the *Caller*. So the evidence isn't there to—"

"But he buried her on Boot Hill! Even though the new cemetery had already been opened. And Madame Trouble—I mean, Margaret—is buried next to her!"

Hazel nodded. "I know. But they were also among the first to die during the pandemic, and everyone was terrified. We know what that's like, don't we? How, in the beginning, no one knows what to think, rumors fly, people are so confused and scared. It's possible the two women were buried in town for public health reasons, not out of spite."

Lace sat back in her chair, crossed her arms, and scowled. She wasn't inclined to let Mr. Owen off so easily.

"There's one more thing." Hazel reached into Mrs. Owen's box, pulled out a small leather coin purse, and handed it to Lace.

"What's this?"

Hazel looked at her. "Well, my friend, like everything else in this box, it's yours. It became yours when you bought this house."

Lace realized that her house had become unnaturally quiet. She had grown accustomed to the creaks and knocks that all old houses have, and to the other noises, too. Occasional soft footsteps, what sounded like humming, a door closing. Always upstairs. Which was why Lace had chosen to live downstairs. But sitting there, at her kitchen table, for the first time she could remember since she moved in, she heard nothing. It was unnerving.

Lace looked at the little purse in her hand and tried to hand it back to Hazel. "This isn't mine. It's Elizabeth's."

Hazel tucked her hands into her lap below the table and shook her head.

"Elizabeth wants you to have it, Lace." Elena spoke sharply. She was sitting up straight, her eyes a deep clear blue, hands folded on the table in front of her, and she was looking so intently at Lace, it was hard to look back.

Lace glanced over at Hazel, who just shrugged.

Lace felt the weight of the little purse in her hand. There was some kind of object inside. She looked at Hazel, then at Elena, then back at the purse, and sighed heavily. Then she opened the purse and turned it upside down.

A simple but beautiful silver ring, with a turquoise inlay, landed in her open palm.

It should have been cool to the touch, and it was. But it generated a heat that filled Lace's hand and spread slowly, up her arm, and then down through her chest toward her heart.

Lace looked to Hazel for answers.

"Based on Elizabeth's diary, I believe she intended to give this ring to Margaret when they got to Paris." Hazel's voice grew very soft. "As a sign of her love and commitment."

Lace folded her hand around the ring and held it in a tight fist. Then she squeezed her eyes shut and felt tears begin to form. The pain of losing Tessa—even if it was her own fault—was so raw. She could not even begin to absorb the pain of these two women. They had come so close to having the love they longed for. They deserved it. And it was denied. Lace did not deserve it. She had proven herself unworthy. But Tessa did. It was all so unfair.

Lace snapped open her eyes angrily and looked back and forth at the two women sitting at her kitchen table. She opened her palm and showed them the ring. "I don't even know what I'm supposed to do with this!"

Elena reached across the table and took Lace's empty hand. "Lace, I don't know any details. But I do know that Elizabeth believes you know who that ring should be given to."

That did not help. It was beyond her power to fix this. There was nothing she could to do make things right for Margaret and Elizabeth. And there was nothing she could do for Tessa.

She panicked.

"But I have made a complete mess of things. I ran out. I let her go. I heard the truck and I didn't even try to chase after her." Words came tumbling out, one on top of another. "I have a three-month rule for a reason. And I can't even do that well. I just don't have it in me. I would end up hurting her. Just like I did to Knox. He gave his heart to me. He took care of me like no one ever had. He was my best friend. And what I did to him, it almost crushed him. I betrayed him. No wonder I never became a mother. Even the universe knows I can't be trusted to love and care for someone long-term. And I couldn't live with myself. I just couldn't. She has already been betrayed by someone she loves. She almost lost everything. And she has worked so hard to get her life back. It would kill me to see her go through something like that again. Oh my God, she deserves *every good thing.* She deserves what Elizabeth and Margaret had, or what they almost had, what they deserved to have, so much more than what someone like me could give her."

When she had exhausted all of her words, she dropped her head to the table and let the tears flow.

"Tessa will understand, Lace."

Lace snapped her head up off the table and stared at Elena. "How…how did you know?"

"Well, I didn't know who it was, until you started talking. I'm not that good." She smiled.

"What are you two talking about? Lace? You and Tessa? What happened? How did I not know anything about this?"

"I don't even know, Hazel. It just happened, I mean, literally, it just happened. Last night. This morning."

Hazel reached over and took Lace's hand. "Take a breath." Hazel waited until Lace had done it. "Okay, now take another one. Calm down. It's all going to be alright. I promise. Now, tell me. What happened?"

"We were just friends, Hazel. I swear. In spite of what everyone was saying behind our backs."

Hazel started to object, but Lace held up her hand. "I know what everyone thought. But it wasn't true. We were good friends. Really good friends. But that was all. We would text and call and have lunch once in a while."

"You were *always* texting and calling." Hazel rolled her eyes. "You would rather sit here and watch a movie with Tessa on the other end of the phone than come hang out with us." She actually sounded a little hurt.

"Okay, fine. You're right. But we were both so busy, and she was so far away. And then—"

"The tasting room," Elena said quietly.

Lace nodded. "The tasting room. That's when everything got so confusing. She was always here. Across the driveway. In my yard. In my house. Here, at my table." Lace paused. "And then, last night. Elena's photo. Angela showed up drunk. I said things I shouldn't have and Tessa heard me. We had a big fight. And then, the next thing I knew…"

Lace dropped her head on the table again with a thud. The next thing that happened was the one thing she never should have allowed to happen. She slept with her best friend—and nothing was ever going to be the same again.

She looked up at Hazel. "I just didn't think about it. I didn't *think*."

"Was it good?"

"Oh my God. It was the best thing that ever happened in my life. But then I…I just *left* her." And that's when the tears really started to come.

Hazel got up and put her arms around her. "Lace, listen to me. I know a thing or two about screwups. Epic screwups. I not only almost blew it with Sena, I almost took down this whole town. But I also know this—and I learned this from Sena's mother—nothing is so broken that it can't be fixed."

Lace broke away from Hazel and jumped out of her chair. "But that's the thing, Hazel. I can't fix this. I don't even want to fix this. I don't want to go chasing after Tessa to live happily-ever-after. I want Tessa to be happy—and that can't happen with *me*."

"Are you open to a question?"

Elena's voice was soft, and she was sitting so still at the table, it made Lace go still, too.

Lace nodded and sat back down.

"You were married before—to Knox."

Lace nodded.

"Then you had an affair and got divorced."

Lace nodded again.

"Now you're afraid to be in a relationship with someone else—including Tessa—"

"Especially Tessa."

"Because you don't trust yourself not to do it again."

"Is there a question here?"

Elena nodded. "Was Margaret a fool for trusting Elizabeth, and being willing to sacrifice everything in order to be with her, even after Elizabeth broke the promise she made to her husband?"

Lace froze. How was she supposed to answer that?

"Elizabeth is asking," Elena said.

A shiver shot through Lace's body and the house came alive again. Upstairs, a door slammed and Hazel jumped.

Elena was unfazed. "It seems to me that one of the lessons this little box has to teach us, Lace, is that life is messy. I'm going to say that again, so you can hear it. Life. Is. Messy. It's also way too short." She topped off all three glasses with the rest of the bubbles. "And the only thing that makes it all worthwhile is love."

Lace took a deep breath, tilted her head back, and closed her eyes. With every exhale, another part of her body softened. First, the area around her eyes. Then her jaw, her neck, her shoulders, her belly. She took one last breath and opened her eyes. "So, what happens now?"

Hazel picked up her glass. "To Elizabeth and Margaret."

Elena lifted hers. "To love."

Lace clinked her glass against the other two and took a long sip.

Then she picked up the ring. It was badly tarnished but could be easily cleaned. The stone was a rare turquoise, easily recognizable because of its vibrant dark blue color and chocolate brown matrix. It could only have come from an Owen Station mine, a rare piece that would have made collectors drool.

She clasped it in her hand and looked up at Hazel and Elena. "I don't even know if she'll have me. After what I did. The way I treated her this morning."

"There's only one way to find out, isn't there?" Hazel smiled. Then she gestured to Elena that it was time to go and started putting Elizabeth's things back into the storage box. "I'll leave these things with you, Lace. They're yours."

Lace shook her head. "I heard you say these artifacts are important to the history of Owen Station. Please, take them."

Hazel looked pleased. "How about if I categorize them as being on loan?"

"Perfect." Lace opened her hand to show the ring, "Take everything except this. I think I heard clearly that *this* is meant for someone else."

Lace hugged Hazel and Elena hard before they left. It was late. She was exhausted. And she planned to be up very early the next morning—in order to be out at the vineyard before sun-up—and she had preparations to make.

But there was one last thing to do before she could embrace the future. She had to let go of the past.

Knox was still the first name on her favorites list. She tapped his number and he answered on the first ring.

"This has become a rare treat! Lace, is that really you?"

"It is." She smiled to hear his voice. Knox had been her best friend since they were kids. Maybe if things hadn't been so hard at home after Dad died. Maybe if she hadn't been so desperate for a safe place in the middle of the storm. Maybe if she hadn't been raised in such a conservative religious environment. Maybe. Maybe. Maybe. Maybe she would have been able to distinguish between loving Knox as a friend and wanting him as a lover. Maybe the slow, rocky journey to her own self-discovery wouldn't have caused him so much pain.

"To what do I owe this unexpected surprise?"

"I'm sorry I've been MIA, Knox."

"No worries. Life has been crazy for me, too."

"I feel bad calling you about this, out of the blue."

"Calling me about what? Is everything okay? Are you alright?"

It was hard not to love Knox. He was so good at loving. "Yes, I am okay. Or at least I think I will be. I just wanted you to be the first to know. I'm going to be changing my name back to Valenti."

Knox was silent for a minute. "It's probably time, isn't it?" He spoke quietly. Lace had been a Reynolds for a little longer than she had been a Valenti.

"Does this mean you're divorcing me?"

Lace laughed. "Well, I think technically we divorced each *other*. And that happened a long time ago, my friend."

"Okay," he laughed. "You're right. Now, how about if you tell me what's going on."

And she did. All of it. Plus what she planned to do in the morning. He was happy for her. He had forgiven her years ago. He told her it was way past time for her to finally forgive herself. He reminded her that they were just kids when they got married. Neither of them knew what they were doing. And that miscarriage? That was a sad thing. The saddest. Unfortunately, it happened to people all the time, for all kinds of reasons. And it was never some kind of a message from the universe. For God's sake, he said, it was certainly not a punishment. Knox wanted nothing more than for her to love and let herself be loved. She had invested her life in helping others find happiness. He said she deserved to be happy, too.

Before they hung up, Lace asked him one last question.

"Hey, Knox, do you think I can be a good wife?"

"Lace, honey, you're going to be *great*."

CHAPTER FOURTEEN

T essa opened one eye.

Based on the muted light outside the small window beside her bed, it was clear that the sun was still only thinking about making an appearance.

But Bleu was already lying at the front door whimpering. Had Tessa forgotten to let her out for one last go before bed? It was possible.

She and Madison had stayed up way too late after Madison convinced her to open a bottle of wine, reminding her that she was almost twenty-one and she wasn't driving. She had been tasting and spitting for as long as she'd been working with Tessa. But just hanging out sharing a bottle was new. Madison had every intention of becoming a full partner at Mujer Fuerte. Tessa had spent the past months watching Madison handle things at the winery while she was building out the new tasting room in town, hearing her creative new ideas to help the business grow, seeing sales numbers climb as a result of Madison's online marketing efforts and her gift for telling the Mujer Fuerte story to guests. She was beginning to get a glimpse of what a real partnership with her daughter might look like.

They shared one of their newest reds, so new the bottle didn't even have a label. It was something Tessa had never done before—a Sangiovese-Tannat blend. Two very different varietals that were absolutely perfect together. It was just as fabulous as she expected it would be. As fabulous as she and Lace might have been together.

But it did mean a late night, and even though she was usually awake by now, Tessa would have loved a few extra minutes of sleep. Especially after the past few days.

She rolled over and smashed the pillow over her head, trying to ignore Bleu's pathetic whimpers. Bleu gave her about ninety seconds, and then started racing in circles, scratching at the Airstream door.

"Bleu," Tessa said in a hushed command, trying not to wake Madison, who was softly snoring from the other room. "Come back to bed."

But the pup wasn't having it. She looked at Tessa and barked.

And that's when the music started. It was coming from outside.

Tessa sat up thinking she might be dreaming. She rubbed the sleep out of her eyes and massaged her face, trying to wake up. When she looked up, Madison was standing at the end of the bed. Strands of light brown hair poked at odd angles out of her crooked ponytail. Pillow creases etched her right cheek, and she was squinting, as if the light was too bright, even though it was still dark inside the Airstream. She looked just as bewildered as Tessa felt.

"Mom?"

Tessa shrugged sleepily.

Bleu bounced onto the bed, licking Tessa's face and pulling on her T-shirt.

"Alright, alright. I'm coming."

Tessa threw off her blanket, swung her feet over the side of the bed, and slipped into her slipper boots. Then she led the way to the door, with Madison trailing behind, and Bleu losing her mind. When she opened the door, Bleu shot through it like she was on the trail of a hundred wayward sheep.

And then Tessa realized what song she was hearing. At concert volume, from the nearest corner of her parking lot, just as the sun was beginning to pink up the eastern sky, Doris Day was singing "Secret Love."

And Calamity Jane was standing there looking at her.

"Lace?" Tessa moved closer to make sure that she was seeing what she thought she saw.

Tessa might have been uncertain, but Bleu certainly wasn't. She was eagerly licking the fingers on one of Lace's hands and wagging her butt so hard that, if she had a tail, it might have taken her airborne.

Lace stepped forward wearing a vintage suede jacket with long fringe, a brown waistcoat, red bandana, layers of leather belts, an old Breton hat smashed on top of her head, and a nervous grin on her face.

She had one hand behind her back and, with the other, she reached into her jacket pocket and pulled out a little remote control—definitely not a Calamity accessory. When she pointed it back at her Bronco, Doris Day's voice slowly got softer, until Lace could be heard over the music. "Good morning."

Tessa raised an eyebrow. "Um, good morning?"

"I brought breakfast."

"I see that."

A blanket covered with all of Tessa's favorite things, and a huge pot of what Tessa could only hope was coffee, was laid out on the ground.

"Lace, what are you doing here?"

"Well, when you put it that way, I'm not entirely sure." Lace smiled crookedly. "I'm never awake this early. And I got zero sleep last night. So I might be delirious."

Tessa raised both eyebrows.

Lace moved closer, until she was just a few feet away.

Madison clicked her tongue behind Lace, calling Bleu, who finally left Lace alone.

Tessa didn't flinch.

Lace cleared her throat and kicked at the dirt. Then she looked into Tessa's eyes and took a deep breath. "I really screwed up, Tess."

Tessa nodded. She wasn't wrong.

"I am a calamity of epic proportions."

Tessa did not choose it, but she couldn't help it, either. She felt herself begin to melt. She closed her eyes, hoping that, if she wasn't actually looking at Lace, standing there in that ridiculous outfit, she could make it stop.

"I am so sorry." Lace spoke softly.

Tessa opened her eyes.

"I hope you can forgive me."

Then, Lace slowly pulled something from behind her back and held it in front of her. She flipped it around so Tessa could see. It was a small hand-painted, wooden sign that read "Calamity Lace and Tessa."

Tessa looked over her shoulder at Madison. She was glad there was a witness because she wasn't sure any of it was real. And, if it was real, she wasn't sure anyone else would ever believe her.

Madison's mouth was turned up at the corners, but it was half-open, and her disbelieving eyes were so wide, her eyebrows were practically on top of her head. She thrust her hands out and swept them in Lace's direction. Like, *do* something, Mom.

A dozen possible next steps tumbled like grapes on the conveyer through Tessa's mind. Take a picture? Ask if she could have a piece of that pie, which she was sure had come from Knox? Take Lace's hand and dance? Kiss the girl?

But before she could do anything, Lace stepped right in front of her, just inches away, set down the sign, and got down on one knee.

Tessa's hands flew to her chest and covered her heart, as if it might leap out of her body and into Lace's arms if she didn't hold it still. It already belonged to Lace. It had for a long time. Tessa didn't know when it happened. She couldn't pinpoint the exact time or place when her heart committed itself forever and completely to the handsome, generous, ridiculous woman kneeling there, wearing an old Halloween costume on a cool summer morning in the hazy moments before dawn. She couldn't even say for sure when she *knew* that had happened. But she could no longer deny that it was true. Lace had her heart.

Doris had finished her song and every critter within twelve miles stopped chirping, buzzing, and foraging. The air was completely still. Even Tessa's racing heart stopped beating for a moment.

The sky was waking up, painted in bright orange and pink, as Lace reached deep into the pocket of her waistcoat and pulled out a small leather purse. She unzipped it and turned it upside down, and a silver ring dropped into the palm of her hand. She stuck the leather purse back in her pocket, took the ring, and held it up with both hands for Tessa to see.

Madison gasped behind her, but Tessa was not surprised. She was strangely calm, embracing the final moments of the best roller coaster ride of her life. After all the upside down loops and terrifying drops, her hair blown in every direction, realizing that she had survived—that they all had—she was gliding toward the platform, feeling whole, realizing that this moment had been inevitable, all along. This was the only place they were ever going to end up.

Lace cleared her throat. Tessa wanted to bend down and kiss her upturned face. She looked so earnest, so vulnerable there on one knee. But as much as Tessa wanted to assure her that it was all going to be okay, that on the other side of her question was a lifetime of happiness, Tessa knew that the question needed to be asked. Lace needed to ask it.

"Tessa, you have been my secret love for a long time. For too long, I tried to keep that secret from myself. Especially from myself. But I can't do that, anymore. I don't want to keep it a secret. Not from myself, not from you, not from anyone. I want the world to know that you are my best friend, my confidant, my movie partner. My soulmate."

Lace paused, blinked, and took a deep breath.

"Tessa Williams, I am asking you to be the Katie to my Calamity. I want us to get hitched. I can't promise it will be easy, but I do promise to love you. To make you laugh. To wipe away the tears when they come. To watch Westerns sitting by your side, into our very old age. To watch the sunset with you every evening and— once in a while, anyway." Lace smiled. "Even watch the sun rise. I love you, Tessa. I love Madison." Bleu barked and, although Lace's gaze never wavered, her grin did get a little bigger. "I love Bleu, too. I want to be a part of your family—and a part of your life—forever."

Lace stood up, so that she was eye to eye, and took Tessa's hand. "I can't imagine keeping any of this a secret for one more day, Tessa, or one more moment." Her voice grew very soft. "Will you marry me?"

Tessa looked into Lace's deep brown eyes, glistening in the light of the new sun. Forever. That sounded just about right.

Tessa threw her arms around Lace's neck, and Madison let out a loud whoop as she threw her own arms around both of them. "This is so sick!" she shouted as Bleu ran circles around them all, barking happily. They were a mess of joyful tears and laughter. And when Tessa's lips found Lace's, they were salty and sweet, a perfect blend—just like the two of them.

After a few minutes, Lace pulled herself away, still holding onto Tessa's hand, with a huge smile across her face. "So, that's a *yes*, I take it?"

Tessa laughed. "Yes, yes, yes!" And she kissed Lace again.

"Okay, then." Lace took Tessa's left hand and slipped on the vintage silver ring. It had an unusual turquoise inlay, and it fit perfectly.

"It is magnificent, Lace. It must have a story."

Lace nodded. "It belonged to Elizabeth."

"Young Mrs. Owen?"

"Yes. Hazel came over last night with Elena. She's finished all her research on the artifacts you found in the carriage house. It turns out, Elizabeth Owen had a secret love, too. A woman named Margaret. Although she was known by her professional name—a name you'll recognize. Madame Trouble."

Tessa let out a gasp. "How do you know all this?"

"Between the diary, old newspaper articles, and other records, Hazel was able to piece it all together. Elizabeth and Margaret were planning to run away together to Paris—one of the few places back then where they could live openly."

"They never made it, did they?" Tessa's heart hurt.

Lace shook her head. "This all happened right as the Spanish flu broke out in this part of the country."

They grew very quiet. Tessa pictured the two lovers lying side by side in bed. And now, on Boot Hill, forever.

"Elizabeth was going to give this ring to Margaret when they got to Paris, Tessa. I hope that if you choose to wear it, it will always be a reminder. For both of us. Life is messy. And it's short, so we shouldn't take even one day together for granted. Because the only thing that makes it all worthwhile is love."

"That is so sweet, Lace." Madison looked like she could float away with happiness. "I didn't know you were a philosopher poet."

"I had a little help figuring it out last night." Lace smiled sheepishly.

Tessa imagined Mrs. Owen wandering around Lace's house, looking for her ring, and felt a little panicky. "Are you sure Mrs. Owen won't mind me wearing it?"

Lace kissed Tessa's hand. "I have it on very good authority that Elizabeth wants you to wear this ring."

Tessa wasn't sure what authority Lace was talking about, and wasn't sure she even wanted to know. But she was confident that Lace knew her roommate as well as anyone. Tessa also knew, better than she knew her own name, that Lace would never knowingly put her in danger. And that was enough.

"I will be proud to wear this ring. First of all, it is an incredible piece of art and history. But I also hope that, wherever they are, it makes Elizabeth and Margaret know that the story of their love will always be told."

Lace took Tessa in her arms. "I could not love you more, Tessa. You have made me the happiest woman in the world today."

Bleu started barking again.

"Okay, you two!" Madison shouted. "I am getting really hungry, and this spread looks amazing. Is it time for breakfast yet?"

Fortunately, Lace had brought a change of clothes because Tessa made her change out of the Calamity costume. Lace explained to Madison that she had worn it to a Halloween party at Delaney's a few years ago, and Madison made her promise she could borrow it one day. Then the three of them and Bleu shared a breakfast picnic together as the sun finally came up over the mountains.

Lace put a playlist on her Bronco stereo, songs she said she had been collecting over the last year, whenever she heard one she wanted to share with Tessa. They weren't all typical love songs, although there were a few of those. Mostly, they were songs about family and friendship. They told stories that touched Tessa's heart or made her laugh or made her want to sing along. They all did sing a few of them together, mostly off-key. And it was perfect. There were a few Tessa decided she would have to learn to play. She pictured many mornings in their future, waking Lace with a love song on her guitar.

The breakfast Lace had put together was a feast. And Tessa had been right, Knox did help. Apparently, the two of them had been up all night, working together to get everything just right. There were berries and croissants, a decadent triple crème cheese, fresh pears, blueberries and blue cheese clustered together with local honeycomb, fresh melon wrapped in prosciutto drizzled with an aged balsamic, Hatch green chili, roasted asparagus croissant tarts. Madison grabbed a chilled bottle of Pommery from the wine barn fridge—Tessa's first vintage, which she had added to her library collection. And the three of them ate until they thought they could never eat anything ever again.

Madison was cross-legged on the blanket, Bleu beside her. "Thank you for including me in this celebration, you two. Lace, I have never seen my mom so happy. I love the way you *see* her, encourage, love, and challenge her to be her best self. In case you haven't noticed, I'm a big Lace fan. And not just because you helped Mom pick out the best birthday present ever, two years ago!" They all laughed and Madison hopped up. "On that note, I'm out of here. You two enjoy each other and this amazing day. My work here is done!"

Tessa's heart swelled as Madison embraced Lace, and then Tessa walked her to the car. She thought about asking Madison to keep the news of their engagement a secret, so they could tell people themselves. But before the words came out of her mouth she remembered Lace's proposal. They were done keeping their love secret.

Besides, Tessa laughed to herself. They lived and worked in a small town. Walt was probably already announcing it on KBIS.

Tessa kissed Madison and let her take Bleu with her for an overnight.

She wanted Lace all to herself.

Lace had already cleared away breakfast and was in the Airstream when Tessa came in. "Can I pour my favorite fiancée another glass of bubbles? Or another cup of coffee?"

"I like the sound of that." Tessa grinned.

"Bubbles…or coffee?"

"I mean fiancée, silly. There's just one problem."

A flash of concern crossed Lace's face.

"You still have all your clothes on."

Lace gave Tessa a playful slap on the butt. "I'm fine taking mine off, but you should stay just like that. You look so sexy in your pajamas."

"Very funny." Tessa was in a cotton V-neck T-shirt and joggers. "At least I'm not wearing deer skin."

"What? You didn't like my Calamity outfit?"

Tessa kissed Lace on the cheek and whispered in her ear. "I will never be able to unsee that."

Laughing, Lace started unbuttoning her own shirt. "Let me show you something to take your mind off it."

They both undressed in under a minute, and Tessa dove under the covers first. Lace climbed in next to her, and Tessa ran her foot down the length of Lace's leg, pulling her closer.

In the loft, that first night, Tessa had been on the edge of climax almost from the moment she felt Lace's fully-clothed body press against hers. She was no less excited now. Every part of her was awake in a way it had never been before. But she didn't want anything about this moment to be short. Sweet, maybe. But they had all day. And Tessa wanted to know everything there was to know about the woman she planned to marry.

Lace pulled Tessa on top of her. With the expanse of Lace's body beneath her, Tessa begin delivering slow, passionate kisses. She moved against Lace, looking for a rhythm that would make them both moan, grinding against Lace's hip bone, and the heat began to build.

Suddenly, Lace rolled her over onto her back and propped herself up so she could look into Tessa's eyes. She raised an eyebrow and flashed a crooked smile.

"You look like trouble."

Lace nodded. "The good kind of trouble, though. I'm ready to play, how about you?"

There was only one thing that could mean from the owner of Arizona's best adult toy shop. Tessa felt a bit frisky and a little naughty. "Where do you want to start?"

Lace leaned over the side of the bed and clicked open a leather case, about the size of a small carry-on.

"How did you get that in here?" Tessa laughed, shaking her head.

"I got skills."

"Oh yeah? Let's see you prove it."

Tessa had never experienced much playfulness or creativity in bed. Olivia was all about Olivia. And Tessa had only had a few other partners since then. None lasted long enough to develop the kind of connection or build the sort of safe space that Tessa would have needed in order to feel free enough to explore.

But Lace was her friend before she was her lover. They had been through business crises, and personal ones. Lace always seemed to know just what Tessa needed to hear, whether it was a word of comfort or a call to action. She knew Lace wasn't perfect. The events of the past forty-eight hours had given Tessa a deeper look at the emotional scars that lay beneath Lace's cheerful bravado. But she trusted Lace to always have her best interests in mind. She had given Lace her heart. She knew she could trust Lace with her body. And she was ready for anything.

"I'll go first," Lace said cheerily. "Have you used these before?" She held up a pair of nipple clamps. "They're old school but one of my favorites."

"Nope. First time. But according to the internet, you're a pretty good teacher."

Lace lay on her back with Tessa beside her and showed Tessa how she liked her chest rubbed. She wasn't turned on by a focus on her breasts, but she loved to have her nipples licked and sucked the same way you would suck a clit or a cock. Lace slipped her fingers into Tessa's mouth and then spread the wetness over her own nipples, stroking them softly and then faster, then pinching them hard, showing Tessa what she liked. Then she took Tessa's hand and guided her, so that Tessa knew exactly what she wanted.

Tessa was completely out of her comfort zone. She had never experienced so many *words* in bed. She had never done much beyond poking around, trying to figure it all out in the dark. And her lovers had done the same. It was always something of a miracle when one of them got it right. And every time she got it wrong increased her anxiety going into the next time. So the first time or two, especially, was always filled with as much apprehension as anticipation. But Lace was lying next to her, being transparent and honest, believing enough in Tessa to share what she needed and patient enough to give Tessa time and space to figure it out. It was a lot like how things with Lace were *outside* of the bedroom. And there was just as much laughter.

Feeling confident, Tessa licked her fingers and made Lace's nipples even wetter. Then she asked Lace to show her how to put the clamps on. They were adjustable, and Lace liked them tight, right on her nipples. When Lace gasped from the pain, Tessa pulled back in concern, but Lace pulled her forward. "That feels really good." Her voice was breathless and husky.

Tessa wasn't sure how long she was going to be able to play like this. Having Lace show her what to do—she was so clear about what made her feel good and so generous in teaching—was a totally new experience. Every inch of her body was tingling, and her pussy was on fire. She rubbed Lace's chest, like she had been shown, while covering her mouth with hard kisses, driving her tongue deep into Lace's mouth. From the side, she straddled Lace's leg and used the knee on top to press against Lace's pussy. Lace lifted her ass, begging for more pressure. Tessa pulled gently on one of the clamps and Lace moaned louder.

"Yank it off!" Lace cried.

"Yank it?"

"Like this!" Lace pulled one off, and then guided Tessa's hand to the other.

Lace yelped in pain when Tessa pulled it off, and Lace pushed her head down on top of the swollen nipple.

"Suck it, Tessa. Hard."

She did. Tessa sucked and licked and nibbled and rubbed, paying attention to Lace's response, doing more of whatever made her writhe in sweet agony. While Tessa continued working her nipples, Lace grabbed Tessa's hand and sucked on her fingers, wetting them. Then she shoved Tessa's hand down to her waist and urged her to go lower. She took Tessa's fingers and placed them right where she wanted them, and then together, they rubbed Lace's clit until she exploded.

Lace brought Tessa's face up to hers and kissed her gently on the lips. And then she was quiet. Tessa snuggled down onto Lace's shoulder, underneath her arm, and lay there while Lace lazily caressed her arms, her back, her breasts. Tessa had been on the verge of orgasm herself, when Lace came, but she was thankful for this in-between moment. She put her hand on Lace's chest and felt it rise and fall.

Finally, Lace's breathing began to return to normal. "You are a very good student, Tessa. I give you an A-plus for effort and an A-plus-plus-plus for results."

Tessa had spent almost her entire life feeling like she was making one mistake after another. Lace's appreciation and praise was unexpected and gave Tessa such a deep sense of confidence and joy. This is what Lace did for her every day. Why would it be any different here, in the bed they shared?

"An A, huh? Do I get a prize for being such a good student?" Tessa's pussy was waking up again, and she was feeling a little wicked.

"Do you have a particular prize in mind?" Lace raised an eyebrow. "Because I can't think of anything I would not be absolutely delighted to give you right now."

"Well, I've always wondered exactly what a butt plug would do for me."

"I have just the thing." Lace reached back into her bag of toys and pulled out a tiny pink plug, just a few inches long, about the size of a thumb. "Since this is your first time, I think we should start with this." Lace grinned. "Tessa Williams, meet Rubyfruit."

Tessa laughed. "Rubyfruit, huh? What an original name! I can't wait to get to know each other better."

Tessa expected Lace to get right to work doing whatever one did with a butt plug. Instead, Lace turned Tessa over onto her side and spooned up tight behind her.

"Before we do anything else, I want you to be as relaxed as you can possibly be. Okay?"

Tessa nodded and settled back against Lace, feeling the warmth of her body and how wonderful it was to be in her arms. She wasn't in a hurry. Lace stroked Tessa's arm, and then her hip, while covering her shoulders and neck with gentle kisses.

"I love you, Tess." Lace whispered in her ear. "I am so glad you said yes."

"Was there every any doubt?"

Tessa could feel Lace smile behind her. "No, I guess not. Wait right here."

Lace reached into her bag again and pulled out a tube of lubricant and a glove, which she snapped on "Now the fun begins."

Tessa's clit swelled, but she also felt her anus tighten. She knew enough to know that probably wasn't good. "Lace, I'm a little nervous."

Lace lay back down, snuggling up close behind her, and spent a few more minutes kissing her and talking softly. She told Tessa how beautiful she was, tracing the stretch marks on her hip. She explained exactly what she planned to do with Tessa's body, and how it might make her feel, and assured Tessa that she would be in total control. As Lace talked and stroked her body and let Tessa feel the full length of her pressed behind her, Tessa felt herself open — her heart, mind, spirit, and body. Lace must have sensed that.

"Are you ready?"

Tessa nodded, and Lace gently turned her over onto her stomach. Using Tessa's hips, Lace urged her to lift her ass just a little. Tessa obeyed, propping herself up and spreading her legs. She had never felt more vulnerable, but Lace was making her feel so loved and so safe, it was dizzying.

The cold lube startled her and sent a shiver through her body. But then Lace began using it to circle and tease her opening. Tessa dropped her head and moaned in anticipation. The next time she felt Lace's slick finger lingering at her opening, she pushed back hard, taking Lace inside of her, and honest to God, she nearly came right there. Lace moved the tip of her finger gently in and out, and the more she moved inside of her, the more open Tessa became.

"I want more, Lace."

Lace withdrew her finger and stripped off the glove. Then she squeezed and rubbed Tessa's ass. She ran both her hands up along Tessa's hips and sides, and then dragged them down along the center of Tessa's back, to her ass again, which she squeezed and rubbed some more. Tessa thought she might die, right there in the middle of her bed, if Lace did not move faster. She opened her legs wider and propped herself up higher, so that she could watch what Lace was doing between her legs. Finally…*Rubyfruit*.

Tessa held her breath as she watched Lace slather the tiny plug with lube. When Lace pressed it gently against Tessa's opening, it felt hard and big. And Tessa *needed* it inside her.

"You're in charge here, Tessa. You decide how much, how fast. You tell me what feels good, and—"

Tessa didn't wait for Lace to finish. She thrust backward, against the plug in Lace's hand, groaning Lace's name as she took it all in. Every nerve ending shot to attention, launching daggers of tingling heat straight to Tessa's clit. Lace grabbed her ass, rubbing and squeezing it, and every movement she made intensified the pleasure. Her pussy was screaming for release.

"Lick me, Lace! Do something to help me now!"

Lace quickly flipped her over onto her back and dove between her legs.

Tessa grabbed Lace's head and pulled it against her pussy. Lace used her soft fingers to split open Tessa's inner lips and, with her tongue, found Tessa's clit. Tessa raised her ass, pressing harder against Lace's face, tightening her legs around Lace's head, and with a few flicks of Lace's tongue, she came harder and deeper than she had ever come before. Wave after wave washed over her, until finally she let her entire body collapse in a heap.

Lace crawled up next to her, propped up on her elbow, and grinned. Tessa couldn't speak. She just lay there, trying to breathe, letting Lace stroke her face, her chest, her belly.

"You're pretty proud of yourself, aren't you?"

"I do okay."

Tessa would never get enough of seeing that smile.

"Are you ready for round two?"

Tessa laughed. "Um, no. Not quite. But I will be later."

Lace did a quick clean up, and then lay down on her back next to Tessa, pulling her into a gentle but firm embrace. After a few minutes, though, Lace's grip softened and her breathing evened out. Tessa smiled into Lace's shoulder. She had been awake all night, getting ready for this day—and had seen the sun rise! Tessa would let her sleep as long as she could. They had the whole day to spend together.

They had a lifetime.

When she was a very young girl, Tessa's very old great-grandmother told her stories from life in the circus. There is a moment, when a trapeze artist is in midair and has to get from one bar to the next, that she has to let go of the one she is holding in order to reach the one she wants. That in-between moment is terrifying, but unless she is willing to risk it, she falls and misses the chance to fly.

It took Lace to help Tessa take that risk. They had done that for each other.

Tessa tucked herself even tighter against Lace, closed her eyes, and dreamed of flying.

EPILOGUE: SIX MONTHS LATER

In the middle of the night, though!" Delaney was poking at Lace's hair.

Hazel had asked—again—to hear the story of when Tessa went with her to Boot Hill for her birthday. And Delaney was just as horrified this time as she was every other time. "You should have known Tessa was crazy for you right then and there, my friend. No one in their right mind would go hang out in a cemetery—in the middle of the *night*—with someone they weren't trying to get into bed!"

Lace swatted Delaney's hand away. "My hair looks fine, already!"

She looked at her friends and felt a wave of gratitude.

"Is that a tear in your eye, Lace Valenti?" Hazel was radiant, and not just because she was so happy for Lace and Tessa on their big day. Hazel had recently confided that, after a year of trying, she was finally pregnant. She and Sena were expecting in June.

"It is a tear, and I'm not ashamed to say it."

"You should be crying, because that haircut I gave you is so absolutely perfect." Delaney jutted her chin up proudly. "Now, let me *fix* it."

Lace gave in and let Delaney do her magic. "I feel like I'm teary-eyed all the time now. I went for a walk with Tessa last night and she was telling me about how the vines are asleep at this time of year, soaking up nutrients from the soil, getting ready for another year of growth. And I started crying, right there in the middle of the field. I've become a big old softy. Tessa laughs and says I always was. Now I can just show it."

"I bet you didn't cry when they hauled old Studly away in handcuffs, did you?" Delaney had been having fun sharing that bit of gossip with everyone who came into the salon.

Lace scowled. "Not even a little. Spencer Taurus was making Tessa's life a living hell. And, it turns out, he was a threat to the whole region. Last week we heard the little cheap ass used shoddy equipment and a construction company that didn't know what it was doing to build his waste management system. It was leaking waste everywhere, seeping into the ground water, and contaminating our most important source of drinking water. And don't even get me started on the conditions those poor cows were living in. They estimate it would take at least twenty million dollars to bring it all up to code. But since he's been indicted for ten federal felony counts and facing prison time, I don't think they'll be operating again anytime soon."

"He didn't know who he was messing with when he took on Tessa, did he?" Hazel asked.

Lace shook her head. "My soon-to-be wife is a badass."

"Did someone say your fiancée is a mujer fuerte?" Knox poked his head into the kitchen, where Lace was making final preparations for the big ceremony.

Lace laughed. "I did."

"Well, I think she's ready for you."

Lace took one last look in the mirror. Delaney was right—her high glossy pompadour was killer. Sena had helped her decide on the outfit—black jeans, a black-on-black paisley printed shirt, and a black bow tie. Her turquoise-colored vest matched the cutouts in Tessa's new boots and ring.

She nodded to herself then turned to Knox. "Let's not keep her waiting."

She and Tessa had decided they wanted their wedding to be just a little different. If they did the traditional walk up a center aisle, would they both walk? If so, in which order? And, if not, who would walk and who would wait? It all seemed complicated, and a little fraught with traditions they weren't sure they wanted to adopt. It also reminded them both a little too much of their first weddings. This was different. *They* were different.

The officiant was standing beneath Lace's favorite cottonwood. It was more than a hundred years old, which seemed a fitting location for a ceremony that would bind her and Tessa together forever. It had been a sapling when Elizabeth and Margaret professed their love to each other and dreamed of their new life.

Mrs. Owen left sometime after Lace proposed to Tessa. Lace noticed that, although the old house still creaked—like anyone would if they were a hundred years old—the upstairs had settled into a comfortable quiet. Elena confirmed that Elizabeth was no longer there. Lace hoped that, wherever she was, she was with Margaret, and they were at peace.

Two hundred white chairs had been set up on the lawn and every single one of them was filled. Sena and Hazel had made their way to the front row, where they sat beside Delaney and Derrick, who both wore enough color to brighten the whole crowd. The form-fitting, royal-blue dress Sena was wearing contrasted beautifully against her brown skin—she belonged on a fashion magazine. She put her arm tenderly around Hazel's shoulder and placed her hand on Hazel's belly. Hazel, of course, had traded her usual pencil skirt for a more loose-fitting jumpsuit. Ricki was there, from the Miner's Hole, in her finest Western wear, sitting with Jorge and Miguel, who wore coordinated guayaberas. Like Barb from the Triple D, they had all put signs on their front doors, saying they were closed "for a family wedding." Elena was there with her family—the Murphys alone took up a whole row, their white faces a sharp contrast against their black, funeral director suits. Dozens of Tessa's wine club members and volunteers were there, all dressed up, but wearing Mujer Fuerte ball caps—there had never been a more loyal bunch of fans. And, of course, Jeremy was there with the whole vineyard crew and their families. Assistant Fire Chief Al Jones, who had recently cut her Afro into a super short buzz, was out of uniform and dressed to rock behind the microphone. She was standing in the back with the

Fireballs, who had their instruments all set up and were ready with the first song as soon as the ceremony was over. Building Jack and Plumber Joe and Caretaker Bud and all the rest were there. This wedding was a town event, and everyone wanted to be part of it.

That's why Walt was there. He was pasty-colored from too many hours in the basement radio station he managed, and he was wearing a wrinkled button-down and an old pair of khakis. He had recruited a volunteer to spin love songs all afternoon, so that he could be at the wedding to do an audio recording. He was going to share parts of the ceremony on a special broadcast he had planned for later, so that neighbors and friends who couldn't make it due to work or illness or being out of town could still feel like they were there.

Their officiant was new to town. Hazel had introduced them after Delaney refused to allow Derrick to do the ceremony. Delaney wanted him to just be her date, sitting with her through the ceremony, which she knew was going to make her cry like a baby. Amanda was a recently retired professor of women and gender studies. She had written a book that made her quite famous back in the eighties, but now she and her wife, Alex, were opening an ice cream slash pet supply store on Main Street. Amanda's unruly gray hair had a huge streak of purple in it and she wore flowing silk robes that matched.

"Is this thing on?" Amanda tapped the microphone hard three times, which got everyone's attention.

Knox, who was standing next to Lace, gave Amanda the thumbs up. She returned it and nodded.

"Alright then! On behalf of Lace and Tessa—Tessa and Lace—I'd like to welcome you to this most glorious occasion!"

The crowd fell silent.

"Bleu, come!" she yelled, making the microphone squeal. But no one minded because Bleu immediately came prancing up the aisle carrying a basket full of dried flowers, just like they all practiced. The perfect flower girl, she set the basket down in front of Amanda, and then sat beside her like she was co-officiating.

Lace looked across the yard at Tessa. They had decided that, instead of following Bleu up the center, they would start in the front, but come in from the sides, and meet each other in the middle, beneath the cottonwood, in front of their family of friends.

It was the first time Lace had seen Tessa that day. She was wearing a cream-colored, crocheted wedding dress and a brand-new pair of cowboy boots. Sprigs of dried lavender were in her light brown hair, which framed her face and fell softly down around her shoulders. Tears filled Lace's eyes. She wasn't sure how she was going to get through the next few minutes.

"Hang tight, Lace. You got this." Knox squeezed the hand Lace had wrapped around his arm. She held on to him like it was the only thing preventing her from sinking into a sea of her own happiness.

Amanda nodded at Tessa and then turned to nod at Lace. It was time.

Tessa took Madison's arm, and Lace held Knox's, and they began moving toward each other. As she got closer, she could see that both Tessa and Madison had tears streaming down their faces. When they reached the middle, Tessa turned and hugged Madison, who whispered something in her mom's ear.

Lace turned toward Knox. His face was wet and his lower lip was quivering. "I love you, Lace," he managed to say. "Be happy."

She got up on her toes—not easy to do in her black harness boots—and kissed him on the cheek.

Then Knox took Madison's hand, and they took their seats in the very front row, right next to Sena and Hazel. Bleu hopped down and joined them.

Lace took Tessa's hands and they faced each other, while Amanda said some words that made people laugh and, Lace heard later, also made them all a little teary-eyed. But Lace wasn't paying attention to anything except all the things Tessa was saying to her with her eyes.

She had been a fool to try to stop herself from falling in love with Tessa. Yes, they were going to have their share of messiness. Life was messy! But life was way too short. This—*this*—was what made it all worthwhile.

Amanda cleared her throat, and then did it again louder.

Tessa smiled and gently shook Lace's hands.

KELLY & TANA FIRESIDE

"You're up first," she said quietly.

Lace nodded, took a deep breath, and prepared to recite the words it had taken her a lifetime to be able to write. "Tessa Williams, I promise to re-up every three months for the rest of my life, to show up every day, and work as hard as I can to be the woman you deserve. To love you, and Maddie and Bleu too, with all my heart and soul. To honor and cherish you as long as I live."

Rivulets of tears fell from Tessa's eyes, but she held them steady, looking at Lace with so much love and gratitude, Lace wasn't sure her heart could bear it.

"Lace Valenti, I promise to hold you to all of that!"

Everyone laughed and a few loud whistles came from the crowd. Lace grinned and nodded. She wanted that more than anything.

When everyone settled down, Tessa squeezed Lace's hands. "I also promise to remember that, no matter what we face in our life together, I am a mujer fuerte—strong, resilient, and resourceful—and because of that, I can and *will* be here for you always, to encourage and challenge you, to cheer you on when you are winning and pick you up when you have fallen, to remind you of who you are and what you are capable of, and to love you the ways you deserve, as long as I live."

Amanda dramatically pronounced them married, in accordance with the laws of the state of Arizona, and in the name of the old gods and the new, and blessed the crowd saying, "May the Force be with you!" Everyone cheered and Bleu ran around in circles barking, and then the Fireballs launched into the first song. As instructed, people in the first ten rows of chairs all got up and moved them out of the way, creating a dance floor under the old cottonwood tree.

"May I have this dance?" Lace held out her hand and Tessa took it, and they held each other tight, dancing slowly to the Fireball's very sexy rendition of "Secret Love."

The rest of the night was a blur. Everyone kept asking the same question—where are you going to live? And they told everyone the same thing. Now that Mrs. Owen had moved out, they were redesigning the upstairs of Owen Mansion to be their home together. Frisky Business needed more room downstairs, anyway. And they were building a tiny house out at the vineyard, where they would stay together during Tessa's busiest seasons.

Maia's food was orgasmic. Tessa's volunteers kept everyone's glasses full. And the Fireballs were lit. People danced until after ten o'clock.

When everyone else had gone home, Lace and Tessa invited their closest friends to stay for one last toast. Delaney and Derrick, Sena, Hazel and Knox all gathered around the counter in the tasting room and Madison poured.

"So, is Lace always such a softy now, or was it just today that turned her into such a crybaby?" Knox asked Tessa.

"You have no idea. Among other things, she is insisting we need to adopt every stray animal in Owen Station. She has that pet finder app on her phone, and every day, it's another one. Yesterday, she wanted us to go get a potbellied pig that got turned into a shelter in Tucson."

Madison laughed. "I can only imagine what Bleu would think of that!"

Lace's cheeks grew warm, but she wasn't ashamed. She took Tessa by the waist and pulled her close. "Can I help it if this woman has melted my heart?"

They all made oohing and ahhing sounds, and Madison told them to get a room.

Tessa grinned and gave Lace a playful slap on the butt. "Oh, we're headed there soon. But first, I want to say something."

Everyone quieted and Tessa looked around the circle at each one of their friends, in turn.

"When Madison and I moved here five years ago, we felt pretty alone. We *were* alone. My family didn't understand and doesn't approve of the way I've chosen to live my life. I had lost everything, including the vineyard that had been my whole life. My heart was bruised and I was so worried about Madison."

Madison reached across the counter and gave her hand a squeeze.

"I was afraid to trust anyone. Even worse, I was afraid to trust myself. I never could have imagined that, one day, Madison and I would have *this*—a family of friends who believe in us and support and love us. Thank you for bringing us into your lives. By showing me how you love each other, you helped open my eyes to what love really looks like. And that—"

She turned to face Lace. "—helped me open my heart to you."

Lace wrapped her arms around Tessa and let herself cry big, messy, unapologetic tears.

"Well, I think that's our cue, friends." Knox slapped Lace on the back. "Let's let these two newlyweds have some time alone."

They all hugged, and Madison and their friends promised they would give them a day or two and mind their businesses for them so they could get ready to leave for their honeymoon.

"Oh! Did you finally decide where you're going?" Delaney asked, clapping her hands enthusiastically. They had been keeping it on the down low and Delaney, Owen Station's gossip central, was dying to know.

Tessa looked at Lace and nodded.

"We're going to Paris," Lace said with a smile. "It's been a long time coming."

About the Authors

Writing duo Kelly & Tana Fireside love traveling, cooking great food, and making music around a campfire. They've been best friends for more than twenty-five years and are still madly in love after fifteen years of marriage. It took them a long time to find their way to each other, and now they're never letting go. After working for many years in public and community service, they are writing stories to help spark a revolutionary love of self and others. They spend most of their time on the road in Howie (their House On Wheels) with a frisky pup named Gabby and her best friend, Chip the cat.

Books Available from Bold Strokes Books

A Talent Ignited by Suzanne Lenoir. When Evelyne is abducted and Annika believes she has been abandoned, they must risk everything to find each other again. (978-1-63679-483-9)

All Things Beautiful by Alaina Erdell. Casey Norford only planned to learn to paint like her mentor, Leighton Vaughn, not sleep with her. (978-1-63679-479-2)

An Atlas to Forever by Krystina Rivers. Can Atlas, a difficult dog Ellie inherits after the death of her best friend, help the busy hopeless romantic find forever love with commitment-phobic animal behaviorist Hayden Brandt? (978-1-63679-451-8)

Bait and Witch by Clifford Mae Henderson. When Zeddi gets an unexpected inheritance from her client Mags, she discovers that Mags served as high priestess to a dwindling coven of old witches—who are positive that Mags was murdered. Zeddi owes it to her to uncover the truth. (978-1-63679-535-5)

Buried Secrets by Sheri Lewis Wohl. Tuesday and Addie, along with Tuesday's dog, Tripper, struggle to solve a twenty-five-year-old mystery while searching for love and redemption along the way. (978-1 63679-396-2)

Come Find Me in the Midnight Sun by Bailey Bridgewater. In Alaska, disappearing is the easy part. When two men go missing, state trooper Louisa Linebach must solve the case, and when she thinks she's coming close, she's wrong. (978-1-63679-566-9)

Death on the Water by CJ Birch. The Ocean Summit's authorities have ruled a death on board its inaugural cruise as a suicide, but Claire suspects murder and with the help of Assistant Cruise Director Moira, Claire conducts her own investigation. (978-1-63679-497-6)

Living For You by Jenny Frame. Can Sera Debrek face real and personal demons to help save the world from darkness and open her heart to love? (978-1-63679-491-4)

Mississippi River Mischief by Greg Herren. When a politician turns up dead and Scotty's client is the most obvious suspect, Scotty and his friends set out to prove his client's innocence. (978-1-63679-353-5)

Ride with Me by Jenna Jarvis. When Lucy's vacation to find herself becomes Emma's chance to remember herself, they realize that everything they're looking for might already be sitting right next to them—if they're willing to reach for it. (978-1-63679-499-0)

Whiskey & Wine by Kelly & Tana Fireside. Winemaker Tessa Williams and sex toy shop owner Lace Reynolds are both used to taking risks, but will they be willing to put their friendship on the line if it gives them a shot at finding forever love? (978-1-63679-531-7)

Hands of the Morri by Heather K O'Malley. Discovering she is a Lost Sister and growing acquainted with her new body, Asche learns how to be a warrior and commune with the Goddess the Hands serve, the Morri. (978-1-63679-465-5)

I Know About You by Erin Kaste. With her stalker inching closer to the truth, Cary Smith is forced to face the past she's tried desperately to forget. (978-1-63679-513-3)

Mate of Her Own by Elena Abbott. When Heather McKenna finally confronts the family who cursed her, her werewolf is shocked to discover her one true mate, and that's only the beginning. (978-1-63679-481-5)

Pumpkin Spice by Tagan Shepard. For Nicki, new love is making this pumpkin spice season sweeter than expected. (978-1-63679-388-7)

Rivals for Love by Ali Vali. Brooks Boseman's brother Curtis is getting married, and Brooks needs to be at the engagement party. Only she can't possibly go, not with Curtis set to marry the secret love of her youth, Fallon Goodwin. (978-1-63679-384-9)

Sweat Equity by Aurora Rey. When cheesemaker Sy Travino takes a job in rural Vermont and hires contractor Maddie Barrow to rehab a house she buys sight unseen, they both wind up with a lot more than they bargained for. (978-1-63679-487-7)

Taking the Plunge by Amanda Radley. When Regina Avery meets model Grace Holland—the most beautiful woman she's ever seen—she doesn't have a clue how to flirt, date, or hold on to a relationship. But Regina must take the plunge with Grace and hope she manages to swim. (978-1-63679-400-6)

We Met in a Bar by Claire Forsythe. Wealthy nightclub owner Erica turns undercover bartender on a mission to catch a thief where she meets no-strings, no-commitments Charlie, who couldn't be further from Erica's type. Right? (978-1-63679-521-8)

Western Blue by Suzie Clarke. Step back in time to this historic western filled with heroism, loyalty, friendship, and love. The odds are against this unlikely group—but never underestimate women who have nothing to lose. (978-1-63679-095-4)

Windswept by Patricia Evans. The windswept shores of the Scottish Highlands weave magic for two people convinced they'd never fall in love again. (978-1-63679-382-5)

An Independent Woman by Kit Meredith. Alex and Rebecca's attraction won't stop smoldering, despite their reluctance to act on it and incompatible poly relationship styles. (978-1-63679-553-9)

Cherish by Kris Bryant. Josie and Olivia cherish the time spent together, but when the summer ends and their temporary romance melts into the real deal, reality gets complicated. (978-1-63679-567-6)

Cold Case Heat by Mary P. Burns. Sydney Hansen receives a threat in a very cold murder case that sends her to the police for help where she finds more than justice with Detective Gale Sterling. (978-1-63679-374-0)

Proximity by Jordan Meadows. Joan really likes Ellie, but being alone with her could turn deadly unless she can keep her dangerous powers under control. (978-1-63679-476-1)

Sweet Spot by Kimberly Cooper Griffin. Pro surfer Shia Turning will have to take a chance if she wants to find the sweet spot. (978-1-63679-418-1)

The Haunting of Oak Springs by Crin Claxton. Ghosts and the past haunt the supernatural detective in a race to save the lesbians of Oak Springs farm. (978-1-63679-432-7)

Transitory by J.M. Redmann. The cops blow it off as a customer surprised by what was under the dress, but PI Micky Knight knows they're wrong—she either makes it her case or lets a murderer go free to kill again. (978-1-63679-251-4)

Unexpectedly Yours by Toni Logan. A private resort on a tropical island, a feisty old chief, and a kleptomaniac pet pig bring Suzanne and Allie together for unexpected love. (978-1-63679-160-9)

Bones of Boothbay Harbor by Michelle Larkin. Small-town police chief Frankie Stone and FBI Special Agent Eve Huxley must set aside their differences and combine their skills to find a killer after a burial site is discovered in Boothbay Harbor, Maine. (978-1-63679-267-5)

Crush by Ana Hartnett Reichardt. Josie Sanchez worked for years for the opportunity to create her own wine label, and nothing will stand in her way. Not even Mac, the owner's annoyingly beautiful niece Josie's forced to hire as her harvest intern. (978-1-63679-330-6)

Decadence by Ronica Black, Renee Roman, and Piper Jordan. You are cordially invited to Decadence, Las Vegas's most talked about invitation-only Masquerade Ball. Come for the entertainment and stay for the erotic indulgence. We guarantee it'll be a party that lives up to its name. (978-1-63679-361-0)

Gimmicks and Glamour by Lauren Melissa Ellzey. Ashly has learned to hide her Sight, but as she speeds toward high school graduation she must protect the classmates she claims to hate from an evil that no one else sees. (978-1-63679-401-3)

Heart of Stone by Sam Ledel. Princess Keeva Glantor meets Maeve, a gorgon forced to live alone thanks to a decades-old lie, and together the two women battle forces they formerly thought to be good in the hopes of leading lives they can finally call their own. (978-1-63679-407-5)

Murder at the Oasis by David S. Pederson. Palm trees, sunshine, and murder await Mason Adler and his friend Walter as they travel from Phoenix to Palm Springs for what was supposed to be a relaxing vacation but ends up being a trip of mystery and intrigue. (978-1-63679-416-7)

Peaches and Cream by Georgia Beers. Adley Purcell is living her dreams owning Get the Scoop ice cream shop until national dessert chain Sweet Heaven opens less than two blocks away and Adley has to compete with the far too heavenly Sabrina James. (978-1-63679-412-9)

The Only Fish in the Sea by Angie Williams. Will love overcome years of bitter rivalry for the daughters of two crab fishing families in this queer modern-day spin on Romeo and Juliet? (978-1-63679-444-0)

Wildflower by Cathleen Collins. When a plane crash leaves eleven-year-old Lily Andrews stranded in the vast wilderness of Arkansas, will she be able to overcome the odds and make it back to civilization and the one person who holds the key to her future? (978-1-63679-621-5)

Witch Finder by Sheri Lewis Wohl. Tamsin, the Keeper of the Book of Darkness, is in terrible danger, and as a Witch Finder, Morrigan must protect her and the secrets she guards even if it costs Morrigan her life. (978-1-63679-335-1)